The Voices of Martyrs

Maurice Broaddus

Other Books by Maurice Broaddus

King Maker: The Knights
of Breton Court, Vol. 1

Anthologies
Co-edited

Dark Faith: Invocations
(with Jerry Gordon)

Streets of Shadows
(with Jerry Gordon)

Early Praise for
The Voices of Martyrs

"Give thanks for these griot, hip-funk, afrofuturist stories of pure horror and complicated hope. Broaddus sounds a deep beat in this true myth of survival: what our heads forget, our bones remember."

—Karen Lord

"Maurice Broaddus has a talent for creating fascinating characters across lifetimes, fierce voices that linger and stay with you. His fantasies, fables, and far out tales come from an imagination as frightening as it is admirable. And whether they come from the past, present, or one of his cautionary futures, you are certain to find a story that speaks to you."

—Sheree Renée Thomas

"An outcast in the distant past struggling to survive. A religious captain rationalizing away the evil of the slave ship he commands. A future biomech warrior in a literal culture war. The stories in *The Voices of Martyrs* again prove why Maurice Broaddus is one of the most exciting writers of today's genre fiction. His vision spans space and time while staying grounded in the stories—in the very voices—which make us fully and tragically and hopefully human."

—Nebula Award-nominated author, Jason Sanford

"Reminiscent of a young Charles Saunders, Maurice Broaddus' *The Voices of Martys* is a fresh blend of science fiction, fantasy, and the folkloric history of the African diaspora."

—Chesya Burke, author of *Let's Play White*
and *The Strange Crime of Little Africa*

"There's a percussive intensity to the stories in *The Voices of Martyrs*. These are not simplistic heroic tales but poignant examinations of the triumphs and losses, the joys and pains, and the deep, rich complexities of a culture."

—Ayize Jama-Everett, author of *The Liminal People*

The Voices of Martyrs

Maurice Broaddus

For Sara

Cover Art by Arthur Hugot
Cover Design by Gerald Mohamed

Published by
Rosarium Publishing
P.O. Box 544
Greenbelt, MD 20768-0544
www.rosariumpublishing.com

International Standard Book Number: 978-0-9967692-5-9

Contents

Past

Warrior of the Sunrise

Lalyani surveyed her surroundings, one hand pressed against her hip in stoic resignation, the other clutching her spear. Half of her spear's length was razor sharp iron and had considerable heft, not easily wielded by a man, much less a woman. Pangs of hunger rumbled her insides, but she dared not chance a bite of what little fruit she spied amongst the sickly branches. Fungus encroached the uninviting copse of trees in slow digestion. The stink of rotting carcasses rose from the murky waters of the fetid pool, discouraging anyone from tarrying too long. A low-laying fog swirled about at the foot of the jutting crag. The Mountain of No Name, a desolate stretch of rock, leered from above the tree tops.

The silence disturbed her, the forlorn and petulant stillness wore on her bones. No bird song, no frog bark, no monkey chatter, no whir of insect, no stir of bushes. The beast had come this way. The muscles in her arms ached from their previous encounter. The scars along her back still oozed though she paid the pain no mind. She nursed her anger, a newborn to be suckled until it could march on its own. She would kill the beast and then its master, such was the simple order in her world. That was who she was now.

Lalyani, the Outcast.

Her name would be whispered on the lips of griots, in poem, and song, and story—sometimes of her adventures with Dinga Cisse and that Greek dog he called a friend—not that she cared about such things. Most times, however, she preferred to go her own way, to wander The Path anyway it bent.

Unbridled and sure-footed, she had the supple physique of a horse, her legs wide-braced and powerfully muscled. Though lacking a man's height, she held her head high, her shoulders always bent in anticipation of action. A broad girdle of bronze beads over black sable skin made no attempt to hide her full-bosomed figure. Her leopard hide skirt stopped a hand's spread above her knees.

Slinging her spear through her kaross, she groped for hand holds along the unnatural ridge of stone before her. The shelf was more wall than anything else; a craftsman had worked too hard to make the imposing edifice appear natural. Her people, the Mo-Ito, were hill denizens, so she climbed the stone spire with keen aplomb. She quickly passed the shattered bones of men scattered along the ridges who had failed their bid to climb the summit.

Hours into her ascent, the cliff wall leveled into a landing. Her hands had grown numb from finding purchase. From the top, she turned westward. The impenetrable forest roof thinned at a kraal. Her breath hitched in remembrance of...

§

...how she struggled in Manuto's presence. The chief storyteller and high wizard summoned her to his hut for his final pronouncement. Manuto let loose a weary sigh as if not knowing where to start and circled her. She imagined he often paced the length of his hut, wondering what to do with her. In better days, she teased his over-protectiveness, rarely admitting, even to herself, how much comfort she took in his attentions. Tonight he bore the mien of his position; his word to the chief's ear was law. Her throat tightened in a dry swallow.

"It is time," Manuto said. A fine sheen of sweat misted his fresh-shaven head.

"Let me see him one last time."

"No."

"You dare stand between a mother and her son?" She stood tall and proud, too much iron in her backbone for some. They met eye-to-eye as he drew near to her slender body, her long limbs somehow seeming out of proportion with the rest of her. Despite her exaggerated illusion of fragility, she possessed a tensile strength, a fierce tenacity of spirit, matching both her raw beauty of exquisite cruelty and her air of cold serenity.

"He nears the age of ascent. And there have been ... whispers." Manuto shifted as if in sudden discomfort. "The tribal code demands that you name the father."

"I cannot. He belongs to another."

"He's married?" Adultery meant fatal punishment doled out by the Tribal Avengers. She hated this dance of conversations. It was mostly for the benefit of the two warriors who stood guard outside of his dwelling. Or the countless other ears straining to eavesdrop.

"Only to his duty and obligation."

He rubbed the keloid along his neck. "Then Kaala has no mother. He has no father. He is of the tribe."

"Like mother, like son." The Mo-Ito were a mixed race people, accepting any who wandered into their community as long as they lived by The Path. Proud and fierce though a near forgotten people now. Lalyani's mother was never named, her father was ... gone. Like her, he would never truly know the embrace of this village. He had to earn his right to be a part of the San tribe. "What will come of my son?"

"Rest easy in this: when it is time for him to walk the journey into manhood, I will stand beside him."

Lalyani nodded. She understood this was how things had to be. All choices had consequences, and she made hers readily enough. The time would not be easy for either of them. She had little stomach for the politics of the tribal ways, but she knew what her fate was to be before Manuto gave voice to it.

"You, however, cannot stay here."

"I know. I will abandon The Path as it has abandoned me." Hers was a conviction that struggled to find meaning. While many in her tribe found comfort in The Path, she knew only her terror and brokenness. Some questions were best left unasked because no answer would satisfy. And Lalyani questioned. Buried doubts and insecurity, an embraced self-deception, meant she would never know the pain again. But the pain cut through the lies. Pain was the Master-Teacher.

"You may abandon it, but you may find that it is not so easily left behind. The teachings remain in your heart." Manuto moved to comfort her, his thick arms opening in embrace. She pressed her palm into his chest to halt him.

"Many things remain in my heart that I can no longer feel."

"Mine as well. The demands of duty."

She knew this day would come and had steeled herself for it. A few tasks remained before night descended on...

§

...the wings of sunset. Lalyani dropped into the gardens. Caution lightened her steps as she glided along the cave wall. The honeycombed mountain encircled a small kraal with a series of catacombs. From the upper ridge, she made out the shapes of huts as well as a byre full of cattle. Off to the side of the kraal proper stood a lone, leather-thatched hut, shaded by an old, leafy marula tree. Like a breeze through leaves, Lalyani moved along the gentle slope of the cavern, treading close to the kraal without disturbing anything. Only when approaching the hut did she realize how large it was.

Slits between sheets of cow hide allowed her to study her enemy's master. The cruel tyrant Harlaramu was renowned for his tremendous rages. A gold band pulled the lank strands of his long black hair into a cord revealing a bald pate. Taut muscles rippled under duress, his skin glistened in the heat, his body sticky with greasy charm medicines designed to repel demons. Scars scored his back. Beside him, an overturned pot—with the last trickle of strong beer draining from it—had drowned his heart and dulled his sullen anger. Mad laughter erupted from him as he talked to the shadows, a shifting silhouette against the tricks of moonlight. With a flourish, he whirled to grab whips tipped with shards of broken pottery and began to scourge himself. Ancient, unnatural words tripped from his tongue. The guttural language wailed in higher and higher tones. His limbs flailed in spasmodic gyrations as the spirit talk threatened to consume him, until he fell prostrate as if struck from behind.

For a few heartbeats, he lay on the floor of his hut. He grabbed a fistful of earth and let the dirt trickle from his grasp. Once. Twice. Thrice. Then he struggled to his feet and entered the next chamber. Fearful of being watched herself, Lalyani scuttled along the side to peer into the room. Harlaramu bent over a coterie of small figures. His body obscured the people, but she heard their thin voices. Once he stepped to the side, she realized this was a nursery of sorts. Strapped to curved pieces of wood, small men—she prayed they were of the Pygmy tribe rather than children, though this was no better a fate for those warriors—whose legs were snapped into positions to encourage deformed growth. Their bones canted at odd angles, their limbs pulled and bowed, suspended in agonizing positions. She counted five bodies in restraints. Harlaramu tended to each one, feeding them, stroking them, whispering to them. The sixth body lay on a table. Its ears mangled, still leaking blood. Harlaramu closed his eyes and uttered a prayer. He jabbed a sharpened stone into the creature's mouth and buried its edge to remove its tongue.

"Now you are truly born," he said with foul pride. A tokoloshe. "Hush now and rest. Soon you will be ready to do your master's bidding."

In that moment, Lalyani's warrior's instinct alerted her that she was ...

§

... being observed. A team of scouts patrolled the kraal at the behest of the great crone. Lalyani trailed them, though, unasked and unwanted. She, too, knew the sting of duty, and one of hers was to the great crone. Perhaps a faint sound broke her reflections, but she brought her spear to bear before her mind realized what disturbed her. Someone stole along the forest line. Branches snapped in the wake of a sinister shadow. Lalyani fought down a surge of panic; its familiar fearsome lope caused most men's hearts to pump water. It stooped in a semi-crouch, its head turning from side-to-side, mouth ajar as if tasting the air.

Then it turned to her.

Lalyani's eyes widened in surprise as the beast was like no creature she had ever seen before. A distorted face—the flesh of its previous victim draped its own, giving the face the appearance of a melted candle—worn as a trophy. Baboon pelts stitched together formed its vest. The decomposed head of a woman dangled from around its neck. All sinew and hair, it hunched over, a malformed man short of stature, its ears raised to a point, almost as a wolf. Its jaw yawned and revealed a gullet of protruding teeth. The snapping of branches and crackling of bushes ushered its charge. Mad laughter careened through the forest in its dash. Despite its diminutive size, it hit with enough force to send her reeling the length of several men.

It should have killed her in its initial rush, but like most men in her experience, it had to demonstrate how strong it was first. Now she had its measure. As it sprang forward, she dodged to the side, but its long arms slashed wildly. Its raking panther talons caught her along her back. It battered the wind out of her. She cursed herself, angry at her carelessness. Its eyes glinted with intelligence. Thrown off balance, she stumbled to the ground but leapt to her feet to face her attacker. It lashed out in frustration. Holding her spear in a two-handed grip, she didn't measure her strength against that of men. She was as strong as she needed to be. It reared in a blur of motion. She tried to sidestep it, but its momentum carried them into the forest when it tackled her. The tokoloshe snapped at her throat until it slowly realized it had impaled itself on the point of her spear. Buried in its fur, the spear pierced thick muscle. Her dark grimace gave a rueful stare as it escaped into the ...

§

... shadows of the catacombs. The rocky path left little doubt the direction it traveled; however, it knew the crags and crevices much better than she. She closed her eyes and listened. The cavern echoed with life of its own, the thrum of rock and pressing presence. She stilled even her breath so she could try to sense it. A void in the darkness hiding patiently, waiting for her to near it only a step further. It was stunned into momentary inaction as she sprang upon it. Her spear whipped through the air, beautiful and frightening, catching the beast across the bridge of its nose. The spear point lanced both eyes like overripe boils.

The tokoloshe screeched in tongueless cries. Blood spurted as it slashed about, seizing her by chance rather than skill. Death was upon her with a snapping jaw and terrible grip. Instinct took over her, her lips drawn back in a crazed snarl, a primal rage burned in her eyes. Reckless, she threw herself into the beast, letting the force of her weight do its work. Its wounds showered her in a spray of blood. She drove the length of her spear deep into its belly, the creature's face tightened in surprise. Its blows grew weaker with each careless swipe until it fell limp along her shaft. She scanned the cavern, her ears alert for any telltale footfalls of guards approaching the fray.

Wiping her spear point on its vest, Lalyani stood over its corpse and knew that the great crone ...

§

... rested a little easier in her grand chair. Daubed head-to-toe in white and red clay, the old woman rocked back and forth. Little more than a skeletal figure, a shawl of antelope pelt cloaked her. Her fierce eyes commanded respect once they opened and focused on the young warrior. The great crone summoned her with a gesture of her message stick. A man's head was carved onto the handle of her stick. It was whispered that it was through him that the gods spoke to her.

"Lalyani." The great crone demanded an austere reverence, one for pomp and pageantry with an ill temper for poor manners and hasty words.

"Mistress." Lalyani resented the bowing and scraping of her assumed tone.

"I want you to kill a man for me."

Lalyani demonstrated nothing approaching surprise at the request. Men and women alike from all tribes and status sought her when their needs so required. "Mistress?"

"Harlaramu. Blood demands vengeance."

"If I may ask, whose blood cried out?"

"As it was whispered to me, Harlaramu suffered from pains in his head so strong, thoughts were harassed from his mind. Only his personal guard, the Krys, seemed safe around him. One day, driven mad from his pain, he shut his favorite wife into a cave alone except for a cow dung fire so that he might watch her tortured expressions while she suffocated to death. Later that night, he raped his daughters and fed them to crocodiles. Yet the maddening headaches still torment him." The great crone reached for her cup of wine and drank deep but with all due deliberation. Lalyani hated the way she had to wait on the great crone's performances. "I trust you knew of the creature that stalked our kraal? The beast comes for me. The weapon of Harlaramu."

"Ah, so it's a game of kill him before he kills you," Lalyani said with a smirk.

"You are too stiff-necked. Your insolent tongue will be your undoing."

"Until then, it amuses me," she said over a mildly derisive laugh.

"I hope your son will be equally amused."

Lalyani's eyes focused into a dagger's gaze. "What say you of my son?"

"No more jokes?" The crone brushed her hair to the side. "Despite the huffing of the chief, your son will be raised as one of our own. He will follow The Path, and perhaps he won't stumble as his mother and father did. He will be the pride of the tribe and will one day lead it to great heights. I will see to his education personally. Once you accomplish your task."

Lalyani parsed the choice before her. She asked for nothing, depended on nothing, and she expected nothing. All she had was honor and duty. She hated to depend on others—a man, an employer, the world—where she'd be tied to life. When things become precious to her, she was always on guard against someone snatching it from her; or worse, she herself destroying it. Life became about fear of losing. And the compromises she made in order to keep what she had. Better to stay unattached. Free. A tribe of one.

Lalyani nodded.

"You remember how to use the charms." The woman handed Lalyani what appeared to be a bone wrapped with twine.

"Yes, mistress." Lalyani held the talisman to her ear. It hummed with the pulse of magic.

"Good, for unprotected, I'd be sending you to certain death."

"The night is my ally and stealth my trade, mistress."

"I trust in your ability to remain silent."

"How will you know if I succeed?"

"These bones will know. And you'll be free. You will be of the Baluba tribe, one of the forgotten, and one day, you may even lead those nomads."

Dismissed, Lalyani ...

§

... crept up the earthen stairs. Weeds sprang up through cracks in the crushed rock that formed the pathway. The cloying moisture of the stones formed a stark dankness with malefic odor. Torches lit the way through the cavern. The walls closed in on her, the passageway narrowing such that only one body could pass at a time. If she knew fear, she pushed it down into the deepest part of her. It was easier for her to act rather than worry, especially in defense of her own. Even if her own would never know of her actions.

Stones steeped in shadows formed the portico of the temple. A series of caged, chattering monkeys screeched in alarm at her approach. Lalyani cursed and then plunged into the deeper shadows of the temple proper. The main chamber was a huge cavity the color of teeth, the walls smooth as if hewn from a single block of marble. From her hiding perch, Lalyani had full view of the passing processional.

Three female agoze, initiates to the dark ways, accompanied the dark priest, Harlaramu. Clad only in a loincloth, a brief garment of antelope hide covered their brown skin. Glazed amber in the eerie firelight, the first carried a macabre drum: a human skull with its top sawed off and skin stretched across. The second illumined the path of the processional with a torch. The last brought a dog to the kneeling Harlaramu. Lalyani stared in horror and fascination as the woman slit the dog's throat. Its spurting blood baptized the shaman. Then the dance began. Harlaramu stomped his foot and held the position until the first agoze began her gyrations. The hollow echo of the drumbeat continued as Harlaramu thrashed about to its rhythm. Faster she twirled about, the frenetic beat riling him to ecstatic exultations until the frenzy dropped him in an exhausted heap. Harlaramu came to a halt between two warriors each bearing heavy swords.

Curiosity suckled at her ...

§

... as she watched from the forest line. The thin barrier of foliage hid her, not that any in the tribe paid her any attention. They had already turned their back to her. The murmur of the gathered throng formed a melancholy cadence, their chants a dull intoning to call to the spirits of the kraal. The musicians occupied the clearing around the central fire. Dancers pranced along, their frenzied steps punctuated by yelps. The drummers caught the spirit of their dance, their wide smiles signaled an increase in the music's tempo. Despite the preternaturally cool night, the tension thickened to that of a storm cloud. Abruptly, the chanting and music ceased, the settling silence a curtain raised for the final act of the performance. The entire village surrounded them, the crowd turning to face the great throne. Manuto brought Kaala before the tribal council, a group made up of Manuto, the high priest, the great crone, the elder, and the chief, the father of the tribe. Manuto engulfed the boy's small hand in his own, his face a sullen mask, except for his eyes, and led him to the great crone. Kaala had too solemn a face. A young boy lost, wanting to cry out, but choosing not to. He would be a fine warrior one day. His chest puffed out, Manuto searched for Lalyani. The great crone nodded. He released the boy into her hands and she, in turn, presented him to the chief. The father of the tribe stood taller than the others, half his face daubed in crimson clay, his arms crossed along his chest. His impassive stare, without scorn, without judgment, turned to the boy. The chief carved a crescent moon onto his left buttock, the tribal scar. He would be accepted for now but would have to prove himself during his rites of manhood.

Lalyani turned, head held high and uncompromising, and strode into the forest maw ...

§

... as if drugged, she swam in darkness, breaking the surface as her eyes fluttered open. Her scattered thoughts took a moment to collect, memories returning in degrees. Her hands tied, a long rope fastened about her, looping under her armpits, terminating around the trunk of the marula tree. She tested the cords that bound her, the realization that she'd fallen not registering with her. Before the idea reduced her to an unfamiliar brand of misery, the sound of feet shuffling on nearby stone drew her attention.

Up close, Harlaramu was taller but slender in a feminine way. With his delicate bearing—hips too rounded, eyelashes too long, and his voice too silvery from his toothy hideous grin—he should have been strangled at birth. Cowerie shells and copper scales decorated his sipuku. He leered at her breasts and legs. Dark eyes burned with intent to throttle her senseless if he couldn't bed her. Men like him bound women, capturing what they couldn't tame. They didn't know what to truly do with a woman other than own her.

"Lalyani. Once of the Mo-Ito. Outcast of the San tribe. Called to the Baluba, the Forgotten Ones." His voice a low mumble, he started and stopped a few times, each time in a different tongue until he found her talk place.

"Harlaramu. Rabid dog in need of being put down."

"You seem none the worse for wear after encountering the tokoloshe."

"I dispatched that abomination for befouling my sight with its presence."

"The great crone chose well in her guardian." He leered at her bosom. "You ... fascinate me."

"Maybe your fascination could have your eyes meeting mine for a change."

"A truce to your jokes, Clever One. Is that what the great crone taught you? Is cleverness the ultimate lesson of The Path? She asks a lot of you and what you have gained in return?

"You don't know what you believe and don't trust what you understand. I could help you, you know. I followed The Path for a while, but I saw it for what it was. I could have been many things to you. The father you never knew. The man that accepts you as you are without question. You could lead the Krys and together we could make this kingdom ours. Show The Path and its followers what it means to live outside of their cages."

Her face tilted, an almond oval in the gloom. Her unwavering gaze studied him. "You are a creature of pain. You have known it in your time and have enjoyed dealing it to others. Your problem isn't that you no longer believe in The Path, but that you fear it might be right. That the reason your hopes and dreams have been dashed to dust isn't due to a failing of the faith, but a failing within you. So you seek to tear down any who might walk the ways of The Path—any who might make a difference in this life—in a pathetic attempt to reveal them as being just as flawed as you. You are weak and a coward."

"I ..." Harlaramu stepped back as if needing to catch his breath. Or not lose his composure. "I don't think you understand the precariousness of your situation." He nodded and three of the Krys stepped forward and hoisted her. She dangled over a donga in the forest, a clearing leading to a pit. Human bones bleached in the sun surrounding a cluster of six great anthills. Harlaramu tossed a piece of spoiled meat into the cluster. At first, only a few ants reared their heads. Then a wave of ants charged, pincers snapping, their barbed legs—each with a sharp claw—scurried across the sand. Their poison sacs seemed swollen with anticipation. "They are called 'Warriors of Sunrise.' They are the largest ants in existence. They can devour a man in long agonizing moments. You are so like them," he said. "Huge. Fierce. Strong." Baleful eyes glared at her. "I offer you what few women get: a choice."

"I'd sooner plunge into the Zambezi. That is my choice." She raised her leg to allow him a measure of a view and grinned with gleeful malice. He could grip himself in the night; she had better things to do than be a man-boy's plaything. Her clamorous voice and mocking tone drew a scowl from him. Little more than a beast, so easily roused to agitated frustration. He slapped her, first on one cheek, then the other, but she didn't cry out. He clutched her jaw, more in a vise than a caress and wrenched her toward him.

"Remove your hand or I'll have your heart," Lalyani said.

"I believe you would." He ran his hand along the top of her breast, but that, too, she didn't feel. No amount of abuse from men could deprive her of her pride and honor. Dignity was her own to claim. She withdrew into herself. She learned to face life's hardships without letting them turn her hard. Except when she needed to be.

With that, he kissed her. The kiss was passionless. He might as well have been kissing a corpse. It wasn't given nor was it his to take. She had never known true love, not that she was unfeeling, but a kiss was ...

§

... too personal, the only bit of love left in her. She stole back into the kraal one last time. She stood over Kaala until the weight of her presence stirred him awake. Though he was the reason she chose as she did, she didn't want hardness to be her legacy.

"Goodbye, Lala." His defiant eyes matched her own. Both were resolved to their fates.

"Shhh, song of my heart." She closed her pain-misted eyes and kissed him good night. A flicker of emotion, quick as a bird taking flight, caught her unaware, like a spear thrown by a hiding coward ...

§

... converging on her. Three of the Krys approached, carrying wide-tipped blades and clubs studded with crude nails. She thought about being broken. Possessed. She detested their leer of ownership as much as the idea of her loss of freedom.

Hers was a craft of subtlety. Her mind was as much a weapon as any spear, so she already out-matched the over-muscled lummoxes who thought only with their sword. Perhaps she hadn't left The Path as much as she protested.

Her lithe arms stretched taut, Lalyani kicked out to gain momentum. The Krys hacked at the ropes rather than go through the dance of torturously lowering her onto the ant mounds. The arc of Lalyani's swing landed her on the cusp of the donga as the knives cut through the cords. She entwined the legs of the nearest Krys and brought him to the ground. Still on her back, she eliminated as much space between their hips as possible and locked her feet tightly at the ankles so her thighs could squeeze his lower ribs. Lalyani shifted her hips to her left then fell towards her right, kicking his legs into the air and using him as a shield to deflect the blows of the second Krys. Heavy blades landed on her shield. The second Krys realized his error and spun off balance which allowed her left hand to under hook him at his shoulder. Her right over hooked at his biceps. She sat into him, straightening her right leg as if stretching to run. She rolled him over his head against her side, then drove her weight into his skull until she heard the terrible snap. She laid on his corpse to allow his blade to free her.

Palming his blade, she head-butted the approaching Krys before she scrambled away. Still weaponless, to all appearances, her eyes narrowed to grim slits. The last Krys gripped the hilt of his club with the fury of emotion. Trembling, the stink of fear rose from him. She met his charge with a fierce desperation, dodging his initial swipe and returning with a kick into his dangling bits. The man gasped and doubled over. Rage bubbled up in his eyes, another man easily led to distraction as he rained blows upon her without forethought or form, an ox yoked about. He disgusted her, little more than brute clubbing, and she parried his clumsy strokes. A deadness in his eyes, his would not be a warrior's death, but an ending to misery. Before his body registered what happened, she slipped within his guard and slit his throat.

Harlaramu had returned to his obscene nursery, treating the wounds of the next tokoloshe. Chain spread-eagled on his table, flecks of blood dotted its face from its earlier wounds. Fatigue and fear characterized its face as it stared vacantly upward. A movement in the doorway focused its attention, causing Harlaramu to turn. His countenance was reduced to an ashy mask of terror, his wild eyes scanning for any exit other than the one Lalyani blocked. She leaned a little too heavily on her spear which had been planted just outside his hut as if awaiting her head to mount. Weary, wounds still bleeding, she took in ragged breaths. The image of her—not the picture of a woman about to pass out but rather one in the throes of barely restrained battle frenzy—was even more terrifying.

Lalyani grabbed him by his hair and forced his head back, setting her blade against his jugular. She pondered the type of death he deserved, but a slit throat was too quick. Her knotted muscles dragged him back to the lip of the donga. She shoved him over the edge. The ants swarmed. Hundreds up his legs. Harlaramu screamed as if he'd been plunged into boiling water. Blood ran down his legs, and he sank into the quagmire of ants. Little more than ...

§

... *an abandoned flower in the dust. Lalyani chanced one last glance at the kraal she once called home, then took her first steps on the Journey to Asazi, the journey to We Know Not Where.*

Rite of Passage

The 3rd of June, 1651

My grave would one day smell much like the odor that haunted me, even now. Loamy, stale, and moldy, the cargo hold captured a bleakness that shriveled my soul. I ran my hand along the rough-hewn planks. Dried blood flaked away like an ancient coat of paint, reminding me of journeys past.

"Captain William Sparke. A civilized man such as yourself shouldn't stay down here longer than he has to," my boatswain, Jeffery Hawkins, said. The owner, my father, fitted the ship as I tarried with my wife and child during my brief stay; so I was still acquainting myself with the crew. As they were with me. Mr. Hawkins, long employed by my father, strode down the cargo hold steps with the swagger of a bully, his cat-o'-nine-tails dangled at his side as his badge of office.

An old hunk of a sailor, surly and grizzled, Mr. Hawkins' every movement simmered with a brooding anger in need of venting. A scar carved upward from his lips, a devil's grin, as if a large hook had caught him in his mouth. The crew made no allusion to it or its origin. Scores of tiny wrinkles circled cruel, uneducated eyes; when he settled them upon you, his gaze produced an increased nervousness within you.

"I was inspecting the hold before we set sail. Were you successful in delivering the ..."

"... Cargo, sir. Think of them as cargo. I'm betting you'll sleep better at night. We're preparing to load, with the Cap'n's permission."

"Tell the lads to step smart and prepare for final inspection."

"Begging the Cap'n's pardon, but we could have set sail yesterday."

"Yesterday was the Sabbath, Mr. Hawkins."

"Of course, Cap'n."

I ascribed my dislike of Mr. Hawkins to his simmering disrespect for me. His cavalier impudence was suffered only because he handled the crew well. He maintained a strict code of conduct. The men scurried as we walked past. Dark as sun-toasted pears and twice as hard, they were a ragged bunch with their shaggy beards and unkempt hair. I awaited the arrival of the Cargo from the main deck.

Jacob's Galley of London, a tall, goodlie ship, was re-christened after my son. I feared, and loved, two things: God and the sea. My whole life I dreamt of the sea. So much so that my father had little choice but to give me my own ship once I completed my schooling. Canoes dotted the sea like surface skimming insects bloated to overflowing with ... Cargo. The launches ported at the boarding area long enough to spew their load. I knew how Charon felt overseeing the arriving dead. This, my first Captaincy, churned my stomach not with anticipatory glee, but with knots of revulsion.

"Stand by the lines to load," Mr. Hawkins barked.

"Some of their own are returning with us as translators," I said.

"No matter, sir, I speak their language."

"What language is that?"

"Pain." He patted his cat-o'-nine-tails.

"While I don't swear by the horrendous tales spread by the naysayers, I won't abide any unnecessary cruelty to the Cargo. I run a clean ship."

"I know you will, Cap'n." He didn't bother to hide the disdain that laced his voice. "The only trouble I expect is while we're still in sight of their land."

The tropical sun glared without mercy upon my ship. The swarms of flies worsened the intolerable humidity. We couldn't long endure the malignity of the air and the diseases that it carried. The males—ironed together with hand manacles and leg shackles and naked save for the white cloth that girded their loins—paused on the loading plank for a last glance at the Whidah port. I left Mr. Hawkins to attend to the details of the loading. I retreated, if only for a brief respite, to my cabin.

The heat from my cabin raked my skin. With good trade winds we would reach Hispaniola in two months. The sooner this damnable trip was underway the sooner it ended. The bill of lading taunted me from my desk with its bold print: viz. 266 males, 134 females. Invested properly, I could retire from the commission on the gross sales as well as receive ten of the Cargo for myself. Better to concentrate on running an efficient ship: chart courses, plan provisions, and judge how close to pack the Cargo.

Amelia's last words to me echoed in my mind: "Why not find another line of work?" What was I to do? Toil at her father's presses? Be chained to a desk? Better yet, work in some field? I would rather risk being accused of not putting away childish things, a boy and his love of boats.

A simple dream spoiled and tasting of ash in my mouth.

§

The 6th of June, 1651

"The cargo is starving itself." Mr. Hawkins delivered the news with an exuberance that belied its ill portent. He paraded in his patched trousers, topless save for the black handkerchief sashed about his neck. "This wasn't totally unexpected."

"What do you recommend?" I asked.

"Best to break the rebellion early, before the practice becomes widespread."

"As you will," I turned from him. "And Mr. Hawkins? You can't go about naked as a savage."

"I didn't know this was a formal affair," he muttered, still within earshot. His hard ways reminded me of my father; as did the way his eyes brimmed with disgust at my presumed softness. The challenge caught in my throat, but I needed his support to control the men. For now. After donning a black vest, Mr. Hawkins applied a special zealousness to disciplining the Cargo. About ten of the Cargo sat around each of the tubs scattered along the main deck, eating boiled yams and rice. Mr. Hawkins snatched a smallish man who abstained from his meal. Two of the crew held the man while the boatswain lit a nearby brazier. The flames of the brazier reflected in the man's eyes. Mr. Hawkins pulled a reddened coal from the brazier with a pair of tongs, passing it to and fro before the hapless man.

All activity ceased.

The coal's heat blistered the man's cheek and his eyes bulged as he struggled to escape. He pressed the coal against the man's lips, Mr. Hawkins smiled a serpentine leer. The lips sizzled like overdone, fatty steaks. The tortured man's shrieks chilled me to my marrow. His arms pinned to his sides, he thrashed his head about. Tears streamed down his face. The smell of scorched flesh stung my nostrils. The hideous scalding and the incipient shrieks slowly subsided. Mr. Hawkins scolded the Cargo through the interpreter, though I doubt any was needed. He savored the moment like a tasty morsel.

The rest of the Cargo ate without incident.

§

"The Cargo is ready for inspection," Hawkins said.

"Good." I had arranged for a doctor to be part of the crew's complement for fear of pox'd Cargo. "Before each morning's breakfast, allow him to examine the privities of both men and women with the nicest scrutiny."

"We can tend to them as they do their exercises."

The doctor treated the Cargo's sores as the crew washed and oiled the Cargo with the casualness of herding sheep. I had heard rumors of their savagery: child sacrifice, orgies to their pagan gods, necklaces of human teeth, cannibalism. Each tale I heard seemed more outrageous than the last. We saved them from their own heathenish ways. I shuddered at the thought of what monstrous brute could ever have performed such deeds against another human.

My heart raced whenever they were on deck. The women and children freely roamed, but leg irons confined the men. The thunderous echoes when they stamped about was a haunting cacophonous jangling that jarred my men to their bones. Downcast eyes feigned weakness and submissiveness, yet I know they eyed the packs of spare harpoons and lances that lined the rear deck.

Mr. Hawkins had peculiar notions of exercise; he forced the Cargo to dance. The display doubled as entertainment for the crew. Despondent countenances fixed on the Cargo during their somnambulant hops.

A queer one drew my attention. With his burnt coffee complexion, his teeth a dazzling white in contrast, he had a noble bearing and fine stature. However, his eyes, joyless and obsidian, bored into my soul. He stood apart from the rest, almost unsure of his role. Mr. Hawkins clarified his role for him with a sting of the cat-o'-nine-tails. He hardly flinched, but his eyes intensified. A controlled burning, like an eclipsed moon, seethed in them.

He began to dance.

He stomped his foot, one solitary pound in tune to the drummer. A few measures later, he raised his other leg and hammered again to the beat of the drum. He chanted in a dialect unfamiliar to my translator, his dreadful drone in tune to the drummer's rhythm. Another voice added itself to his. Then another. Before too long, a chorus of the men sang out. The women and children stopped to watch. He continued his steps, and only then did I realize that the rest of the Cargo synchronized their movements to his. He increased his methodical thumping, followed by the rest. My heart fluttered at the sight of them, alarmed by his energy. The crewmen, with the fear of a possible mutiny, stood back, paralyzed. The romp devolved into a mad frenzy of twisting and jumping—a fiendish, indecent writhing with an energy of its own, still chanting their pagan psalmody. The first man stretched out his arms beyond his chains, beyond his shackle mates, beyond the ship, beyond the seas, in his mind, touching the ends of the world. To touch home.

"Enough, you muckies," Mr. Hawkins screeched. He kicked the drummer over to gain everyone's attention. With a gesture, he ordered the crew to return the Cargo to the hold. "I don't blame you for standing windward, Cap'n. The lot of them smelled worse than rotten codfish."

"You seem to know these people well, Mr. Hawkins. What of that one? The dancer?"

"Njinga. Future 'ozo' of the Igbo," he said with a smirk.

"It never occurred to me that they had names."

"I only know it because he was singled out to me by my procurer. I guarantee that one will be trouble."

"All he did was dance. Bring him to my quarters." I could not be persuaded to entertain the thought of needless barbarity, especially to creatures who—except for their want of true religion—may have been as much the work of God's hands as us. Heaven have mercy on us all, Presbyterian and Pagans. Mr. Hawkins brought Njinga before me, and his aged eyes peered into me. I placed my copy of the Holy Writ in his hands as I spoke to him. "Son of darkness, I must do my duty by you, concerned as I am for all the souls on my ship. I fear you cling to your pagan ways, but you could lead your people from the fiery pit that awaits you."

Njinga stared at the book in his hands with uncertainty, like it was a serpent threatening to strike. I thought for a moment that the light of understanding flickered in his eyes, and, for a brief moment, hope welled within me that maybe Providence had me here for a reason. That there was a purpose, a meaning, to this business.

Then the black bastard dropped God's Word, the Book landing with a slap. I shook with fury and reached for the nearest object to grasp. An unopened bottle of New England rum sat on my desk. I brought it down upon the man's temple with as much force as I could muster. Mr. Hawkins burst in at the sound of the commotion and stayed my hand from further blows, before he removed the heathen from my presence.

Alone in my cabin, my mind betrayed me with remembrances of the Cargo and our treatment of them. I wondered whether Mr. Hawkins was once a religious man. Compared to the eternality of their souls, what matter their physical duress. Besides, I have a responsibility to my crew, my backers, and my family. I feared that I knelt before a new altar, to this god of economics.

That night I dreamt of Negro bodies bobbing around me, like jutting placards from wrecked ships, with capricious waves tossing me to and fro. I bound the bodies together by their loin clothes, shaping them into my own makeshift raft. Their mouths gaped, wordlessly screaming into the oblivion of waves.

And I feared for my black-stained soul.

§

The 8th of June, 1651

Great tragedy and waste ruined this night.

The rigging creaked with the vitality of life at sea. The sails unfurled with the snap of freshly laundered sheets. With the blowing breeze, we made splendid time. I escorted a few of my crewmen for an inspection. The air below deck was stifling, close like a whale's belly. When I reached the seventh step, the noxious stench of effluvia overtook me. Had my men not received me, I would have collapsed into the hold. It was no wonder that the Cargo was in such high demand: Living in harsh climes made them a hardy lot. However, hardy or not, the hold needed fumigation. The possible danger of the tar igniting when it boiled over the tin pots had the crew of the mind that allowing the Cargo to suffer was better than risking destruction by fire. Though the operation would spread my crew thin, I ordered it anyway. The men filled small tin pots with tar and marlinespikes, then plunged glowing red irons into them. A dense smoke arose as the men scrambled from the hold, coughing into their tightly clutched kerchiefs. The hatches on the hold were sealed for two hours, time enough for the Cargo to exercise and eat while the tar smoke sweetened the air.

A few days ago, we ran out of rice and yams and forced the Cargo to eat horse beans. They detested the boiled pulp, especially the "slabber sauce" we prepared them in: palm oil, flour, water, and red pepper. The Cargo sat with their pained grimaces and huddled postures around the tubs. Then shouting commenced. A man threw his beans at another, presumably for some wrong done to him during the night. My crew chuckled as one of the Cargo slapped at another while beans trailed down his face. The whole scene left me torn between laughter and wariness. During the brouhaha, about ten of them jumped up, their gaunt frames filled with renewed vigor. My lads took a few lumps as the Cargo lashed out—more an act of desperation, since none knew how to pilot my vessel—like the last gasp of a dying man who didn't understand the nature of his death. A few men fired their muskets past them. Most of the rebels settled down. Two jumped overboard after yelling something in their native tongue. The remainder cheered.

"Bring the ship to," I said. "Mr. Hawkins, please have your men retrieve the Cargo."

"Cap'n, you may want to see this for yourself." Hawkins called me to the edge of the ship.

I pushed past the men staring at the sea in slack-jawed silence. The seas churned in white foamy billows where the men leapt in. We spotted an occasional shark fin, but I heard no cries. A maroon track extended shoreward, widening then fading.

I don't know if I can do this business much longer, I thought.

"There go 100 guineas to the sharks," Mr. Hawkins replied, winking at me as if we shared some common joke. The crewmen, after going through the trouble of fumigating the hold, seethed with undeniable anger. Mr. Hawkins gnashed his teeth with a spiteful gleam in his eyes. Mr. Hawkins related the tale of the last ship he served on. The ship dropped its anchor at its destination. The air was still, like the wind was attending its own wake. The cargo hold was silent. No sobs. No groans. Despite their bruises, sores, and other illnesses, they held their heads high. A woman emerged from the hold, an Igbo leader. She marched alongside her people, and they fell in step with her. Guards directed them toward the auction barracks, but she turned and marched into the sea. The entire cargo followed her: men, women, and children, preferring to drown rather than become slaves. "Cap'n, unless you want more trouble, some must be made examples of."

"Why do you rebel?" I asked, pacing in front of them, my translator doing his best to keep abreast of me. "Your treatment has been most humane. Not perfect, but humane. Some of you were in famine, but here you eat well. Most of you were captives of your own wars. I've heard tell what you do to your prisoners. We take you to where it's in your owner's best interest to give you the best possible treatment."

A voice shouted from the back. Without seeing, I knew it had to be Njinga.

"What did he call me?" I asked.

"Hard to translate," the translator offered, "'a great rogue,' perhaps? Yes, you are a rogue to snatch them from their homelands."

"Is that what you think of me? A rogue?"

"You see with the eyes of a crocodile, not seeing where your path takes you," Njinga said through the translator. "Or us. Your magic may have stolen the earth, for there are no trails to follow in the water, but we can still find our way home."

"Don't bother reasoning with them, Cap'n," Mr. Hawkins said, "it's only a waste o' breath."

"Fine then, I'll leave the matter to your hands." I had prayed that the Cargo would have responded to our efforts to lessen their duress with some measure of gratitude. They had no idea how hard we worked for them.

"I am *your* hands, sir, that way you don't have to get yours dirty."

Mr. Hawkins seized Njinga. I doubt he was any more involved in the unrest than anyone else, but the others looked to him for guidance and strength. That and Mr. Hawkins held a special grudge against the African. The sailors hoisted Njinga up the mast, dangling him by his chains. Mr. Hawkins pranced along the deck, in his patched pantaloons and ridiculous black vest, stomping his feet below Njinga. Njinga's dark eyes fixed on him, fierce, but cold. Mr. Hawkins twirled his whip with practiced ease. The tips of the tails glinted in the light. He had embedded shards of glass into them. The air crackled as the whip tore through it. The tips caught in Njinga's back then ripped free. Stored cruelty vented to the cheers of his men. Njinga never cried out. His quiet defiance only aroused Mr. Hawkins' passions and heightened his creativity for expending his vengeful energies. He took a thin plank of wood and tamped around Njinga's wounds causing profuse bleeding. Mr.

Hawkins splashed brine on the wounds until the man cried out:

"May worms hatch inside your belly and devour you slowly from the inside," my translator offered.

A vicious grin crossed Mr. Hawkins' face. He left the prince in his chains for an hour. By Mr. Hawkins' reasoning, a living Njinga advertised the price of rebellion. In addition, the crew dared not object to his next action for fear of being next.

Mr. Hawkins pulled two more men at random, one a presumed cheerer, the other a conspirator. He ordered them both decapitated and their bodies tossed to the sharks that trailed our ship like faithful dogs after their master. He lined the remaining Cargo up to return them to the hold. As each got to the door, he stopped them and placed one of the severed heads in their hands. He forced them to stare into the dead man's eyes, grip the head by the still moist stump, and kiss the lips.

I retired to my cabin. I filled a quarter of a cup with New England rum, studying the cup as if I divined dark clouds. In one swallow, the alcohol dashed against my skull, an anchor hitting sea bottom. I tossed about in bed, lost in the soft susurrus of sound as the rataplan of the pelting rain finished the day.

This is how we bring heathens to Christ?

§

The 9th of August, 1651

The black cloud formed gradually on the horizon, then galloped toward us like the fourth horseman. The heavens released a mournful downpour. Lightning pierced the darkness, streams of fire threatened to cage us. The crew had voyaged through their share of storms, but none like this judging by their confused shouts barely heard over the deafening thunder, the shrill wind, and the roaring sea—the elements taking arms against the ship. Spreading the awning, the men left the crowfoot halyards slack to catch the rain in its center. They filled eleven large casks to replenish our waning provisions, since the journey had lasted longer than we anticipated. The men, on short rations, grumbled about having to maintain the Cargo at all, but I'd be damned before I let this voyage be in vain.

Steam trickled from the edges of the vents. The hold grew intolerably hot, its confined air rendered noxious by the effluvia exhaled from their bodies, but the air vents had to be shut during turbulent seas lest we take on water and it all be for naught. With the men scattered, busy about their duties amidst the fury of the storm, I couldn't chance the Cargo on deck.

The dreadful bang of thunder quaked the ship. The wind cast our ship on waves that foamed like a rabid dog until the wind our mast began to crack. Newly-freed rigging whistled past me.

Then suddenly came the unnatural calm.

A woeful cloud of melancholia draped the ship, an unseen funeral shroud while the men carried out their duties with a regretful muteness. A sickening colonnade of bodies of the morning's dead formed along the deck. Sharks, increasing in number with each day of the lengthening voyage, trailed in the bloody foam of the ship's wake. Though the howlings of the cargo hold alarmed me, when we first set sail, its absence now haunted me.

"Damned ignorant creatures," Mr. Hawkins said.

"Who, Mr. Hawkins?" I asked, though his deprecations were only ever aimed at the Cargo.

"You don't understand them like I do. This silence is something to worry about. They're a troubling lot that needs to be broken."

Some of the women carried beads though a few of the women draped themselves with some of the crewmen's kerchiefs. A somber woman—once one of the more ebullient women who often led the others in singing during the afternoon exercises—now wore a haunted look about her countenance. A striking woman, beneath the purplish bruises and despite the recent lash marks that striped her back. She cradled her kerchief with unbridled contempt. Spitting into the cloth several times, she then tied it around her long hair, and wandered the deck with a beguiling casualness. Without a sideways glance, she threw herself overboard into the waiting maws of the teeming sharks that cascaded after us—though she let out not so much as the slightest shriek as they rent her to pieces. The blood foam, the freedom of death, beckoned even to me. However, I had a job to do. When all was gone, the damnable job still called.

"Mr. Hawkins, have your men construct a latticework of rope yarn to keep the Cargo from jumping overboard. There will not be a repeat of this."

"Yes, sir."

"Do you know why some of the women have the crew's kerchiefs and trinkets?"

"As either guilty or grateful payment, sir. A new day has a way of casting a different light on midnight reveries, eh, Cap'n?" Mr. Hawkins smiled like a contemptuous serpent.

"If your ... reveries were behind the incident today, we'll put an end to them right now."

"Cap'n, you've got to give the men their ease when they're off-duty."

"I have to do nothing except instill in them discipline and bring this ship to port."

"Begging the Cap'n's pardon," Mr. Hawkins' tone slithered from his toothy smirk, "I take it that you will not be needing a belly warmer again tonight? I can't bring her myself, I've a Cargo net to construct."

Serving to distract me from the shaming sting of Mr. Hawkin's words, the sky darkened by degrees. Never had I seen so severe a squall. The water mirrored the dark skies, and warring elements entombed it. Lightning shot through the sky with a brazen temerity that struck even the most hardened among us with terror to our souls. The wind, a devil's howl, spat torrents of rain upon us. We brailed our sails, preparing to furl them though the waves tossed us 'til the deck nearly met the water.

I sought solace in my cabin, to spend yet another contemplative evening wherein I struggled to reconcile what we might have wrought with this dreadful business. Duty compelled me to see it through. I filled a cup halfway with New England rum. When I embarked in the business of slaving ... when a man senses a wrong, a wrong he finds himself every bit the culprit, he strives to cover up his suspicions, even from himself. I had reached the improbably sage conclusion that a man's soul was one thing, his trade quite another.

Dead men visited my cabin at night while I dreamt, peering with sightless eyes and brine-rotted skin. They bade me to follow them. My worn mattress felt stuffed with corn cobs. I awoke to find that a woman shared my bed with me. My belly warmer. The sheets failed to hide the smooth curves of her feminine frame. My hand reached for the soft curls of her hair, while my other hand rested near the small of her back. I leaned over her. The bed was damp. I pulled back the covers to see blood pooling into my bed. Her back was cross-hatched with open scars from which small maggots, like so much boiled rice, wriggled loose.

The woman with the kerchief rolled over.

Purplish bruises covered her sunken chest, and her empty eye sockets peered into my soul, chilling my heart. Her jaw strained opened and closed. I heard her voice, though her movements did not match her words. "No one will know. No one listens. No one cares."

That morning, I ordered the men to scrape our name from the hull of our ship. We await Death and Judgment. Let other ships think us outlaws. Better we sailed without a name, especially a name that reminded me of home.

The latticework proved a vain endeavor.

I was stirred from the fitful respite that passed for slumber—the hold beckoned me. As I crept down the stairs, the immensity of the silence struck me like a physical blow. Only the planks thundered overhead with the crew's trampling feet. None of the men dared enter anymore for there were no midnight revelries to be had. Sallow torchlight created looming shadows. The smell of sweat and unwashed bodies mixed with expelled waste assaulted my nostrils. I imagined the heaviness of bowels that it must have taken, the extreme need to relieve oneself, yet being taunted by a lone bucket too many strides away. With barely enough room to sit up, to have to crawl over rows of bodies while chained to another, it was better to ease oneself where he slept.

What remained of the Cargo waited on Njinga. Barely moving, content to lie in their blood and mucous, their emaciated bodies grated against their sleeping berths, the motion of the waves scraping away their flesh. They still didn't make a sound, not wanting to give any ears the satisfaction of their moans. A low mumbling drew my attention. I made my way to the rear of the hold only to find Njinga chanting to himself in whatever tongue he spoke. I recognized the reverential tone as a prayer. Suddenly, I could hear his words in my head.

"Father, let our bodies die that our spirits may go home free and receive us. Let their magic steal the earth. Ours shall steal the sky."

His eyes flicked open, coal black peering into me—as if his spirit flooded my soul and engulfed the hold with a crypt's quiescence.

I am the first to realize that we will never see home again.

§

The 30th of October, 1651

Damn this ship of death. Almost five months at sea, the last two weeks spent drifting after the storm broke, the wind dropped, and the waves calmed. We spread every available bit of canvas during our few good winds, but most days, the sails hung limp. Lifeless. The three masts of my once beautiful ship now only reminded me of a forlorn Golgothan hillside. We were a floating sarcophagus, an entity of desolation and fear, on a voyage to hell with a freight full of good intentions.

By my calculations, we were spitting distance from the shores of Bermuda, but no mewing gulls signaled nearby land. No black skies, no raging seas, only endless mist guided our days; an interminable gray, an imperfect misty dawn that heralded only further considerable horizon. A preternatural stillness matched by that of the cargo hold. Only Njinga remained. Sitting in the silence, eyes piercing the darkness with his faraway gaze. He cursed us, I know he did. Him and his heathen ways. I sealed him in his tomb of pressing bodies, the hold no longer my concern.

We had become a ghost ship that haunted the seas. I watched my own men grow sick and die. Mr. Hawkins was the last. So afflicted with a case of coast scurvy, his whole skin grew transparent with his swelling. His eyes sunk into his skull, his suffering was agony to witness. My fate would not be the same. I raised my pistol to my head. I heard Njinga's laughter in my head by day and by night. I feared that he might not let me die.

And I was out of rum.

Ah Been Buked

Monologue. Spoken by Viney Scott. Recorded at Parsons, Indiana, by John Henry Freeman, June 1935

It's best to leave some things forgotten.

Lord have mercy on my soul. Have mercy, have mercy, have mercy. I don't know why you want me to talk about all this in the first place. This here's a spirit stone, and I come out here to make sure it ain't been covered up. Things need tending to. No, I suppose not all things ought to be forgotten. Feels like I done been around here some thousand years or some such; moving, settling down, and moving again. 'Course I ain't been around quite that long, it just seemed that way when I got to thinking back.

§

I was nine years old when I watched my Poppa be whupped to death.

You ever been to a zoo? It don't matter none iffen you couldn't see the bars or chains. Look into their eyes and you could see that even beasts of the field know when they ain't free. Being in a cage did funny things to the body's mind.

§

"What you staring at, nigger? Don't you go on get no ideas about running off." Young Marse Chapman would say to me when he caught me staring off at the hills. Then he'd crack that whip. Let it land right next to me to give me a start. I was the same age as young Marse Chapman. He had a special hate in him, even then. I tried to stay away from him in case his hatred was a-catching.

Lord help a colored who ran off, iffen they caught him.

Old man Marse Chapman was always away on business. He left the young marse in charge. Used to be that we had a colored overseer, Uncle Moses, running the field coloreds. Though black like the rest of us, with a little bit of authority, he forgot who he was and where he came from. But young Marse Chapman was coming of age and was eager to prove himself. Told Uncle Moses he was too soft on us and took over. Young marse was generous with the bull whip.

§

35

I did little jobs to help the field coloreds: toted brush and bark, rolled up little logs, carried water around to our mens folk, and swept the yard. Mrs. Annalynn, old man Marse Chapman's wife, took a shine to me early on, and I spent many a day on her lap. With my thick braids of hair and my knobby-kneed li'l self sticking out of the burlap sack that passed for my dress, she said I was the smartest colored in the Ohio River Valley. Few of us coloreds had anything to do with no reading or writing as weren't no schools for us back then. And I wasn't one much for figuring anyhow. My smarts were in keeping my eyes and ears open and my mouth shut. Sometimes I wondered whether Mrs. Annalynn was trying to make herself feel better by taking me on. Owning other folks twisted a body up inside as much as it twisted up those you owned.

Mrs. Annalynn straddled her horse like a man, one leg on either side, and I rode behind her. Old man Marse Chapman hated it, saying that it wasn't none too lady-like. Mrs. Annalynn told him that he never seemed too terribly interested in ladies. Then she asked how Miss Clara rode. Not that she said, "Miss Clara"; but the dead need respecting and I don't speak like that. They never spoke much about it after that.

§

Aunt Clara.

We called everyone aunt and uncle out of respect, but Aunt Clara really was my kinfolk. After Mammy was sold, she watched out for me. When I asked her about the mole under my left eye, she said it was a black tear drop. I "cried for all of us," she said.

The field coloreds called Aunt Clara a conjurer.

One time, Uncle Moses tied her up to be beaten. There she was, all spread out for everyone to watch. Even those who resented her light skin didn't want to see her whupped. They feared for anyone who had to face the whip. But I saw her eyes. She weren't scared none. She just stared all boldly at him, practically daring him to whup her. Then Uncle Moses turned and walked away, like he forgot where he left her. No one was allowed to touch her.

One day, a cough settled in old man Marse Chapman's chest. A fever burned him up dead. Folks said he became a haunt, swore they saw his spirit walking about the shotgun houses. All I know was that Aunt Clara's eyes weren't so bold after that.

§

I opened the gates for Mrs. Annalynn, then rode into town with her to buy supplies. Afterwards, she wanted me to sit with her in the kitchen. That turned a few heads, because field coloreds never was allowed in the house, and house coloreds never worked in the field. But Mrs. Annalynn said that I had "special dispen'sion."

I think I was like a doll to her, someone safe for her to tote around and be her friend, who didn't talk back, but could keep her company. I was still surprised when she asked me, "Do you want to live with me in the big house?" She had an odd, dreamy sort of look in her eyes, as if she were already lost in special plans. Or hopes.

"I want to be with my Mammy." I don't know what got into me. My Mammy had long been sold off. I couldn't even remember her eyes.

Mrs. Annalynn grew red-faced, like I'd slapped her. Betrayed her worsen if I stole her prize cow and sold it to the neighbor she feuded with next door. Something cold replaced the light in her eyes. I knew that look from Uncle Moses' face. That was the last time she *asked* me anything.

I couldn't hate her, though. She just wanted a child to call her own again. No shame in that.

Only hurt.

§

Most days blurred into the next. Lying in my pallet on the floor, I slept until the guinea fowls woke me up. Well, until the roosters joined in. An old bell donged on some plantation up the road a ways, then more bells added to it, like the clanging was on a morning stroll up the road. By four in the morning, young Marse Chapman straddled his horse, a big, monstrous, wild-eyed beast that had a devil in him. Riding down to us, young Marse Chapman picked ham out of his teeth with a long shiny goose quill pick. The rising wind carried the smell of sow belly frying past the shotgun houses. The smell of hoecakes and buttermilk soon followed. The kitchen from the main house had different smells coming from it: cakes, hams, chicken and poke, taters and good egg and pone bread. Most times, I was lucky to get li'l pieces of scrapback each morning. We worked from sunup to sundown in family groups, that way we could help each other when someone got behind.

§

No, a spirit stone wasn't like a head stone, though sometimes it feels like a grave marker. Aunt Clara taught me about them. A spirit stone kept a part of a person's spirit so that they were bound to whoever owned the stone.

I dreamt that ivy took hold of it and dragged it away from me.

§

Hills bumped up all around the Chapman house, and the land stretched on far as the eye could see. A creek, cold and bubbly, crept through two caves before it passed through the property. It separated the row of shotgun houses the coloreds had from the rest of the estate and emptied into the river.

The Chapman's house, white and proud with all of its columns and iron gates, stood right along the road. A porch ran the full length of the house.

Old man Marse Chapman rocked back and forth on the porch, sipping at his glass of lemonade while Aunt Clara fanned him.

I don't know, maybe I was sixteen about then.

My favorite place was where the creek passed through the caves. It was near dark, but I wasn't worried none. I was supposed to be fetching water, but folks knew I had a way of lingering whenever I went. Whispers carried on the breeze. I tell you what, my poor little heart pounded so hard, I thought it was going to jump out my chest and swim upstream. I knew they could only be one thing: patrollers.

Sometimes we called them buskrys, poor white folks who had no slaves of their own, but who tracked runaway coloreds. Iffen they caught a lone colored out by themselves with no pass—'cause you had to have a permission slip to be off or away from your Marse's property—they would catch you and whup you or just sell you to a trader themselves. Iffen they returned you to your Marse's, he'd turn around and give you a proper whupping for running off.

So, I held my breath and crept along.

I listened carefully, trying to figure out where they was coming from, then I heard this woman speak with a slow, deep voice that made you snap to attention. I recognized her voice, which boldened my steps to find out who she was meeting with. I crept and I crept, not noticing the drop off til I was already tumbling down.

"Land sakes, Viney," Aunt Clara yelled at me. "You gave us a start. We thought them patrollers had us for certain."

As I dusted the leaves and dirt from me, a round-faced little boy crouched behind her.

"It's all right, Frederick, it's just Viney. She's clumsy and noisy, but we're safe. Me and Frederick were trying to figure out how to get this here paddle boat 'cross the river. Think you could get him to the other side?"

Aunt Clara only worked in the house and wasn't used to no real work, leastways so I thought. Maybe she worked one of her charms on me as she was so good at getting out of work.

"That li'l thing. I rowed bigger'n that for Mrs. Annalynn. I'm stronger 'n most men after working in the field for so long."

"His mother's waiting for him over the river."

Frederick's big brown eyes would haunt my dreams forever iffen I said "no."

The current was strong, but it hadn't rained in a spell, so we weren't in for too much paddling. My skinny, little arms trembled every time I set my oar to water. It wasn't the cold that sent a shiver up me and gave me goose flesh, it was the whupping I knew young Marse Chapman waited to give me should I get caught. Too scared to dare whisper to Frederick, I locked my eyes on the nearing shore, focusing on what Aunt Clara told me to tell them when I reached it.

As I neared the bushes on the other side, I realized I never even thought about what might lay across the river. Never had no account to since my whole world was Marse Chapman's farm. The world may as well have been flat with us threatening to fall off the edge. Other slaves talked about the other side of the river like it was the Jordan River and all freedom danced beyond it. I figured whatever was on the other side probably had marses and bullwhips and traders like anywhere else.

As soon as the boat bumped the shore, I started praying. Frederick clutched the back of my dress, wrapping up in the folds as if they were curtains. The dark had a funny way of pressing in on you from all sides. Even tree limbs seemed stark and unfamiliar in the gloom. I knew I wasn't alone.

Hands reached down and started to pull me up. I swooned, nearly dead from faint.

"Menare." I yelled what Aunt Clara told me. She said it was from the Bible. "Menare. Menare. Menare."

"Shh, girl," the bushes whispered with urgency. "We heard you the first time. Who else would be out here?"

That was when I first saw him. Zias.

Zias was a great big buck of a boy. No scars ran along his fine, dark skin, near as I could tell. And his soft, brown eyes had a sparkle to them. Full of hope. And freedom. Weak as I was, I slumped in his huge, strong arms.

"You hungry?" he growled. His gruffness held a gentleness in it, like he didn't know how to sound tender. But he tried.

"Yes'm" was all I trusted myself to say. I trembled as I ate. I don't know why. I wasn't cold, and I no longer feared young Marse Chapman's bullwhip.

I rowed poor colored across the river, most every Saturday afternoon and Sunday night, just to see Zias.

§

Aunt Clara taught me lots of things about men and women. Told me that some Marses handed out permission slips for colored to get married.

§

I only knew Zias once. It was beautiful, and I didn't need no marse's permission for it.

§

Young Marse Chapman, not so young by then, was quick to stop men. "Whose colored are you?" he'd always ask. Iffen the slave was reedy or sickly looking, young Marse Chapman would say, "You can't see my gals. You ain't good stock." Zias belonged to Marse Chapman's Uncle Silas, who started sending him around. Marse Chapman took one gander at Zias, tall and husky, like he was bigger and stronger than a horse. Normally, he'd have planned to use him as breeding stock, studding him worsen a horse. But Marse Chapman didn't like how Zias and me snuck glances at one another. His eyes got full of the devil whenever Zias came around.

Young Marse Chapman's big, mean self studied me. Not like he watched the other coloreds, but like I was a flower that he waited for the right moment to pluck. That worried my li'l soul. Nothing was more frightening than the devil showing mercy.

There was no room in his foul heart for anything close to love. Some folks whispered that young Marse Chapman intended to have me for himself. Maybe that li'l shriveled thing Marse Chapman called a heart pumped more of its hate through his veins not standing for anyone around him to have what he couldn't. I was his prize, and he meant to have me.

Not long after dark, he came around the houses. The door to our shotgun house creaked open, waking all of us. We all knew what the midnight creak meant. Old man Chapman slipped in on more than one occasion, usually when Aunt Clara was on her monthlies. It was a roll of the bones who would be selected. I hadn't been of age and had not aroused their attention. But now, he saw me with that look men got when they were heated up. He stood over my pallet. The other women rolled away, turning their backs and closing their eyes. Sorry for me, but relieved they hadn't been chosen. He crawled on top of me, all pawing hands, his weight pinning me as he grabbed at me. All I could think about was the stirring in my belly. I clawed and gave him what for. He came away from the houses, like a scalded bear. Folks whispered about it all through the night. But all I could think was that, if you wounded a bear, you better kill it.

Lord Jesus, have mercy on this poor, old soul of mine.

§

Every colored in the field knew that Marse Chapman was a thunder cloud waiting to break wide open and rain anger on us all. His eyes followed me everywhere, burning worse than the noontime sun. No one dared get near me, like I carried a "whupping plague" they could catch. He waited, patient as the wily serpent he was. Lord, how cruel that man was.

One day, without warning, young Marse Chapman spat and cussed something fierce, yelling about how we coloreds have forgot who was in charge. Leaping down from that big horse of his, he went after Zias. He didn't care that Zias wasn't one of his own. He was property, and Marse Chapman could always settle up what he owed. All the ruckus drew Mrs. Annallynn and Aunt Clara from the house.

All I thought of was how Poppa ...

... was a big man, strong and tall like an oak tree. When he took my hand, he swallowed me up like Jonah and the whale. Poppa worked leather, and, on that day, as Poppa fixed Marse Chapman's riding harness, the heat got to him. He fell over and tore the harness beyond repair. Now, iffen Poppa had been in his right mind, he'd have known Marse Chapman would have just had him make a new one. Uncle Moses had already gotten a talking to about damaging Marse Chapman's valuable coloreds. With his heat-addled mind, all Poppa knew was that bullwhip.

So, he ran.

Uncle Moses got out those loud, slobbering hound dogs and chased after Poppa. He caught him down by the caves, trying to lose his scent in the water. Dragging him in front of all the field coloreds, Uncle Moses took a piece of iron with little holes in it what he called the "slut." He filled the holes up with tallow and shoved it in the fire 'til the grease got sizzling hot. Then he held it over poor Poppa's back and let that hot grease drip on his hide. Every time I close my eyes I could still hear that scream.

After that came the whupping.

Uncle Moses brought his arm up high and held his bullwhip there. All the field coloreds gathered around. We'd recognized that delighted glint in his eyes, like a preacher caught up with the Spirit. He waited until he had our full attention, and ...

... let that whip fall hard on Zias' back. The first stroke of that whip was always the loudest, the one that made everyone jump. Lord Jesus, that first lick. He let loose a soul scream, crying out for all of us. His skin split open, a busted seam along his back, sputtering blood like a gutted hog.

Zias' back arched, drawing away from the bite of the whip. His knuckles turned white as he gripped the air. Tears rolled down his face.

Marse Chapman whupped him with the passion of a man knowing his wife.

Some turned away, they knew how things usually went: the thirty lashes, rubbing salt over his wounds, throwing the poor colored in the stock house, maybe chain him up a couple days with nothing to eat iffen the punishment was to be more severe.

Zias stared up at him, his soft eyes fading. Only two words formed on his lips. "Pray, Marse."

Young Marse Chapman paused when Zias murmured that. From the confused look on his face, he wasn't sure what Zias meant.

"You coloreds have forgotten how to work, and I aims to teach you."

Young Marse Chapman hitched Zias to a plow. Slipping a bit into his mouth and jerked him about by it, he worked poor Zias like a mule, beating him bloody and sore. Zias never ran off, neither. I read it in his eyes: he feared iffen he left, Marse Chapman would only turn on me.

Suddenly, Zias' big body slumped. Zias was dead.

Marse Chapman told us to leave him where he lie, as an example, and, iffen we moved him, he'd do the same to someone else. So no one touched him.

§

Lord have mercy on my soul.

§

To hear Aunt Clara tell it, when the universe was created, powerful stones soaked up the magic of creation. Like lightning striking the earth, they fell, bringing with them sparks of magic. Life and spirit fused, things of power. Lord, how she'd hunch over one of her chosen stones, painting it, doting on it like it was a baby. I wanted her to help me make one not too long after Zias died. It was a way to capture a piece of a person, to always remember them. I asked, "How do you know which stones have power?"

"You'll know. It's like the stone chooses you," she said.

§

Marse Chapman wasn't through with me, especially not after he noticed the swoll of my belly. The devil was patient.

"Soon as your baby comes. I will have you. And then you'll know The Swing."

When it came to cruelty, he studied better than a scientist. Marse Chapman had heard tell of other farms using something like it to punish their coloreds. They stripped a body before they whupped them, always trying to find different ways to take your dignity. They wanted the world to see you naked. I knew Marse Chapman would take special joy in tearing off my clothes in front of the other field colored, leaving me plum naked and humiliated.

"And then I'll sell that little nigger baby of yours."

§

The midnight creak didn't send a shiver through me. I'd snuck out like I was due to help someone across the river. Instead, I went to the big house. Aunt Clara let me in but didn't meet my gaze. I slinked up to young Marse Chapman's room. Marse Chapman snored lightly beneath me, undisturbed by the creak because he never had to be. He slept sound, wrapped in his privilege of being born a Chapman. He'd known birthdays, his Poppa, his Mammy. He'd never tasted a bullwhip. He might find a love and have a child and be able to know them in peace.

He was allowed to dream.

The stone grew heavy in my hand. I smashed it down on his head hard as I could. Marse Chapman raised up out of bed, his arms flailed in his sheets like a ghost flapping in the breeze. I brought the stone to bear again, but the light had gone out of his eyes. He tumbled forward, toppling off the bed, bashing his head against the night stand.

I was certain he went to hell, even though I didn't know how the devil could stand him.

§

No, I don't know how I felt. Sometimes you were better off not feeling. Feelings could grind you up, leaving you nothing but ... I feared the hate. I feared that hate might one day eat me up. The truth had a way of coming out, no matter how long you let a lie settle into you. So, I vowed I'd always remember how easy it was to hold a life in your hand and what not cherishing life could drive a body to do.

I waited all the next day for them to come round me up. I prepared myself to cross the Jordan and meet my Lord. But no one came. Mrs. Annalynn found him. Told everyone that he had a spell and fell out of bed. She walked right by me, glanced at my belly, and moved on.

§

My spirit stone chose me, and I chose Marse Chapman. It was Zias' grave marker since Marse Chapman wouldn't allow no proper grave. So, now he watched over Zias.

§

Lord Jesus, it was an awful business belonging to folks body and soul. Then one day, one of them Union boys, all tired and pale, came up to us.

"You're free," he said.

"No, you just having fun with us," I said. I don't think I understood what he was trying to tell us.

He didn't have much patience for my foolishness. "You're as free as I am."

Lord, how we sang and danced. I wanted to move across the river to put the plantation behind me and explore the world. But the Chapman house was all I knew, and I was afraid to leave it behind. It broke and bowed everyone. They never walked the same, a bent to their spirit as if they'd never be quite whole. The fear would always haunt me. That fear of the night reaching out, covering my mouth and dragging me back to that life. At night, low moans and cries might snap you fully awake, each sob picking a scab on your soul. Just cause some law said we weren't a slave no more don't mean everyone obeyed it.

So I stayed, ministering to my spirit stone. A memory kept for safekeeping. A pain so deep, it lost all meaning. A bit of Marse Chapman's spirit bound to it. to remind him that he was bound to me. Kept. Owned. In the cool of night, I could still feel the heat of his hate, but that was all right. I brushed the leaves from him and let him rest.

Lord have mercy on my soul.

A Soldier's Story

July 23, 1895 – Parsons, Indiana

"There are things ..." he started to say, but how do you begin such a horrific tale to one so young? "Once upon a time, there was a town under the spell of ..." Of what? Unsettling madness?

He casually stroked her downy, blonde hair, as if appreciating her beauty for the first time. Her small wood hewn bed framed her like an idyllic picture, just as he always imagined it would. Though it was the dream from a different life, he mentally pictured this very scene a hundred times. It inspired him to labor on when he hand-crafted each piece. He knew the nine months would pass too quickly when he started working the wood, and he wanted it to be perfect. Whittling away long, devoted hours on the headboard alone, he lamented that his skill didn't match his passion. Translating what he imagined into what he carved: a broad willow tree in a field of blooming flowers. Where better for his child to lay her slumbering head? She slept, innocent against the backdrop of violence, mayhem, and blood. It always came back to blood, so much of it on his own, still trembling hands. A miasma of despair, grief, and guilt, he only distantly recognized the hollow sounding voice as his own. He pressed on with the telling of the tale anyway.

"I've committed some awful things. Deeds of which I am not proud. Things a child ought not to hear. But things which I must tell you anyway.

"It hurts to remember, like a dull headache you get when someone wakes you too quickly from a nightmare. The story begins with Holten Owensby. That opportunistic devil."

She grimaced in her sleep, furtive sounds escaping as she jostled her blanket. Only then did he realize how sharp his words had become. No matter how many generations down the line she may be, she was still kin.

"I'm sorry," he whispered as he brushed her head with his hand, "but I have known the truth about that demon in men's flesh for far too long and kept silent. He couldn't wait for his father, a good man, mind you, to die before he started spending his money. A few financial setbacks had put him in a state most foul. He was one of the investors in the railroad endeavor through Parsons that slowly proved itself to be a Pyrrhic race. You knew, for those who wanted to know or cared to look, from the leer in his eyes that he had killed in his time. And that kill was still on his mind. Deep-set grey eyes, like murky reflecting pools hidden by shadow. His spare silver hair combed back to vainly disguise his bald top. His face swirled of shadows and distrust, helped in no part by his overgrown mustache that gave him the appearance of a character from a dime store western.

"Parsons was a sleepy little hollow, with aspirations of being a city. The last shot from the Civil War still echoed in the air as people moved there.

It was the perfect place for a man with a history he wished to forget to lose himself in. Free Negroes and escaped slaves settled the area just outside of the town. A few log cabins and meager shanties, more of an encampment than a town, but it was theirs. As Parsons boomed, so did the Scott settlement. That was all they wanted. We should've seen that. And they knew their place. Most of the time they contented themselves doing the jobs that no white man wanted to do. It was not as if they did not know that the Sheriff and his boys could come in and settle any disputes any way they saw fit. Such was the relationship between Parsons and the Scott settlement, like a town and her shadow. With the arrival of the trains, Parsons expected its growth spurt to continue.

"But there were only so many train jobs."

She slept, undisturbed in the glow of pale moonlight. Angelic. An ideal worth protecting.

"I was not worried about myself. I kept to myself, never wanting to draw too much attention. You live a life as long as I have, you learn a few things. I was tired of wars, whether they were revolutionary or civil. It was on such a field of battle where I was changed. It was easy to hide and feed among such death. Soldiering was all I knew. No, that wasn't true. Mine was the business of death and I was tiring of it. I tried to change, and I returned home. Folks didn't care about my peculiarities of habit and hours kept because I was the best furniture maker in these parts, 'cept'n maybe them folks in Amish country. Plenty of call for me, too, with all the newfound money people were making, not to mention the old monied families desiring to expand their interests. My neighbors, my friends, however, they worried for their jobs, their futures, and how they would take care of their families. People only grumbled, as they were wont to do, when jostled on the street, feelin' too pressed in by the Scott settlement. But that fear always simmered underneath. That 'it could all be taken away' fear; and just cause times were good and no one was goin' hungry don't mean that fear had gone. Fear that Holten preyed on.

"It was an election year, and, of course, there had been some lively electioneering going on in these parts during Cleveland's campaign. Folks knew that all of those Republican-voting Negroes were going to turn out in hordes come election day. That didn't sit well with many folks, especially those who already believed that with all the Negroes migrating here, they were going to vote away jobs from the local people. People thought they were going to lose their jobs. They thought ... what was said about their women and children ... terrible things. It was no excuse, I just wanted you to understand. You would think they had enough to fear with the things that moved in the night. The creatures they whispered about around the hearth fires. But fear blinds men to their reality. Fear snakes through them, takes hold of their heart and drives them to do dark things in its name. That was the nature of humanity.

"The sun, bold and bright, made for only a cool, sad day. We crammed into the courthouse, miserably hot because so many concerned citizens showed up. We had people at the door that only allowed Parsons locals in. Labor leaders fine-tuned the organ of resentment for Holten to soon come play. Rumors tore through the town presenting problems only politicians promised to fix. Rumors that more Negroes were due to be imported in from others states, to steal men's jobs. The mood became more hostile as the sun squat in the sky.

"Then that devil Holten stood up.

"'Parsons has changed,' he said, 'and is no longer safe for *good* folk. Right now, in our jail, sits an animal guilty of murder.'

"'Murder?' 'Who?' The whispers scattered like crickets in the night.

"Holten paused, letting the weight of his words carry, his fingers deftly dancing along the organ. He slowly revealed how earlier that day, Samuel Demory, an ax buried in his neck, was found dead. The blade did not match the savagery of the wound, the veins almost mutilated in the frenzy, but that didn't matter. The ax belonged to his long time workman, Ezekiel Walker. The same man guilty of … deeds most vile against Samuel's daughter, Rebecca. She still rested in shock, being treated by her mother at the Demory place. Rebecca Demory. She had spark,, that girl did. Her aristocratic manner she used to try and put on never once hid the gentle soul that did not hesitate to reach out to people. She stirred things within any who saw her. Made it difficult for them to keep their hungers at bay, no matter how God-fearing or disciplined they were.

"'Our women, our daughters, are not safe. How long will the good folks of Parsons suffer this?' Holten asked. 'Our women desire protection, and this is the only way we'll get it.'"

The man paused, stroking the curls of the sleeping girl. The rise and fall of her chest came in regular, even breaths. The way the moonlight fell on her face, swathing her like a shroud, only made her seem more winsome. More vital.

"If it hadn't have been this, it would have been something else. I know it in my soul. When you have a room full of blasting powder, the kind of spark doesn't matter. By late afternoon, the paper ran an editorial: 'Nab Negro for Attacking Girl.' The fact that he was already 'nabbed' and in jail eluded everyone. The article demanded—without actually calling for—the lynching of the Negro that very night. It ran beside a cartoon of Negroes bribed with beer, chicken, and watermelons carted in to be new voters to the area and steal jobs.

"Because apparently the flames apparently needed a little more fuel.

"Holten deputized everyone. It didn't seem to matter that he couldn't deputize his big toe much less anyone else. 'Niggers were guilty of crimes against whites,' he shouted to any doubters, 'that was all the authority I need.' The women, in their Sunday dresses—all calico and sunbonnets—paraded alongside us as if on their way to a show. A town full of good people, decent people, now overwhelmed by the sudden conviction of the rightness of their actions.

"My convictions, I thought, were unshakeable. I lived by a simple code which kept me alive for so long. To hear people murmur, there was no doubt that, come the next morning, they would be able to stand by what they did to that 'rabid beast,' Ezekiel. No one felt any sorrow over righting that wrong. But their shame was soon coming.

"Apparently, word had escaped to the Scott settlement about the storming of the jail and the justice to be carried out on old Ezekiel Walker. The people of Parsons didn't care. They wanted the Scott folk to know that any one of them could be next if they stepped out of line or forget their place. Even as the good people of Parsons were dispersing after our ... bonfire ... word got back to us that the Negroes were arming themselves. For a war. Can't say that I much blame 'em really, folks just defending themselves and their families. But niggers with guns? No one could have foreseen that. The very notion of that was disconcerting. A stand had to be taken. There had to be respect for the rule of law.

"Night dusted down to the song of dusk. A hot, sweaty dusk. The night color gave courage to many men who had been different during day hours. Men swarmed about, the hour too late for respectable women and children. It was a motley collection of overalls, thick tan shoes, and felt hats. They weren't thinking any more, not in the way men usually think. It was as if they were seized by a feeling, almost a presence, bigger than themselves, bigger than Holten Owensby, maybe bigger than Parsons. Like worker bees rushing about serving an unseen queen bee. I don't know what their intentions were, whether we wanted to secure our town or rush into the Scott settlement with the common goal of beating every Negro in the area. I really think we believed it was more of the former.

"They reached the crest of the hill where their meager cabins sat like Christ seated in judgment over our town. The people of Parsons labored beneath a feast of a moon. Between bolts of pine trees, oil lamps swayed in marched unison to the flop of their feet along the dusty road. Caught up in the urge that first made Cain splinter his brother's skull with a stone.

"The pull of blood. I recognized the quickening of the pulse. The metronome of the hunt. The taste of copper on the tongue. Blood drew them like a thirsty man to honeysuckle.

"No, not them. Us.

"The plaintive cackle of chickens first announced their presence as they neared the first farm. A shadow peered from behind the henhouse.

"'Evenin', gen'lmen,' Jim Archer said, his old shotgun, reminiscent of a Confederate provost's musket, cradled in his arms like a bouquet he'd come a-courtin' with. He tanned hides down at the Pruitt Shoe Company. A good man. Never tried to cheat you. He should've been running a middle buster, plowing his field, not challenging them.

"'Where you going with that gun, nigger?' Holten asked. I heard the voice as clear as day, yet it sounded as alien as anything I had heard. Angry, distorted, little more than a growl, not in control of his own faculties. Like a puddle of quicksilver, each of them was a drop that pooled together in one unseemly mass. One voice speaking for the whole.

"'Thought I might stick around. Use it iffen I have to,' Jim said in that steady, unintimidated voice of his. By light of day, this might simply have been a man protecting his family's farms, but that night, right then, he was only a nigger threatening white men with a gun. Part of me wanted to cry, 'Put the gun down and run, Jim. Don't be so damned proud.' But my silence, the conspiracy of silence which kept secrets long buried like cancer eating away from the inside continued to hold reign.

"'We takin' you down, boy.'

"The thing about quicksilver is that once you drop it, it scatters in little drops that you have to sweep up.

"But you could never track all the drops.

"Men pounced on Jim from the surrounding shadows. They jerked his gun high, with only a single shot fired off. Two men held him while others beat him. Others set his henhouse, and then his own house, ablaze. He must've sent his family to a neighbor's house. I could almost hear his wife pleading with his stubborn mule self to join them. Now, the only voice heard was an unsteady, terrified one that cried out to Jesus.

"'Southern niggers deserve a genuine lynchin'!' Holten coaxed, in mincing school mistress fashion, as if to school boys with their primers, all dirty grins and horrid chuckles. He danced about overturned chairs, climbing atop Jim's hay-filled wagon for a better view. Holten against the flames, the very picture of the devil incarnate, his features, dark and twisted in a wrathful shade of red.

"Frenzied whoops of carousing, between their cheers, their howls, and their imprecations arose at his suggestion. Even as the smoke seared my nostrils, through the tumbling smoke, buried in the flames, Jim was no longer Jim. No longer human, but some vague threat wrapped in flesh. Clubs smashed his head open with brutal efficiency, the poor cuss. Bloody, unconscious, near death. Lofted into the air, they passed from man to man, a battered ragdoll no one wanted yet everyone wanted a piece of. 'I got some rope,' someone yelled. A noose slid around Jim's blood-slickened neck. As he was hoisted into the air, the rope broke.

"'Get stronger rope,' another voice bellowed. It sounded like one of my neighbors, but again, the voice was distorted. Ugly. Barely human. Jim, however, was none the wiser and long past caring. In order to put the rope about Jim's neck, someone (I?) stuck his (my?) fingers inside the gaping scalp and lifted his head. What monsters we had become, to think nothing of the fact that my hands were awash in the man's blood. To drink deep of the violence to quench the thirst for blood.

"'Grab hold and pull! Pull for Parsons!' Holten yelled. We pulled Jim about seven feet off the ground and left him hanging in a grove of mulberries and locusts, a blood-smeared, sambo scarecrow. I drew water from his well. Tepid water, tasting like beech trees and old bucket, but it was wet in my parched throat. Though my thirst remained unabated. The evening had barely begun.

"We set afire the shacks of poorer Negroes who lived in the surrounding area. The flaming wood skeletons painted the night in amber hues. We stoned and clubbed Negro men, women, and children, whoever we came across. We were a mess of people tramping about in the mud; muddy, despite the fact that it hadn't rained in quite a spell, but you stomp enough people, your boots'll get wet just the same.

"I don't know if you knew or not, but I was a gunner in the war. Worked as swift as we could. Focused, we were. The labor was meticulous, or so it seemed to the other calvary men. We was always asked, 'How do you remember what all you have to do in that confusion?' I became numb to it, if I were ever truly conscious to it to begin with.

"The key was to concentrate on the work. Experience which came in handy that night. We destroyed any saloon or business that catered to

Negroes. We overturned the tables, drank the liquor, broke the windows, then torched the place in view of hundreds of spectators.

"As the night wore on, the creature we had become had to find new ways to amuse itself. Make no mistake, on the fringes of the chaos, I fed. Blood smeared my lips and dappled my neck. But the blood on me was out of thirst. Primal necessity. No one glanced a second time in my direction. In the shadows of night, however, neighbor reveled with neighbor, spurred on by their own blood sport. We was all a-whoopin' an' a-hollerin'; having a gay, ole time of things. We were heady on the intoxication of that night's pursuits, emboldened by the fine liqueur of fear. I was blood drunk. Fear—ours and theirs—swept us along. Fever infected our brains, and we were a brigade of possessed madmen—grinnin' devils, teeth looming large and yellow in the amber glow of the torches, going about the business of hell.

"The frightful din of windows breaking. The clutter and clang of fences being knocked over. The screaming. The caterwauling. Babies crying, mewling, like they were past scared tears and simply awaited what they knew was coming. Or worse. Eyes wide open taking in everything that they saw, they were just too young for their brains to know what to do with the information. Not crying a bit, just staring, with dead eyes, eyes no child should have.

"Shooting residents as they ran through smoke and flames became a game, monstrous fun, if one were to judge by the laughter, hollering, and clapping. One Negro, in particular, gave us quite the sport of a chase. That crazed fool dashed from his burning home. We fired by the score, not to hit him, only to scare him into running. I kept waiting for a fox hunting bugle to be blown. He zigzagged between the few buildings that remained untorched. The men fanned out, more amused than perturbed, between the shacks and sheds, eyeing the crawl spaces and nooks that our quarry had to know far better than we. Some men had been foolish enough to follow him directly and were soon tangled up in trash.

"Unfortunately, for him, his panic at our proximity took him down an alleyway. The nearest three men or so followed him in. He regained his senses long enough to use his head. He smacked the first man on him, knocking him clean out, which gave the rest of them pause, pause enough for him to scamper past them.

"I found myself rooting, even praying, for him, but only the way you cheer for the hopeless horse in a race. God heard my prayer as well as any made for myself the night I was cornered trying to fight past just as ancient a hate on that fated battlefield so long ago. Only the Negro's fate was more merciful. All it took was one well-aimed shot. The Negro leapt into the air, his sprawl met with our shouts of approval. As the flames crept toward his body, he writhed, attempted to get up. A few warning shots kept him low. The flames marched on. He looked up at me with his yellow eyes, desperately searching out hope. His veiny hands pulled him away from the flames' grasp, faster than the fire moved to catch him.

"Someone shouted that his arms should be broken, see how fast he'd crawl then. A man stepped forward and brought his heavy boot down upon the Negro's arms. He stomped until a bone poked through the flesh. The terrible snap it made."

The scrape of his boots as he paced along his wood floors drew him out of his revelry. The old, rocking bed creaked as she rolled over in her sleep. It neared dawn now. Soon she would wake, full of hope and promise. So often he'd visited those of his line from when he was human. Not to watch over them but to see what he'd missed. To touch, to rekindled, whatever remained of his humanity.

The story was almost done now.

"The soft glow of the burning moon showered the Negro shanties, a mournful luminescence over the ashen countryside. The low murmur of wind whispered through the tree branches. We had cut a bloody swath from one side of the Scott settlement to the other. I don't know how much was left. I only knew the one cabin that stood in front of me. Mocking as all of the Scott settlement had mocked Parsons and what we stood for.

"The single log cabin room was built of logs split open and pegged together. From my window-side vantage point, one window, two doors. The wind whistled through the black cracks of the wall boards. The black earth along the floorboards crunched beneath soft footfalls. A woman hummed as she tended the black iron kettle that swung above the fire. She pressed her delicate hand against the small of her back to ease whatever back strain she may have had. The backdrop of the fire against her robe revealed how full with child she was. She slumped wearily into a chair, the sole furnishing in the room except for the pallet in one corner and a spinnin' wheel and loom in the other.

"She had a wheel an' loom in one corner of the cabin. Her son scrambled into her lap, enthusiastically clutching a tattered hand-me-down children's story book. An oil lamp burned unsteadily above them as they stole a moment to read.

"Their brown eyes strained against the fine print. Her pointed nose, straight and long, set against her high cheekbones. Her skin, the color of leaves in the fall, she kissed her son with the loving affection I'd seen your mother so often show you.

"That was when we heard the scraping sound.

"They looked up out the window. I scrambled out of view as I heard the sound. I wondered why I chose to get out of sight, though I had no reason to hide. I knew the all too familiar sound, but maybe she didn't. So far away from everyone else, she may have been too far removed from 'the trouble.' Or maybe her husband had left her there while he went out to protect them. Maybe that's who she thought she heard approach as she excitedly scanned the surrounding woods. But I knew. The woods were deathly still. A throbbing silence. A womb song. Interrupted only occasionally by the rustling of leaves caught up in the night's breeze. And the scraping sound.

"The scraping sound drew nearer.

"Apprehension must have fanned the embers of dread in her soul, with the dawning realization of the scraping sound. The sound of men on a mad march, like papal warriors on yet another unholy crusade. The scrape of gun barrels against tree branches, the early dawn of nearing torches from all sides.

"'Manna?' I heard the little boy ask. He clutched her desperately, perhaps sensing her own fright. Fear-dilated eyes frantically scanned the room.

"Holten was the first to enter probably because he knew her folk was away. 'What have we got here?' he said with a devil's drawl.

"'Nothin', suh,' she said. I truly feared for her in that moment. My soul filled with an unspeakable dread. The loose pile of bedding shifted behind her.

"'You lyin' ta me, girl?' he said. His shotgun issued a single report.

"Executed for her crime of hiding her child. I felt her deep-set eyes poring over me, accusing me, as her limp and lifeless body collapsed into a heap on her floor. Her blood mixed with the dirt, making it look like she bled mud.

"The wee boy was torn in two by the second report of the shotgun. Blood sprayed the cabin walls. Shot just because ... The room filled quickly with the odor of blood. Blood smells. The hovel smelled of a butcher's shop, at the time of an animal's butchering. The thick, musky, biting aroma of blood and the earthy odor of slaughtered meat, that was what I smelled that night.

"'Look what we got here, boys,' Holten said, spying the risin' in her belly.

"'What you reckon we ought'n do with it?' someone asked.

"'Someone here needs a doctor,' Holten said, pulling out his hunting knife, 'and looks like I'm the nearest surgeon.' The flesh made a horrific sound as it was torn, not unlike the gutting of a hog. Her open eyes were long past caring. Her insides ripped open as she lay in a pool of her blood. He paused for a moment then found my gaze. And he smiled the same terrible grin he gave me when he spied me hovering over Samuel Demory's body, my mouth buried in the open rictus of the man's throat. No revulsion, no horror, only the light of damnable opportunity in his eyes. He resumed his carving until a small purple fleshy mass was pulled from her, sputtering mewls as it gasped for breath. Holten carried it outside with the casual disdain of a man carrying one of his dog's newborn pups. 'It's over, boys,' Holten jabbed his knife through the infant into a willow tree, letting it hang. And he stared at me with knowing eyes. Leaving it for me, scraps for a dog from his master's table. 'Let's end things.'

"It didn't take long for the fire to consume the cabin. The tongues of flames wagged, swollen with the gossip of hate, serenaded by the morning song of whippoorwills. The crackling and spitting of logs, like mocking laughter. They tossed the woman into the fire. Blood splattered their shirt sleeves as if they labored at an abattoir. It was then that I realized that in the light of morning, with time to reflect on what they'd done, they would be able to meet one another's eyes without care or remorse. Unashamed. Plastered with mud, shivering in the pre-dawn air, my time drew near, an empty sort of fear all over, so I ran to beat all.

"Holten blamed the whole affair on 'Negro agitators.' The conspiracy of silence consumed everyone. From the town leadership down, no one wanted to press the matter. No copy of the newspaper that riled so many of us could be found, not even in the archives. It was as if the paper skipped a day in its publishing history. The state attorney in Jefferson County claimed that he couldn't prosecute anyone because he was unable to find a single person who witnessed any citizen committing violence that night. No one had that look, that tainted, guilty look of barely-held, barely-hidden secrets.

"I'm tired of the hate. I'm tired of the unceasing thirst, that soul ache, which can drive someone to depths they'd never imagine. Even those that prey in the night trembled before the malice of the human heart unchecked.

"It is almost morning. I had it in my mind to drain you. Prevent you from growing up in this cesspool. But who am I to judge.

"I'm so tired. And the sun will be up soon. It will be a beautiful view."

Shadow Boxing

The roar of the crowd burned in Lee "Stagger" Jackson's ear, a hornet's nest of hate and catcalls. He closed his eyes beneath the blindfold, making himself undistracted by tricks of the light. And he waited. At the hollow clang of the bell, Stagger retreated to his corner. Hastily-strung ropes formed a twenty-by-twenty canvas-topped "ring." Four other gloved men, also Negroes, skulked around its breadth and width behind their own blindfolds with no obvious plan beyond flailing about. A hilarious spectacle for the jeering audience who watched them. His opponents fought solely from fear, and, though it was a powerful motivator, fear also gave them away.

Tall, thick-bodied with the power of a 90-horsepower automobile, Stagger listened for the drag of heavy foot falls against the canvas. His massive upper body chiseled from the heart of a mountain atop his oddly slender legs, Stagger stood upright. His generous nose and thick lips would have made tempting targets for a sighted opponent, though he kept his fist steadily cocked, a spring-loaded weapon in need of release. The same way some folks had music in their soul and couldn't help but give voice to the song in their hearts, Stagger fought to fight. He also understood that commitment to his craft didn't stop with the match; they demanded he put on a show.

As they always did, his thoughts idled to the last memory of his father. The frantic, desperate thrashing as he fought the men determined to slip a noose around his neck. How his legs kicked and strained, dancing about without purchase, struggling against the twin implacable foes of the rope and gravity. And how the harder he fought, the louder the crowd cheered. Cutting through the din of the audience, Stagger focused on the shuffle of feet. The echo of closeness. The heat of pressing bodies.

This wasn't Stagger's first battle royal, though he hoped it would be his last. Hopping the freight, he'd ridden through Memphis, St. Louis, and now Springfield, grinding out enough dollars to live on. Tonight, a three-dollar purse hung in the balance. The fight would be fairer if he were the only one blindfolded. At his last battle royal, the four other fighters were friends, so their plan was to rush the stranger, agree on a winner, then split the purse. It ended the same way this one would.

"They call you Stagger 'cause that's how I'm gonna leave you." The first man painted a bull's-eye with his tongue. A roundhouse to the jaw stopped the jibber jabber.

"They call me Stagger cause that's how I left your momma last night." Stagger was as good with his mouth as he was with his hands, often terrorizing his opponents before they had a chance to throw the first punch.

The nearest man actually growled at him as he threw his slow wind-up of a punch. Stagger side-stepped the arcing whoosh and countered with a devastating shot to the head. Two opponents down in two punches, the others rushed him, bumping into each other, panicking them to step back and start swinging. The crowd roared in rising delight.

A disconcerting presence fluttered at the edge of his senses, the notion that someone else was in the ring with them struck him. At first, he feared a con similar to one he was subject to back in St. Louis, when someone hid behind a curtain, and, whenever he brushed by, an unseen assailant pummeled him in the back of the head. Stagger chanced opening his eyes to count too many shadows against the wan light and, as if surprised by his own reflection, began dodging and weaving.

The shadows coalesced back into two figures, and his vision's clearing left him feeling foolish, as if he had been caught doing something unwholesome. A shot to one of the remaining men's midsection dropped him to his knees; Stagger imagined the man's face, eyes no longer focused as if lost in prayer. Tottering like an ill-balanced sack of potatoes, the last chump's body realized all the fight had fled him and fell.

The dock warehouse's closeness left the cloying taste of sweat and cigar smoke on Stagger's tongue. He stalked the last man around the ring. The laughable melee came to an end with a flurry of punches as Stagger trapped the last man in a corner against the ropes, making it difficult for him to break left or right. Flashing a foolish grin, he took off his blindfold. The crowd threw coins into the ring, a gratuity for a good show. He shook the image of his father's bulging eyes staring back at him through the charred mask of his face. And the disturbing memory of the children who ran around selling bits of his father, his fingers and toes, as souvenirs of the evening. In the end, this was a fight, and the coins spent better than pride. He had sought attention all his life. Now everyone knew his name.

Stagger Jackson.

§

The cellar smelled of decaying mushrooms and other things that thrived in the dark, but it served well enough for their purposes. Stagger pummeled a heavy bag, sounding like swatting a wet mattress. Nan ran him through his paces. The old man's raspy cough, a phlegmy death rattle, didn't hide his gin-soaked breath. Rheumy eyes studied Stagger's movements as a sparring partner riddled him with blows. Stagger barely flinched, training his body to absorb blows faster. Once the last of his workout fury was spent, Stagger settled into his rubdown.

"What'd you think, boss?" Nan asked, as his spidery fingers, with wrinkles like fine webbing, wound their way along his back muscles. With a mixture of beef brine and borax to pickle his skin, he massaged Stagger's head and neck twice a day.

"I think I'm tired of scraping for chump change when there's real money to be made out there," Stagger said, despite the fact that he always earned on top of the purse by betting on himself. The youngest of seven children, three of whom died before they reached school age, he knew from poverty and spent his life making up for it.

"That was quite a thump you put on. We'll get there." Nan kneaded his shoulders.

"When? I feel like we're barnstorming for hayseeds. Who's up next?"

"Baby Doc."

"Again? That lump of coal couldn't stun flies with his punches." Stagger turned his head.

"No, suh." Nan kept rubbing, unmoved by Stagger's bravado.

"Can you give your 'yassa boss' routine a rest? It's giving me a headache."

All of his familiar black rivals had been beaten two and three times over. Called Mysterious because he always found a new way to cheat, Tobias "Mysterious" Williams lost to him three times. Marcus "Mule Kick" Harrison was always good for a four-round knockout. The last time he fought Miles "The Abilene Wonder" Louis, he was kneed in the groin for his trouble and won due to foul.

"We gonna be ready, boss. Maybe in Chicago."

"Yeah. Maybe."

"What hole did you crawl out of tonight?" Imogene Watson strode into the room with nary an announcing sound. The milky skin of her face drew too tightly across her skull, her haunted eyes always chased the next thing to hold her attention. Her arms looked uncomfortably thin, and she had no ass to speak of; but Stagger could see the hurt in her. Some women measured their lives in self-destructive inches. Though the flame was fit to singe her, she gravitated to the life. She exchanged hard glances with Nan as the old man didn't like any woman breaking their routine. Smoking her cigarette, she hugged herself to stave off a chill of her spirit in the warm evening.

"Dock yards. Battle royal."

"You need a well-connected manager. At least a better connected one." She took another drag of her cigarette and blew it in the opposite direction of the men, an excuse to not have to look at them. "Tell me I'm wrong."

"Look at you, trying to wear some pants." Stagger sat up, and Nan draped a robe around him.

"Someone ought to."

"Watch yourself now. Don't start speaking out of turn." Despite his gleaming smile, a hint of threat undergirded his words, a mild bark to settle her down. He wasn't going to be talked down to, even by a white woman. His prize, as if he'd won yet another bout in life.

"Do you remember what you promised me when you asked me to come with you?" Imogene asked.

"The life. The sporting life."

Imogene studied each wall in turn then took another drag of her cigarette. "There's someone I think you ought to meet."

§

The Black Belt of Chicago ran just south of the Loop and down by State Street, some thirty or so odd blocks. A world of Negro entrepreneurs catered to the needs of their own. From Eighteenth to Twenty-second streets, between Federal and Halstead, was the Levee District, where vice (such as blacks and whites mingling together) was tolerated. And nowhere was vice more tolerated than at Out. A series of joined three-story houses, Out catered to the elite of the sports, the dream child of one Harlem Williams.

The sauntering, towering figure of Stagger Jackson certainly cut a dash in his new togs: green waistcoat, fresh creases in his pantaloons, and patent leather boots. An ermine silk scarf over a tasty double-breasted suit, Harlem had set him up just fine. Imogene clung possessively to his arm. Draped in an elegant black dress, she, too, shone in the Black and Tan club. A mosey of a walk allowed bystanders a chance to admire them.

"Stagger, Stagger, Stagger. Glad you could make it." Harlem turned to Imogene, took her hand, and kissed it. "Baby, you know you're welcome at Out anytime, anytime."

"You want me to wait here?" Imogene withdrew her hand and held it to her chest as if to suppress a cough.

"I don't have to daddy you 'til at least my third drink." Stagger dismissed her, a stray to be handed off. He set his suede, pearl gray afternoon gloves next to his drink and leaned his cane against the table. He turned to Harlem. "I want a shot at the champ."

"Straight to business, huh? You think you gonna get a whiff of the white man's belt after what Jack Johnson did? You box in his shadow. Even got a white lady on your arm like you ain't learned a gotdamn thing."

"What can I say? I learned to walk upright. With pride." Stagger smiled, his teeth capped with gold, and diamonds duffed his cuffs and fingers. The long-schooled coloreds didn't lead an easy life either, not one they could call their own. The weight of the whole race bore down on them at every turn. He knew how they were seen, no matter their pedigree. Brutish apes with savage, unintelligent eyes, without the mind for higher society but fit enough for menial labor. Thick lips drawn back to reveal threatening teeth ever eager to tear into soft, white flesh. Large hands and swinging penises ready to grope and penetrate their precious white women. Then they spent their energies trying to convince white people how gentle and civilized they were.

Not the shadow he brought with him, but the shadow white folks planted in him. It grew, deeper and more tangled, a spreading kudzu across his soul.

"Then box your pride 'cause that ain't the way things work. And you know that ... so I don't know why you got your chest all puffed out." Harlem tamped the bottom of a box of cigarettes, sizing Stagger up during his little ritual. "Now, I got money. And, as long as there's at least one crooked bone in a man, money has connections. I can set up a meeting."

"That's all I ask."

§

A knife scar etched Tolliver's left cheek, a souvenir from a bar fight gone awry. Unlike the champ, Tolliver crossed the color line: he fought whomever for whatever as long as the money was guaranteed. Stagger could have taken Jack "Little Sullivan" Tolliver in the first round if he were so inclined. Tolliver took six, seven, eight jabs before his guard went up and fought from a bit of a crouch which made him appear smaller than he was. But Stagger needed to draw things out.

"You punch like a woman," Stagger chatted to the crowd and other corner.

"Fight like a white man, you yellow cur." Tolliver kept jabbing though he never connected.

The bell pealed. A short, red-faced man appeared apoplectic with Stagger's continual taunts. "Get the lead out," he cried out to Tolliver. Stagger never sat down between rounds, a tacit jeer for them to deal with. Let them measure his manhood that way. Searching for Imogene, he scanned the crowd. A colored man sat along the swiftly constructed fence. A wave of vague unease washed over him, though the details of the man's face were obscured by distance. Mouth agape, he bulged his eyes like a coon from a minstrel show in an accusing glare. The look of his father, shaped by the sting of a whip. The wildness driven through his mind by the taste of a bit in his mouth. The sullen emptiness of waiting to be bought out of slavery. Defeated, broken, and chained, even when the jangling no longer echoed with his every step.

The bell tolled for the start of the next round, drawing Stagger's attention back to the bout. Jogging to the center of the ring, his left arm leading, he measured the distance like a scope on a rifle waiting for the shot of his devastating right jab. From the corner of his mind, as he sensed the movement rather than saw it, he knew the colored man had stood up. As Stagger circled, the man pivoted, his left arm extended and his right hand cocked.

"Who told you you were a fighter?" Stagger cuffed Tolliver to wake him up, then bumped him to throw the timing off his punches.

"I'm going to send your nigger balls into your mouth," Tolliver muttered.

"I guess I'll find out what your wife's been tasting."

Stagger let loose a barrage of punches, sloppy and without technique, only to spy a matching flurry of motion. His mirroring fan became his anchor: when he swayed to the right, his doppelganger swayed to the right; when he ducked Tolliver's awkward, slow roundhouse, his admirer also ducked.

"Nigger." The voice lulled, clear in Stagger's ear like he were right next to him. "You ain't nothing but a nigger."

Distracted, Tolliver caught him with an uppercut which lifted him off the ground. Shaking his ferrous skull sadly, Stagger dabbed the blood with his glove and hunched his shoulders. Showtime was over. The crowd grew silent as Stagger slowly dissected the man with punches where he stood. The Indianapolis Freeman later reported that Stagger danced around the flat-footed white man all night, never taking a punch and that he sealed the deal with a "right in the kisser" in the ninth round. When Stagger glanced up, his dark twin was gone.

§

"Was all that signifying worth it?" Harlem chomped on a too-large bite of catfish, chewing in wet gulps.

"They weren't going to give me a fair shake no how. It was worth it to see their faces." Stagger made peace with the "you'll fight who I want, when I want, for what I want. If you want to fight at all" rant from the superintendent by calling it an opportunity. With enough fights he hoped to shame the champ into a bout, even if it meant just the two of them in a cellar.

"Next time you in a mood to get us lynched, let me know so I can skip the meeting."

"I don't take orders from no one."

"You one of them 'New Negroes.'" Harlem pointed his fork at him, needing to swallow the last bite of food in his mouth before speaking further. "Thinking you all but free."

"I need to believe that I have some sort of say over my life." Stagger jabbed a wayward piece of his steak. He'd gotten two steaks and three beers during the course of this verbal spanking. He'd eat an entire purse's worth of food if he let the man ramble on.

"You got boundary issues. You don't know how to pick your spot and work within it."

"I don't know my place?" Stagger raised the question and wanted to believe the iron of his indignant tone. "Good."

"We don't want to get above ourselves."

"If we were any less above ourselves, we'd be underground."

"But you got nothing. Just living the life of a sport," Harlem said.

"Better than most." Stagger smiled his gold-capped, toothy grin at the passing waitress. She returned with a beer and a shot of whiskey, both of which he downed under Harlem's baleful watch. The banter flared without heat. He studied his shadow as it danced along his plate. Reaching for his glass, the near translucent cast struck him as a pale reflection of himself, intimately bound up with his life. His soul.

"See, that's your problem: you think you a pimp. When the day comes, make it a bout, but make no mistake, when we say it's time, you swallow that cold, dark thing you call pride and lose that fight."

§

A jagged scar of a man, Luke "The Stackhouse" Kutchner was a hard-eyed white bruiser of the first order. Uninterested in the finer aspects of the art, he charged opponents and usually pummeled them mercilessly within a few rounds. Kutchner immediately re-thought his strategy after his initial assault swiped nothing but air and received two quick right jabs and south paw in the jaw for his troubles. Now he circled Stagger with quiet, menacing assurance.

"We need to get their hopes up, drive the fervor to have a white hope beat this uppity fool down. Be the villain you need to be," Harlem had ordered. *"This keg of beer was a chump, but you need to make a show of it, so let it go a few rounds."*

"I'll trim you good," Kutchner snarled, saliva mixed with blood over his protective mouth bit. The pink-tinged drool dribbled along his chin.

Stagger remained silent. No taunts about Kutchner being used as an outhouse. No chatter about the man's mother, wife, or sister and the dreams they had of bedding such a black stallion. No jibes aimed at Kutchner's corner or even the row of reporters who rendered his every comment into pidgin English despite his literate affect. Only a cold, pale silence as he listened to the Shadow.

"You're a tough nigger," the voice said, low at first. A movement in the stands distracted him and allowed Kutchner to graze his temple with a glancing shot. The crowd erupted, jubilant that Kutchner had finally landed anything solid after three rounds. Stagger searched the crowd. The darkness moved, an ebon shark amidst the sea of white faces.

"You're a clever nigger." The walking blot oozed among the onlookers, drawing strength from each stained soul it touched. An explosion of flashbulbs temporarily blinded him, leaving Stagger's vision playing tricks on him. The crowd was rows of pale pickaninny dolls, with leering eyes, too big for their heads. Their teeth wizened to points, in grins of frozen rictus. Open mouths ready to rend. Sweat stung his eyes. The ring canted beneath him, the corners not meeting at proper angles.

"You're a pretty nigger." The voice neared and filled his ears like the roar of an ocean crashing against a galleon. Tauntingly near, yet just out of reach.

Kutchner made his move. A snap of a punch caught Stagger square in his face and exploded his nose. Splattered blood filigreed Kutchner's face, to his delight. Buoyed by the crowd, he led with his left hand and countered with his right jab, Stagger absorbed every blow, as if savoring every bite of a succulent meal.

"At the end of the day, that's all you'll ever be. Just another nigger."

"Wake the fuck up," Nan yelled at him from the corner.

Stagger fell into the ropes. Kutchner, too confident, bought the feint. He waded in with a full-fledged attack. Stagger danced under his roundhouse and landed an uppercut connecting flush with Kutchner's jaw. It sent him flying through the air and left him unconscious for ten minutes after the ring cleared. While Stagger collected his purse and winnings from betting on himself, the crowd booed Kutchner when he struggled to his feet.

§

News of his final fight came down from Harlem. A clubber named Ronald "The Dock Saint" O'Leary, a solid opponent who'd racked up enough wins to be credible, but he was no champ. Not even a true test, with Stagger being the clear favorite, as he should've been; but the arrangement Harlem struck with the superintendent demanded that Stagger go down. In the eleventh round would be good, so additional money could be earned by replaying the match on movie reels. Stagger brooded in silence, haunted by could've beens.

Imogene didn't bother to hide her disapproval at the half empty bottle of unlabeled whiskey. Her low slung breasts filled out her evening dress. With a forlorn face of uncried tears, she skulked about as if on a barefoot walk atop shards of glass. Her left arm crossed her chest almost propping up her cigarette-clutching right hand as if protecting her, or blocking his view. He hated the way she looked at him, with a mix of pity and resentment.

"They all use me," he began, not really talking to anyone in particular. Stagger had let his conditioning slide. Still firm and imposing, one could still see hints of flab along his once finely cut flanks. "Some people see me fight and win and feel good. Some people want to cheer for my defeat to feel good. No matter what I do, I'll make people happy. If they ain't got whatever they need by now, all my boxing ain't going to help nothing."

"So, you took the money," a slow cloud of cigarette smoke encircled, her voice clotted with disgust. "You have no soul if you can do this."

"Fifteen thousand is a lot of money. We can live the sporting life for a while on that." He wanted to be somebody powerful, somebody with clout. To be the man worthy of the way she used to look at him, with stolen glances smoldering with admiration and spent passion. "Look at you: drawn to the life, bought, and traded by the players. Might as well be on an auction block your own damn self."

"So, you blaming me now?" Imogene drew her hair back behind her ear and finished her cigarette.

"I don't think you're hearing me." Stagger sighed. The moment passed. Eyes hardening, he straightened then fixed his gaze on her. "You giving out misery like it was on sale."

"Like you're so different. You're just mad because you're theirs and you just won't admit it. You've turned us both into niggers. At least I've accepted it."

The back of his hand raised. She flinched, knowing terror lit her face, and he hated himself for being the cause of it. An apology bubbled up as his hand lowered, but his throat grew thick and choked it off. Anger still managed to squeeze through. "You see what you almost made me do? Go on now, get out."

In the gloom, Stagger resigned himself. Some things were meant to be, though he had only a dim notion of what he should do.

§

Movie stars, gangsters, politicians, sports, and up-and-coming boxers filled the stands. Every seat sold out, the aisles choked with gangs of rowdies and howling pandemonium. Little boys climbed out over the rafters of the pavilion, anxious to see the fight.

O'Leary came in at 190 pounds, Stagger at 209, with "The Dock Saint" being the taller of the two by half an inch and having a two-inch reach advantage. The Irishman was flat-footed while Stagger could cut off the ring. The tall clodhopper, with wisps of reddish blonde hair and a toothless smile, was discovered harvesting beets. He had the bearing of a school bully, the kind of boy who abused opposing players and accrued constant penalties for misconduct during sporting events.

Escaping the latrine smell of cellar runoff, every name was hurled at Stagger as he approached the ring. With a resolute grimace, Stagger hardly blinked. Fighting in front of hostile crowds killed the dream of fair treatment, not that it mattered.

"You flat-chested coon." O'Leary was a mockery of everything he was about.

Coming out quickly with his hands up, Stagger moved under the punches, then countered with a left hook followed by a series of jabs. Despite the hard banging to his ribs, O'Leary could take punishment and keep coming. He threw a combination, but Stagger deflected most of the blows with his gloves.

O'Leary's shadow moved independently of him, countering Stagger's shots. The shadow, despite the lights, withdrew into O'Leary, winding itself around him. All trace of O'Leary disappeared, his skin darkened in a penumbra of hate. Features flattened into unrecognizable shapes except for eyes that became white slits of anger, The Shadow's maw revealed shark-like teeth, rows upon rows, ready to grind his flesh and chew his spirit. A roundhouse right connected with Stagger's face; the blow heard at ringside. His legs buckled some, but the ropes caught him.

Strong, impervious, fast, patient, the unrelenting Shadow showered him in punches, each blow jolting him. Stagger's face burned. He was no longer able to feel his feet. In the next moment, he found himself sprawled out on his back. The crowd counted in unison.

"2 ... 3 ... 4 ..."

"No witty rejoinder?" The Shadow asked. O'Leary couldn't have spelled rejoinder on his best day. Stagger merely glared at him as the ref checked him out. "Say something, damn you."

Stagger willed himself to his feet. "My name is Stagger Jackson."

Dancing in and out before the Shadow could react, Stagger worked its body. The Shadow's sides heaved for breath in jagged sears. But by the eighth round, a sinking feeling of despair settled on his corner. He was losing points with every round.

"Box, damn you," Nan begged, his fists clenched as if he was ready to hit Stagger himself. "Let him come after you."

"I can get him." Blood trailed down Stagger's face. A cut had opened over his eye during the fifth round when he dodged into the Shadow's uppercut. The ringside doctor battled to stem the bleeding.

"Not if you don't jab. I'm going to throw in the towel." Nan's gaze was dispassionate and unfamiliar. The thin veins of his eyes a maroon frieze of rivulets.

"You throw that towel, I'll kill you myself. You just do right by my family. And Imogene."

In the twelfth round, Stagger felt two ribs go with a roundhouse he wandered into. The Shadow continued to grind him down one punch at a time, one round at a time. The Shadow drilled the cut over his bunged-up left eye with surgical precision opening up the wound into a geyser. The scent of blood only further fired up the crowd.

"4 ... 5 ... 6 ..." A tapestry of hoots and hollers, the crowd counted the next time he hit the canvas. He remembered the bonfire underneath his father, the flames crept up his body long after he stopped dancing. The flames licked the rope, and the remains of his body, a charred shade barely recognized as human, tumbled into the pyre. All to the renewed cheers of the crowd.

After every trip to the floor, Stagger came up smiling. Hands slack at his side, he'd walk into another haymaker, cheered by ring-siders—in the full throes of their bloodlust—every time he got up.

"Just stay down," Nan yelled. "They'll kill you."

"My name is," he said between swallowed breaths, "Stagger Jackson."

Blood poured from his shattered nose and busted lip. His face reduced to lacerated welts of raw meat, he hardly looked like a man anymore. The murmurs of the angry dead, a susurrus of voices rose to a dull chorus in the back of his mind. The Shadow reeked of smoldering wood and overcooked meat.

"6... 7 ... 8 ..." The crowd became little more than a mob. A contagion of madness spread among them. No matter their station in life, they thought and acted as one, shadows of themselves, ready to sell souvenir bits of him for the asking.

In the seventeenth round, he was slower to get up. His ghastly, bloody mouth spat out another gold capped tooth. The Shadow still punched with the strength of a mule's hind leg. Stagger locked him up, feeble jabs working its body, to stall out the fight in a clinch. The creature carried him to punish him. The ref had been paid well and didn't once move to stop the bout. Nan had already cleared the ring. A big, awkward left hand landed.

"My name is ..." Stagger took a drunken step backwards, his eyes rolling up in a stunned, hopeless gaze before he spilled forward.

"7 ... 8 ... 9 ..." The crowd cheered. "10."

Stagger's leg twitched a few times before it stilled. With the erupting pandemonium in the ring, he slipped into the waiting darkness and dreamt of where he's move to spend his pieces of silver since he bet against himself. Someplace bright with no room for shadows.

Present

The Ave

Muffled cries woke Prisoner #935579 from the light slumber that masqueraded as sleep. The deck lights illuminated the upper tier of Cellhouse C; enough for the Correctional Officers to measure their steps, but they reduced the cell dwellers to shifting shadows. The brutish shade in the opposite cell hunched in familiar fashion.Knuckles whitened on the bunk rail as the recent arrival in Derrick Mayfield's cell took an involuntary ass pounding. His own fault, really—only a few days in, he failed to grasp any of the rules of survival. He smiled, he chatted, and he trusted—the same get-along/polite maneuverings that served him well on the outside but marked him as a wounded gazelle to the hyenas that stalked these corridors.

Some men were destined to be punks.

The smothered screams echoed through the night. Prisoner #935579 eyed Officer O'Reilly, who ignored the ruckus though his station was only a few cells away. A bull of a man and former Navy, O'Reilly was reknowned for his harshness—another schoolyard bully who found a profession to vent his cruel streak. A scar snaked up from the corner of his mouth along the side of his face, contorting even his mildest grimace into a demonic sneer. An inmate gave him that gift the last time he interrupted a midnight tryst. "Animals rutting in the night," as far as that hack was concerned.

Prisoner #935579 buried his head in his pillow. That was life on the Ave.

Allisonville Correctional Facility. Level Four. The A-V. The Ave. Prisoner #935579 remembered the day he walked the forty-three steps of the loading plank, in handcuffs and leg irons. Rows of black faces lined up for inspection, like an auction block manned by hostile hacks barking orders. First they took away his name, then told him when to eat, when to sleep, when to shower; but the chains were the worst.

The Ave allowed few emotions, but Prisoner #935579 knew the hate. He hated through clenched teeth, the kind of hate that scratched, kicked, and lashed out at the world in blind fury, if only to break the tedium. The kind of hate that led to the fight between cells earlier this evening, ending in frustrated men hurling their own excrement at one another, staining the bars and cells yellow and brown, stinking up the whole tier. Officer O'Reilly swore to let them stew in their filth until breakfast.

Sleep without relief eventually claimed him. The incessant jangling of metal cobwebs shattered the night-time tranquility of the forest. Prisoner #935579's tongue traced the bloody bruises in his mouth. He drew his chain-weighted hands close, studying the scars left by the metal cuffs. His back, scarred from the many-tailed whip of a man with a scar reminiscent of O'Reilly.

Steam rose from the chorus of men that marched alongside him. Tribesmen, familiar as brothers, stumbled through the forest not cooled by the still air. Branches of thick underbrush scourged them as they trod along the path that no outsider should know, but the Scar-Mouthed One did. Few chose to come to the sacred forest, a place of mystery to the faithful, peril to the unbelievers. A forlorn, gnarled tree grew at the center of a clearing—the Tree of Forgetfulness. The Scar-Mouthed One spoke in the tongue of the Igbo people. The Scar-Mouthed One commanded them to march around the Tree seven times. The men dragged themselves around the tree, their legs robbed of the strength to move. One man wept as he staggered.

The Scar-Mouthed One knew the Igbo well. None walked around the Tree except to sever their memories, or have them stolen. Memories— of their family, their village, their motherland—gone. Another man cried out, met by the wail of the many-tailed whip. The man stumbled, tripping Prisoner #935579. On his knees, Prisoner #935579 clutched a handful of dirt from mother La's bosom. He stood, ready to curse mother La and die, then he heard the voice—the voice of his father and all the fathers that had been.

"Listen, son of our sons," the voice whispered, a breeze through tree leaves, a roar only Prisoner #935579 heard. "The leopard and the hyena hated each other. No one remembered why, but the hate was ancient. One day the hyena was about his hunt, when he came across the leopard sleeping beneath the shade of a tree. The hyena attacked the leopard from the rear. The hyena proved too much for him. As the leopard lay bloodied and battered, he said 'you can destroy my body, but my spirit will be free.'"

"What would you have me do?"

"Reclaim your name. Never forget who you are."

Prisoner #935579 woke up to the thin cries of the broken fish.

"My name," he whispered, "is Ashanti Tannehill."

§

"Prisoner #710001. Prisoner #935579," Officer O'Reilly introduced the two, escorting them from the newcomers tier back to Cellhouse C. He shoved the man to start him along. "You two are now roomies. Ashanti here will help you acclimate to your new home."

Wintabi Freeman.

The hacks obviously thought it amusing to pair up the convicts with African sounding names. *Anything to fuck with us,* Tannehill thought. He studied Wintabi with a cautious glare. Older, at least judging from the gray sideburns and burgeoning bald spot. His eyes flashed with a warrior's fierceness. Wintabi was different from the other fish Tannehill had seen walk the halls. He wore the prison-issue blues—blue pants and blue shirt over a white cotton T-shirt—with the dignity of one noble born. He carried his bedding and toiletries with an easy gait, confident yet threatening—the menace of experience.

"Your house, youngblood, which bunk?" Wintabi deferred when they reached the cell. Even with this gesture, he retained control.

"I'm cool with the top."

"Lettin' you know what's what, I'm a lifer," Wintabi said, setting his things on the bottom bunk. "I'm gonna die up in here; ain't got no illusions about that. Seen the insides of Leavenworth, Marion, and am just up from Angola."

Tannehill would've sighed, if he allowed himself to show any reaction. Lifers had nothing to live for, and worse, nothing to lose.

"Jus' so we clear, I don't wanna be peepin' your ugly loc ass anymore than I got to," Tannehill didn't want to let a lion in winter set the rules, but his bravado rang a little hollow to his ears.

Wintabi smirked. "Just so we clear, I ain't one o' your dawgs, prags, or niggas. We stuck in here together. I'm just lookin' to do my bit in peace."

"A'ight, then, we understand each other," Tannehill said. "Welcome to the Negro Warehouse. What'chu in here for?"

"What's it to you?" Wintabi folded the corners of the sheets under his mattress with deliberate care. "You lookin' to bond with me? We gonna stay up and do each other's hair later?"

"Just like to know the quality of motherfucka I'm bunkin' wit." Tannehill looked around his house with fresh eyes. The same 10x12 room with a metal toilet attached to a metal sink in the rear. In the first five minutes of his incarceration, he knew every inch of his space. He peered through the metal bars, scoping the activity of the other prisoners.

"They say I killed two white men," Wintabi said finally.

"I heard that they made that shit illegal now."

"Not in this case." Wintabi went about the work of setting out his things among Tannehill's clutter. "These two peckerwoods broke into my house like they had a right to be there ..."

The words touched a memory in him. Tannehill reached back to steady himself. The bare walls of the cell grew dark, as if Tannehill listened to Wintabi from within a tunnel. The cool metal bars felt moldy, scraping his fingers like wooden boards. Though hearing Wintabi's words, Tannehill found himself imagining (no, remembering) hesitant shadows, imposing only in their presence at such a late hour in the ship's cargo hold. His heart beat with the controlled fury of solemn drums.

An ominous scent pierced the fetid, still air, growing heavier with each step nearer to the partition that separated the men from the women and children within the ship's hold. A woman's voice cried out. Drunken hands groped about in the darkness, and hers was not the only one startled and fearful. Children retreated into scared huddles in stifled whimpers.

Tannehill's hand curled into a ball of impotent rage at the sound of the whip cracking. He pounded the hull. Only then did he remember who he was: ozo of this lost Igbo tribe. The maniacal cackle of the Scar-Mouthed One rose above the flogging. He snarled with the savagery of a hyena, the heaving, haggard breaths of fat, slavering men pummeled the cries of the despoiled women. The Igbo men wailed to cover any trace of the sounds. Tannehill wanted to cup his hands over his ears but didn't stir an inch until the men skittered like vermin up the stairs. Sobs filled the night air, like the scent from a fresh kill on a cool night. A familiar voice drew him back.

"... raped my wife and my daughter. Motherfuckers had the nerve to brag about it. Weren't even charged," Wintabi said. "Youngblood? You all right. You look like you faded on me."

"I ... naw, that shit's just fucked up." Tannehill glanced in the mirror. Sweat drenched his forehead. His face, drained and sallow, appeared ashen.

"That was the last time they did that shit. Different time, different era.

Today, my ass would be on Oprah, off on temporary insanity, but, in 1952 Georgia, I'm lucky I made it to trial. What about you?"

"Down on a trumped-up charge for twelve years. Five-o tryin' to get me to roll on my boys." All his life he prepared to jail. A stretch in prison was like attending the college of the streets, with the Ave being Harvard: You were only sent there after fucking up everywhere else. "I done dirt comin' up, corner work, so I knew shit would catch up to me sometime."

"I seen enough of you corner boys in my day," Wintabi remarked as he studied Tannehill. Then he just exhaled, like he had taken the full measure of the man and decided to relax, though he didn't drop his guard. "Me, I'm just tired of the game."

"What game?"

"All of it. The cycle. The system. The bullshit. No one tells you that you don't have to play."

"I don't get you." Tannehill trusted few people other than his mom. He'd seen niggas shoot each other over dumb shit. His cousin popped some fool simply for laughing at him. However, the weariness in Wintabi's voice was old, like his father coming home from a long day at work and collapsing into his chair. Old and trusted.

"Well, well, well. Look who we have here," Frank Connolly said, suddenly standing in the open cell. "What's up, Winnie? Winnie, the nigger." Tannehill kicked himself for allowing the redneck to get so close to him without noticing. They shared history. Connolly, a member of the Aryan Brotherhood, gave him a casual eyefuck but focused his attention on Wintabi. Connolly's clean-shaven head glistened above his groomed handlebar mustache. Tattoos stippled the side of his neck and coursed over both shoulders. Connolly's dieseled body leaned against the guard rails outside of Tannehill's house.

"Fuck you, Connolly," Tannehill said, a little too defensively. A primitive part of his brain reminded him that, unless he wanted to be referred to as Mrs. Freeman, Wintabi's prag, or a punk, he'd best leave Wintabi to fight his own battles.

"Let it go, youngblood," Wintabi said, earnest, yet without reproach.

"I heard we had a rat problem."

"You always tryin' to start shit," Tannehill said, despite himself, while glancing at Wintabi. The only thing worse than being a rapist or a child molester was being a snitch.

"Why else you think they transferred him from Angola? How the fuck did he get outta Marion?"

"He ended up here, didn't he?" Tannehill said. "Let me ask you somethin': Do all you Nazi motherfuckas cut off one nut to be like Adolf?"

"Fuck you. You don't hear him denyin' it."

Wintabi stood in silence.

"We got a problem here, Connolly?" Officer O'Reilly approached the cell.

"Naw," Connolly raised his hands, "just jawin'."

"Then get your ass gone."

"This ain't over. You can't hide in your cell forever," Connolly stage-whispered. "We know how to deal with vermin."

"Bitch ass can't even spell 'vermin.'" Tannehill watched Officer O'Reilly encourage Connolly. "What was that about?"

"Don't know, don't care." Wintabi returned back to his bunk.

§

That night Tannehill tossed in his bunk, not quite inured to the smell of grown men sweating in the night. The wooden sleeping berth scraped against his shoulders and ankles during his sleep. He dreamed that blood-slickened chains connected his wrists to Wintabi's. Tannehill ached with longing for home. A noisy fly buzzed about his head. He fought the heaviness in his bowels all day, waiting for some measure of privacy to dump his business.

"The funny thing about prisons is that, no matter where you go, they always feel the same," Wintabi's voice whispered from the shadows. "Losing everything can have a purifying effect on your soul—stripping you of your freedom, your privacy, your dignity. You learn what you really are."

"So, what have you learned?"

"That most men become animals when you chain and cage them, but the true measure of a man comes in how he carries himself despite his chains." Wintabi's voice took on a faraway, dreamy quality; he no longer spoke directly to Tannehill. "Can you hear them?"

"Hear what?"

"The drums. The heartbeat of our people. Our ancestors. Calling out to us." Wintabi's voice no longer sounded like him at all. His voice grew deeper and more ... ancient. "Let me tell you a story: A tiny village sent its children to the fields to gather the harvest. They filled their calabash bowls at the river for the journey home. A young man stepped from the reed and asked them to give him a drink of water. They did and in return, he gave them a pitcher of honey. They invited him to return to the village with them.

"On their journey home, the young man grabbed one of the children and disappeared, saying, "If you tell anyone of me, I will come and kill you all." When the children arrived at the village, their parents asked what happened and where the missing child was, but the children were too scared to say or do anything.

"Finally, a young boy, whose wounds still bled, told of the man. A great rumbling shook the earth with the man's voice thundering, "Why do you expose me?" He sprang from the forests, and they realized he was an Iimu, a great devil from across the river. He swelled to the size of an immense serpent. Fire burned in his mouth, flames fell to the ground like spittle. The men grabbed their spears.

"'You cannot kill me,' it taunted, 'for you must use your own bones to grind mine into powder.' The Iimu started to devour some of the men, the children ... and the women. It destroyed much of the village while caught in the throes of its lusts. The men realized the riddle of its words: That they must sacrifice themselves to destroy it. And they did. As they and the Iimu lay dying, they saw their family and kinsmen again. All had been restored."

With that, Wintabi's voice faded to silence. Tannehill knew sleep would be long in coming for him.

§

"Shakedown!" Officer O'Reilly yelled. The prisoners stepped out of their houses as the hacks went in to ransack the cells. The ostensible purpose was to search for contraband—drugs, weapons, or what have you—but the real purpose was to remind the prisoners who was in charge. Officer O'Reilly lined up the prisoners and shouted a series of orders as if narrating a surreal workout video: "Run your fingers through your hair like your mothers were grooming you for lice.

"Open your mouth. Stick your tongue out. Lift it and move it from side to side.

"Lift your dick and your balls.

"Turn around, bend over, and spread your cheeks."

A beating, Tannehill could take—a man took a beating—but the daily, heaping servings of pinprick humiliations, the constant reminder that he was owned by another, that reality slowly consumed him.

Navigating the politics of the cafeteria often proved nearly as treacherous as negotiating the yard. Each gang set had their own territory, and one had to step wise if one wanted to survive chow. Wintabi and Tannehill respected the color line but ate at the fringes of it.

"You feel it, youngblood?" Wintabi asked.

"You ain't gonna start with that drum bullshit again are you?"

"What are you goin' on about? I'm talkin' 'bout the air. It's got that vibe."

"I feel you," Tannehill said, unsure whether the other man remembered his "drums" soliloquy, "like somethin's 'bout to jump off."

"You see your man, Derrick?" Wintabi nodded toward him as he sat among his brothers. "You gonna make a move on 'im?"

"If there's gonna be a stickin', he's welcome to try," Tannehill said.

"Just make sure that you remember who you are. You're still a man, they can't take that away from you."

"What was Connolly goin' on about the other day?"

"Old ghosts. Most times, it's about who hurt who last. I knew his father when I was at Leavenworth. Me and him got into it pretty bad. Someone dropped a kite to the warden ..."

"Didn't know anyone up at Leavenworth knew how to even write a letter."

"The kite detailed a conspiracy to kill a couple of hacks. They took it seriously. Next thing you know, hacks shakedown Connolly's old man's house and found a shank. He ended up in Ad-Seg and died there."

"They thought you dropped the kite?"

"Ask me, he sent the kite himself to get himself away from *me*. Don't matter none. Even in Ad-Seg, you can be reached. Got me moved to Marion."

Tannehill felt hate like it was his birthright, the bondage of this life passed onto the next, with chains as his legacy.

Connolly approached as the two stood up to dump their trays, bearing a scornful eyefuck that Tannehill couldn't let pass without reciprocating. He was so intent on his posturing that he didn't notice Connolly letting his filed toothbrush slip from his sleeve into his hand.

Connolly turned and jammed it into Wintabi's back. Blood darkened the old man's prison blues. Connolly handed the shank behind him, and that person passed it along until its final owner was unknown.

"Where's all your jigaboo prancing now?" Connolly raised his hands as the hacks rushed toward them.

"Get down! Get down!" Officer O'Reilly shouted. Other hacks pinned Connolly against the wall as he smiled.

"Why can't I feel my legs?" Wintabi asked to no one in particular. He stretched out his bloody hand searching for purchase on Tannehill.

With enough imagination, anything could be turned into a weapon. For Connolly, it was a toothbrush. For Tannehill, it was a bedspring, unwound with its edge sharpened. Tannehill pulled it from the waistband of his pants. The cycle tightened like a noose about his neck. If he had any inkling of hope, he watched it fade with the pool widening about Wintabi. Their eyes locked, the light fading from them even as Tannehill brought the bedspring to bear. The hacks pushed the men along, preparing to escort them to Ad-Seg. No one thought to keep a closer eye on Tannehill, not especially known for being a trouble maker. He buried the shank in Connolly's chest, right through his cloverleaf tat, before the stunned COs had a chance to react.

"Get the fuck to your cells!" Officer O'Reilly shouted. "Lockdown!"

§

Administrative-Segregation, Ad-Seg, was a prison within a prison. Most of its inmates were snitches in danger of being shanked in the yard, prisoners too dangerous to roam "free," or incorrigibles awaiting a transfer. However, even within Ad-Seg, there was a prison, the secure housing unit known as "The Hole." Twenty-three hour a day solitary lockdown with two hacks that escorted each bound-in-chains prisoner to the concrete exercise yard during his one hour of rec time. Hacks cut the lights on or off at their discretion, most leaving them on and forgetting about them.

Ashanti Tannehill sat in the middle of the floor and admired his handiwork. He crafted a mural of misery from the only media at his disposal: his own blood and shit. The buzzing flies didn't bother him. Their company dispelled some of the loneliness. After the first three years, his family, one by one, wearied of doing time with him.

His frayed braids fell into his face. He wanted to brush them out of his face, but he was cognizant of his shit-stained hands. A fly buzzed past his ear and landed on his eyebrow. He fought to ignore the crawling of tiny legs along his body. A sole fly circled his head in its own curious orbit. Soon, two engaged in aerial combat chasing each other through the ravines of his body. The flies swirled around him, their wings' hum haunted his ears. More flies gathered, a pooling swarm of wings, legs, and bulging red eyes. They scurried along the walls drawn to the stench and filth. They crawled along Tannehill's body, despite him brushing them aside. A maddening buzz, incessant voices that formed words.

"Ashanti."

He cocked his head to the side, uncertain that he heard the name from his dreams. He pushed aside the gnawing nervousness as if the nesting army of flies swarmed solely in his imagination. The flies gathered around him in a thick cloud, whorls and eddies, blown about by an unfelt breeze. He dared not breathe for fear of inhaling dozens in a careless gasp. I n n u m e r a b l e feet itched his flesh in their passing. Tannehill covered his face. Still more flies settled along the mural, their bodies glistened as light reflected at impossible angles from the black sheen of wings. A figure took form along the mural. From within the head of the figure, red embers burned to life. Its voice, like terrible thunder, echoed through the beating wings of its mouth.

"Do you know what I am?"

"An egwugwu," Tannehill said, not knowing how he knew, "an ancestor spirit."

"Yes," a tremulous voice covered in raffia replied. Tannehill dared not stare into its face. A sickly odor hung in the air about him, cutting through the filth, like the rot of diseased fish left in the sun. "I have come from the underworld. My journey has been long, and my stay will be brief."

"What do you want?" Tannehill asked, sure that this time his mind had finally snapped in the bowels of the Hole. He wouldn't be the first to go mad in solitary.

"'Ike di na awaja na awaja'—Power flows through many channels. As long as your head is not separated from your body, your ancestors will guide your spirit home. Let your body die that your spirit may be free from these chains."

The flies flew tight circles around his form, each competing for space to claim. They skittered across his eyes and crawled into his mouth. They climbed along his nostrils. Flies crawled along every inch of Tannehill's body. His flesh glinted in the moonlight like shifting shards of shattered glass. He imagined the flies consuming his body, grinding his bones to dust to float away.

Home.

Family Business

Nathan Bratton was always closing his eyes to something.

Though only 16 kilometers separated Montego Bay from Maroontown, an eternity passed in the dips and sharp turns of the hillside roads. He forced his eyes shut. He hoped to sleep—if God so chose to favor him—but mostly he didn't want to watch. The taxi driver expertly (Nathan prayed it was expertly) wove along the road. With each heave or lurch of the car, Nathan's mind registered a flood of images. The taxi honked. Kids laughed and yelled. Branches whipped the car. Tires squealed as they skirted what Nathan knew was the edge of a steep drop off. The taxi honked. A passing car returned the honk. The din was like mating sheep being run over. Nathan opened his eyes for a moment. A bus passed excruciatingly close at its own breakneck speed. He tugged at his seat belt. Again.

Nathan reconsidered his reasons for coming back to Jamaica, although that made it seem like he had a choice. Nathan's mom was born in Maroontown. She left when she was a teenager. She visited often, bringing Nathan with her. She wanted him to know where he came from even if he didn't. Jamaicans struck Nathan as a proud people, proud to the point of arrogance. They acted like their culture was superior to everyone else's, their ways made more sense, their history somehow richer. Those beliefs were shoved down Nathan's throat. He took it for granted, the foods, the stories, his heritage, until his mom died last year. Only then did he realize how little he knew about her. And himself. He was a tabula rasa, part of his identity was missing. He'd planned, or meant to plan, a pilgrimage to Jamaica. Then yesterday the phone rang with news of his grandfather's death. This morning Nathan found himself on a plane bound for Jamaica. And as much as an outsider as he felt, he knew he had no choice but to come.

He was summoned.

"How much?" Nathan asked, tugging his suitcase free of the car seat.

"Five hundred dollars." The driver's thick accent clubbed his ears. Nathan watched as the driver studied him in his rear view mirror. Even with the $40 Jamaican for $1 U.S. exchange rate, the price seemed high. Nathan hated to haggle, but the word "tourist" might as well have been spray-painted across his forehead.

"You must be mad," Nathan said, believing that the key to effective haggling was in the attitude. "That doesn't even sound right."

"Five hundred dollars," the driver repeated.

Nathan spied a familiar face pulling alongside the taxi. He removed a folded photograph from his vest pocket. A wedding photo of his mother's sister, Karen, and her new husband. The photograph was little more than a month old. "You must be Uncle Edward."

Edward filled his police Jeep with his massive build. He opened the door and put one freshly polished black boot on the ground as he waited for the transaction to finish. Stiffly pressed Navy slacks with two red stripes running down the side and an equally pressed light blue shirt was the uniform of a ranking police officer. A sense of menace exuded from Edward like a sinister shadow. Staring into his black eyes was like being raked by shards of glass. The taxi driver locked eyes with him momentarily. Edward nodded.

"I'm sorry. How much was that ride?" Nathan repeated.

"Fifty dollars," the driver muttered. He gripped his steering wheel like a drowning man to his life preserver. "Respec', corporal."

"Respect, man." Edward dismissed the driver. He looked about conspicuously, then pulled his black cap curtly to the front of his head. He approached Nathan in arrogant strides. Though Edward's hands were soft and manicured, there was a heaviness to his handshake.

"It's good to finally meet you, Uncle Edward."

"It's good to meet some of Karen's American family." Edward's words rang with exaggerated enunciation, as if speaking slowly for Nathan's benefit. It was only mildly condescending and was better than the sing-songy, frenetic accent that sounded like it could have been as easily Chinese as English.

"I'm happy to hear someone I actually understand," Nathan said.

"Oh, surprised to hear my command of the English language?" Edward's voice bubbled with a self-satisfied haughtiness. Nathan was swept along in the intimidating charm of Edward's serpentine grin.

"I didn't mean any offense."

"None taken. Not everyone speaks in ignorant patois." Edward gestured toward his Jeep. Nathan quickly learned to hate the silence. Edward spoke in a loop, as if he had rehearsed only a certain amount of topics. Any lull in conversation was filled with Edward recapping how important he was. As senior Justice of the Peace for his ward, he knew everyone. He was well traveled. He'd been to America, England, and Canada and had no trouble driving on either side of the road. His authority was such that he could have anyone jailed, for no reason, for three months. Nathan listened amiably, a forced smile plastered across his face. Edward droned on, in love with the sound of his own voice. Either that or he was simply used to people hanging on his every word. Every so often, Nathan caught Edward glancing at him, trying to read him. Nathan smiled, continuing the dance of first impressions. The radio distracted him with jingles for Prima milk. IRIE FM was the main station received in the country. The trip took a surreal turn as a reggae version of "We Are the Champions" played.

"How much longer to your house?" Nathan masked the impatience in his voice as travel fatigue.

"It's just around the corner," Edward chuckled to himself. "Everything's 'just around the corner' out here. You can go 10 miles around that 'corner' and still not be there. But if I honk my horn from here, they'll have the gate open by the time we get there. Supper will be ready."

"By the way, thanks for letting me stay here."

"No problem. Family takes care of family."

§

"I'm full." Nathan pushed his plate to the side. His palate, too weak for ackee and saltfish, felt fairly safe picking at the curried goat, boiled bananas, and yams. The food sat in his full stomach. The heavy bass of Beenie Man's "Betta Learn" thumped from down the street. Many people slowly gathered for the funeral though it was not until tomorrow. The gerriae, which Nathan likened to an Irish wake, started the day of his grandfather's death. The music, dancing, and food would not stop until his burial. Friends and family were flying or driving in from all over, though no one else dared ask to stay with Edward.

"Before you make good food go to waste, 'mek belly bust'" Edward scraped the untouched ackee and saltfish onto his plate.

"Aunt Karen always did cook enough for an army. I guess she had to, I mean, granddad did have 37 children."

"You mean 36," Angela said. Angela McGhie was Aunt Karen's daughter from her first marriage. Nathan and Angela bonded immediately since they were both in their early twenties. Her mocha complexion only deepened the melancholy that girded her face. Long braids of thick black hair framed her oval face. She possessed a hustler's eyes and a rogue's heart, but everyone in the family had a bit of The Scoundrel in them.

"No, 37. Here's the notice." Nathan fished in his briefcase, past a flurry of Post-It notes and scraps of paper, to reveal a folder. Most of what he knew about his grandfather he learned in the obituary column. "See here, he was survived by 37 children, 139 grandchildren, and 3 great grandchildren."

"Yeah," Angela paused meditatively, the names ticking off in her head. "We forget 'bout Hubert. He was a baby when he died."

"Yeah, crib death. I heard." Nathan attempted to wrap his mind around the idea of 139 grandchildren.

"Hmph." Angela's fork clattered noisily against her near empty plate. They sat around the table as Aunt Karen fussed in the kitchen. Edward's son, Saul, quietly ate. Nathan watched as Saul surreptitiously dropped a piece of meat for one of the dogs to eat. The other dogs perked up with interest.

"What are your dogs' names?" Nathan asked.

"Names?" Saul asked.

"Don't they have names?"

"No, suh. We call 'im 'puppy,' an' 'im come. We call dat one 'puppy,' an' 'im come."

"Who name dem dogs?" Angela interjected. "Dat's like fe name your chickens."

"But we eat our chickens," Nathan said. "They don't run around the yard."

"We 'ave our dogs jus' fe mek noise at night. Fe tiefs."

"He nuh 'ave dogs in America?" Saul asked.

"Yeah, but dey 'ave dem all in dey bed wid dem."

"It's time for bed," Edward cut short the conversation.

"Come on." Angela reached for Saul's hand. "I'll tell you a story."

"Can I listen?" Nathan asked.

"Come on."

Angela told Saul the story of Brer Ananse saving Brer Buffu from Brer Snake by tricking Brer Snake into his own trap. Nathan listened intently, jotting down the story onto one of his Post-It notes. "An' he and Brer

Buffu went off fe de village," Angela concluded, "leaving Brer Snake for de woodcutter's axe."

Saul grinned broadly, then rolled over. She leaned forward and kissed him. She ran her fingers softly through his hair.

"Was there a moral to that story?" Nathan whispered.

"Poppa seh, 'de same knife wha stick sheep, stick goat,'" she said, looking down at the soundly sleeping Saul. "Why you interested in stories?"

"My mother used to tell me the same stories when I was growing up. Over and over. Oh man, they got on my nerves. Then, when I grew older, I realized I had no stories to tell. I miss them, especially the duppy stories."

"Duppies dead out."

"Ghosts don't die out," Nathan said.

"People don' believe in dem. Dey nuh scared of dem."

"That's because there are more frightening evils among the living."

§

Nathan tossed fitfully in his bed. Aunt Karen placed bottles of Jamaican Rum Creme on the dresser, in case Nathan wanted a midnight nip. A curtainless window opened against the night heat, allowing shadows of the burglar bars to play along the far wall. Several mosquitoes buzzed too close to his ears. Nathan flung the sweat-soaked sheets to the other side of the bed. He prayed that sheer exhaustion would carry him to sleep. The wind murmured its dirge through the banana trees. The wind-whipped leaves produced a sound easily mistaken for rainfall.

The dogs growled. Again. The snarls usually signaled a dispute over sleeping arrangements that ended in yelping. This time was different. The tenor had changed. Nathan grabbed a bottle of Rum Creme and headed outdoors. It tasted like a vanilla milkshake spiked with rum, albeit 200-proof rum. The house was an anomaly along the street side. Their neighbors dwelled in little more than tin-roofed shanties. Edward's home hid from the road behind a grand concrete wall, ornately decorated with roaring lions. Iron gates enclosed the veranda. Even Nathan heard the rumors of how crookedness swirled around Edward like an inescapable odor, but he dismissed them as the gossip that generally accompanied all Jamaican police.

Nathan circled around the house, enjoying the night air outside of his stifling room. Hundreds of stars flecked the night sky, freed from the cloak of pollution. The crickets hummed like overhead power lines, interrupted by the occasional cry of "ka-ka" of passing birds. As Nathan approached the side of the house, the dogs whined, as if disturbed, then abruptly stopped. Fear fluttered briefly in his chest like a vulture disturbed from its perch. Nathan heeded that primitive part of his brain sensitive to danger, though he overrode the urge to flee as he pressed himself against the house wall. He peered around the corner only to see the dogs sitting in a perfect semi-circle. Their attention seemed engaged on someone in the middle, engulfed in the shadows of the trees.

The unseen presence charged the air around him. Nathan gulped courage from his bottle. The figure defied recognition from so far away, so Nathan crouched alongside the wall and edged closer. Hidden behind the rainwater barrels, Nathan chanced another glance.

The shadow-enshrouded man reached out toward the dogs, mimicking a petting motion. The dogs wagged their tails merrily. The wind died, an eerie stillness settling on the scene. Faint traces of marijuana smoke emanated from the neighbor's home. The gerriae revelers had long turned in for the night, readying themselves for the funeral tomorrow. No traffic rumbled along the street. Nathan fumbled with his bottle as he neared the distracted dogs. Each footstep firmly set itself along the pebble-strewn path. The figure's haunted face was familiar to Nathan, though he only recognized it from a yellowed photo crammed into his bedroom mirror like a mute guardian: a younger version of Nathan's grandfather. The essence of his grandfather flickered in the gentle eyes eclipsed within the hardness of his face. Except that the figure stood taller than Nathan recalled. Too much taller.

He hovered above the ground.

Nathan dropped his bottle. The shattering glass splintered the silence. The man's eyes bore into Nathan. The figure melted into the night as if a spell had been broken, little more than a memory captured from a fleeting dream. Nathan's hand grappled for anything to steady him. The Rum Cremes must've been more potent than he thought.

§

"Don't sit there. That's Poppa's chair," Aunt Karen said. Nathan froze in mid-sit down, not sure if she was serious. She patted a nearby chair. "Sit down over here."

"Uh, okay," Nathan tried to keep an open mind. He wasn't conceited enough to consider himself sophisticated, but his mind often wondered whether or not his people were backward. It was bad enough that they spent the morning of the funeral fretting about the house. Death was little more than a chore that needed to be attended to. Aunt Karen shuffled outside to collect the laundry from the line. That unnerved him more than any foolish superstition. "But why save his seat for him. He's probably not going to need it again."

"Oh, but he might," she huffed over the basket. Nathan ran over to grab it, but Aunt Karen brushed him aside with her don't-make-me-box-you-over look. "He was a powerful obeah man."

"What do you mean?"

"Me seh he worked obeah, set duppies," Aunt Karen said as she folded the laundry. "True, true. 'Is people dey come trouble 'im, all vex up 'bout dem neighbor or someting. He work obeah on 'em, an' seldom asked fe anyting."

"Really? Interesting."

"You an obeah man, too," Aunt Karen said. "Yes suh, you 'ave faith, so if an obeah man tried to work obeah on you, it wouldn't work."

"So, if you believe in it, it works on you. If you don't, it won't."

"Mostly people wit grudges seek out obeah men. Some obeah are real," Angela interrupted from the doorway. She cut a sensual figure, even in her mourning outfit. Nathan rose, taking his cue to leave. "*Most* are con men. Li'l more than thugs. If they say someting bad will 'appen, dey may do it demselves."

"How can you tell a real obeah man?" Nathan asked. Angela led the way as they walked along the gravel path that headed toward the church. It was a short walk cutting through the property.

"Real obeah men seldom look you in a de eye. Dey carry a basket or whatever dat 'olds 'is tings. Dey of'en wear a red flannel shirt or someting. He 'as fe kill a member of his own family as the final rite to become a true obeah man."

"You ever been to one?" Nathan asked Angela.

"Once. 'Im read me up."

"Told you your future?"

"Yeh. 'e tell me, me not gon keep no work unless me let 'im give me a guard ring. So me ask 'im, 'How much is de guard ring gon cost?' 'Im say, '$8000.'" She bugged her eyes out in mock amazement. "'Je-sus,' me seh, 'Me no 'ave no $8000 fe pay you.' 'Im say me fe give 'im $4000 as down payment. If not, 'im seh me gwon dead in a two week time."

"So, what happened?"

"Me no know. That was three weeks ago." Her laugh was as free and easy as it was infectious. Her laugh trailed to silence when she glimpsed Edward sauntering toward the church. A somber pall settled between them. She whispered as he passed, "Do you ever wonder 'bout Edward?"

"Wonder what?" Nathan asked.

"Sometimes me tink he did someting to Poppa." Angela cast her eyes downward, as if not wanting them to betray her to Edward. "Death's shadow is 'pon 'is face. You no see it?"

"What? Obeah?" Nathan smirked, thinking himself cuter than he was. Angela was less than amused.

"Shh. Ne'er mind. The funeral soon start."

They made their way to the front of the church. Everyone stood as the coffin was brought up the steep, rocky steps to the church. A gray shroud covered the coffin. Once the coffin rested before the pulpit, the casket lid was opened so that Poppa was visible during the sermon. His appearance was waxy, dehydrated. Rumors circulated all week as to the cause of his death. Some said he only had diarrhea but was too embarrassed to tell anyone. Some said he was poisoned. Some said a rival obeah man worked powerful obeah on him. He seemed so small, almost lost in the silken linens of the casket.

The church filled to standing room only. The doors in the back of the building were opened so that the overflow crowd could catch a glimpse (and be seen). It was quite a spectacle. Poppa was a retired district constable, so many off-duty Montego Bay policemen lined the walls, decked in full regalia. People were there from all over Maroontown, even as far as Garlands. Angela explained to Nathan that it was because of more rumors. Word spread that the will had been revised to divide the farm among the family. That rang true to Nathan. When his mother visited, she brought all manner of goods and merchandise from America and left all that she brought, even her own clothes and luggage. "Family took care of family," she said.

When it was time, a Rastafarian—with a huge nest of dreadlocks tucked under his multi-colored hat—crawled into the sepulcher to receive the coffin.

Whispers churned among the gathering, since only family was allowed to gather immediately around the sepulcher. And Rastafarians never went near the dead.

"Nathan, I think it's time we talked. Man-to-man." Edward beamed with malevolent intensity. Angela shook her head "No." An uneasy chill stirred in Nathan's gut.

"Sure, Uncle Edward."

The night was unusually frigid as a wind sliced through the lush hills. Brooding clouds encroached the baleful eye of the moon. A distant rumble disquieted the sky. Suspense reduced Nathan to halting breaths.

"What were you and your cousin whispering about this morning?"

"Oh that?" Nathan was tempted to breath a sigh of relief. "Nothing. She was telling me tales of obeah men. Do you believe in that stuff?"

"I don't have time for that necromancy foolishness."

"Why do you ask?" Nathan still waited to exhale.

"I just didn't want you meddling in my family's business."

"Our." The word leapt from Nathan's mouth before he could stop it.

"What?"

"*Our* family's business." Nathan heard his voice, though his mind wanted his mouth to shut up. Words kept tripping from his tongue. "We are in the same family now."

"Let me ask you something," Edward half-smiled, as if enjoying some game. He reached to his side and unsnapped his holster. "Have you ever fired a gun?"

"No." Nathan eyed the holstered gun. His armpits itched ferociously. A nervous perspiration dampened his forehead. His mind raced, mapping possible escape routes. All of a sudden, Nathan counted all of his dumb mistakes. He let himself be convinced to meet this virtual stranger alone. He didn't bring a weapon with him. Nathan's eyes followed as Edward drew the gun in mock-gunslinger style. Nathan flinched, but remained rooted.

"Take it. Go on."

"Okay." Nathan held the gun with the tips of his fingers.

"How does it feel?"

"Heavy."

"How does it make you feel?"

"What do you mean?" Nathan asked.

"I'll show you. Feel the gun in your hands. Aim it over there." Edward pointed to a distant hill. He spoke slowly, almost seductively. No lights glimmered along the valley. "Pull the trigger."

The gun cracked with deadly authority, jerking in Nathan's hands. His ears rang as the discharge was louder than he imagined it would be. An acrid odor, like burnt ozone, assaulted his nostrils. He held the gun where he fired. Nathan didn't know what lesson he was suppose to glean from this exhibition. Edward continued his baiting smile.

"It's about control." Edward grabbed the gun at the barrel and turned it and Nathan toward him. "Right now, you hold my life in your hands."

"I don't think...."

"How does it make you feel?" Edward's eyes burned with a devil's luster. He wetted his lips. Nathan was unnerved enough to begin trembling. His stomach churned with imminent queasiness. He could only stare along the sights. He itched with mosquito bites that he didn't remember getting. His palms slickened against the grip. Edward reached for the gun. He removed it from Nathan's grasp. Nathan's hands still cupped the air, not daring to move. "Control. Power. No fear. Don't cross me."

Just then, a sound pealed in the distance. Like a thunderous snort. Rain poured from the skies hitting the corrugated tin canopy next door with such fury it resonated with the roar of distant applause. Beneath the din was the sound of jangling metal getting nearer.

"What was that?"

"Nothing. Thunder. Let's go inside." Edward's voice wavered. It was slight and quickly covered up, but Nathan heard it and found it comforting. A few moments later, another grunt bellowed, shaking the floor. Aunt Karen scurried to the living room and called from the window.

"G'wan fe bed," she ushered Nathan to his room, "an' don' look outside."

Nathan retreated to his room, not bothering to turn on any lights. Outside the window was a terrible tramping, as if some behemoth trudged along the banana groves. It occurred to Nathan to peek outside, but his aunt's warnings echoed in his head with the urgency of angels to Lot's wife. The clanking sounds of metal coalesced into something familiar. Like chains. It sounded like something bowled over the banana trees and ate the gungoo pea stalks. With each hideous snort, the house warmed up like a make-shift furnace. Nathan sat on the corner of his bed wondering if this was some sort of Jamaican fire drill. He had come to Jamaica to answer one nagging question: Who am I? Yet, all he had seen left him no closer to any real answer. The figure and the dogs. Angela. Duppies. The funeral. Edward. The gun. Obeah. If a destiny awaited him, it had to come to him.

The chains rattled outside his doorstep before fading into the night.

§

Last night seemed like a nightmare induced by a bad batch of goat belly soup. No damage had been done to the groves. He woke to the usual bleating of goats, though the dogs were nowhere to be found. He found Angela washed blood from the house walls with a casualness that stupefied him. The blood was smeared, almost sprayed. A garish display that felt more like a warning than anything else.

"Look how de duppy kiss me last night," Angela laughed, as she pointed to a bruise on her arm.

"Oh, really?" Nathan asked, unsure if she was even joking.

"Shut yo' face gal wit dat nonsense," Edward scolded. He seemed more on edge than ever. He glanced at Nathan and regained his composure. And his unaffected speech. "I'm sure our guest doesn't wish to hear such ... foolishness."

"Me love fe chat, it don't mean nutting."

"You love chat too much," Aunt Karen yelled from the porch. "'Ere comes Saul. Mek 'im put on 'is school clothes."

Aunt Karen, often lamented that none of the current generation wanted

80

to farm. It was, after all, the family business. So, Saul had to work in the field before he went to school. The banana exports were due soon. Saul headed straight to the house from the field. What was once Sunday dress pants was worn to feather-thin, dirt-encrusted fringe. His tennis shoes were barely soled, and his New York Knicks jersey was soiled to inscrutability. He brandished a machete that was over half his size. Angela followed him into his room to hurry him. Nathan trailed behind her.

"All right, what was that last night?" Nathan asked.

"You mean de rollin' calf?" Saul giggled. "Aunt Karen tol' me de tale las' night."

"A what?"

"You *did* wan' a duppy story," Angela said. "It obeah man duppy."

"It come 'roun' between Christmas an' New Year's," Saul called out from the bathroom. "It a huge someting wid chains 'roun' 'is neck an' fire in a dem eye. You can't look in a dem eye. Its breath kill you dead. He can't trouble you on de straight road or in shadow of a tree. Otherwise...."

"Anyting dem meet in a dem way, dem kill." Angela finished.

"Bye, uncle." Saul threw his backpack over his neatly pressed, khaki-colored school uniform. Nathan silently thrilled at the respect shown by being called "Uncle." Saul shook his hand with a fearful trembling like he wanted to warn him. He looked over his shoulder, toward the door, and thought better of it. Angela grabbed Nathan's hand, escorting him along, leading him back to the kitchen.

"You are quite fortunate to marry a man like me," Edward said, noting Nathan and Angela's return. "You are lucky to have a man who has breakfast cooked by the time you get home."

"Me know, me know," Aunt Karen said.

"Now, I cleaned up the kitchen when I cooked. I expect it to stay that way."

Edward raised his hand, only to pat her shoulder, but she shrank back like an oft-scolded dog. He headed toward his bedroom. Aunt Karen ate her breakfast in solitude. Angela waited a few minutes then gestured for Nathan to follow, leading him down the porch steps behind the house. She stopped below Edward's balcony. Angela cocked her ears toward the opened window.

"What're you doing?" Nathan asked.

"Shh."

Edward's distinctive baritone echoed as he spoke on the phone.

"Yeah, man, the property's practically mine ... banana farm too ... I know ... she got it all ... he never had a chance to change his will ... sure she'll sign it over to me ... interest of British importers ... not often an opportunity like this comes along." Edward loosed a chilling chortle, its echoes scraped across their souls like gnarled fingernails.

Nathan lacked Angela's surefootedness; he stumbled over the jutting stones of the house base. Edward awaited them on the veranda. He dropped a basket of laundry, apparently for Angela to hang.

"Nathan, you'll never fin' a woman if you keep 'round your cousin. You carry on like a couple in love. You two are aware you're family?"

"That never stopped you." Her words sliced like daggers through her teeth as she turned to pick up the basket. Nathan's heart stopped in his chest. Silence reigned for an interminable span of seconds. Edward shifted noisily before turning sharply on his heel. His voice was a tyrannical rumble, like crashing waves.

"Don't poke around my business."

§

Nathan sat along the beach edge, fascinated by the water's clarity. He stamped his foot underwater just to watch the sand stir about then settle. His hands dug nervous holes in the sand next to him. Storm clouds gripped the hills of Maroontown in a terrible grasp, a view best appreciated from Brighton Beach. Vestigial winds whipped sand particles across his back like a stern taskmaster. Angela delighted in Nathan's suggestion to visit the beach. He found it difficult to watch Angela in her own element. She enjoyed the liveliness of the beach. Her playfully flirtatious manner made her quite popular. However, she quickly tired of the attentions of the crowd.

Nathan felt relieved to see her walk toward him. Despite her joviality, Angela carried herself with a melancholy air, a profound sadness that saturated her every movement. The only time it didn't haunt her was when she played with children. Even then, the sadness transformed only to a longing. Maybe that was why Nathan felt so protective of her. She was at once fragile and hardened. Angela sat close to him. They watched the events of the beach like it was their personal stage. Two young boys, not quite teenagers, shadowed a tourist who might as well worn an "I'm a Tourist, Please Rob Me" shirt rather than his orange and turquoise flower print shirt.

"See those two pick'ney behind dat white man?"

"Yeah?"

"They're pickpockets."

Closer to them, a Rasta performed his own show for three college frat boys giving them a "Jamaican Experience" to tell the folks back home. He sang for awhile, breaking his routine to sit for conversation. He borrowed one of their Walkmans to provide extemporaneous commentary on their music. One of the frat boys sat up in attention, extremely entertained.

"'E betta be careful," she said. "'Im tek 'is time moving farther and farther away as he dances. Soon, he take off wid it."

"Ain't that the same Rasta who pulled Poppa's coffin into the sepulcher?"

"Yeh, dat's Bigga. He didn't even go fe 'is own mother's funeral. Dreads seh, 'When dey dead, dey dead.' Won' have anyting fe do wid dead bodies."

"Why not?"

"Dead bodies are unclean. Like pigs."

"They don't eat pork either?"

"No, suh. You give 'im a box o' animal crackers, he'd even pick out de pigs befo' he ate dem."

Bigga noticed their laughter. His scruffy blue jean shorts, along with his red-yellow-green crocheted hat, flapped as he danced next to his knapsack. He sang along with whatever melody overtook him, occasionally casting a sideways glance toward the prying eyes of Nathan and Angela. One of the men got up for a drink run. He brought back four bottles of Guinness: one for him and each of his friends and one for his dreadlocked acquaintance. A few minutes later, Bigga wandered toward Angela and Nathan, neither of whom hid their nosiness.

"Irie."

"Irie, dread," Angela said

"Why you watch me so close?"

"Just watching you entertain folks," Nathan said

"Wha', you wan' be like this Rasta?"

"Yeh, Rasta," Angela mocked, "jus' like you, some mawga foot dread. Move yo'self, you too facety."

"You wicked, gal." Bigga turned to Nathan. "No suh, what you need is fe eat a plate of steamfish, drink two Guiness, and smoke two spliffs. Thas how you 'andle a big gal like this'un. You do dat, and you break a woman six times before you break once." Nathan and Angela looked at each other and burst into titters. Bigga took another spiteful swig of his Guinness.

"I'll have to remember that," Nathan finally said. "Too bad you don't know anything about obeah."

"Obeah. It jus' science," Bigga nonchalantly said, knowing eyes peering over his tipping beer bottle.

"What, you an obeah man, too? Like my granddad?"

"You wan' me fe read you up?"

"Yeah," Nathan offered Bigga his pen. Bigga fitfully wrapped his hands around it and closed his eyes. His face contorted with some unseen agony. He winced, tilting his head to the side. To Nathan, it seemed quite the performance, but his skepticism gave way to apprehension. Feigned or not, Bigga's apparent fretfulness caused anxiety to creep into Nathan. Angela stared with equal, but silent fascination. Bigga set the pen down and foraged in his knapsack.

Overturning various accoutrements—feathers, beaks, horns, bones, hair, dried herbs, balls of clay bound with twine—he decided on a small ball, little bigger than a clear marble. Nathan's rising anxiety returned to cool skepticism.

"I look in a it fe see who trouble you," a fearful grimace of confirmation soon flickered on his face. "Here, take this. This will help protect you."

Bigga tied a tiny leather pouch around Nathan's neck. Nathan often watched his life play out like he was little more than a spectator. Of all the things to happen on this trip, this was the first to feel natural. The pouch necklace felt right. He asked the only question he was capable of mustering at this point. "How much?"

"Nutting," Bigga said sharply. "You 'ave potential. Only need ta be taught. Keep it, man. It's a gift."

That evening Nathan found his suitcase perched on his bed, spilling its contents like a disemboweled stomach. The papers of his briefcase were scattered across the room. All of his belongings had been thoroughly rummaged.

"Where's Edward, Aunt Karen?" Nathan demanded.

"Whas de matta, boy," she flustered, "he went out fe visit Poppa's grave. Him vex 'bout someting."

Nathan stormed toward the door, until Angela blocked his way.

"You can't go. Thas what he wan' you fe do. Meet on 'is terms."

"Well, I wouldn't want to disappoint him, now would I?"

"You no easy, cho," she sucked her teeth disgustedly at him, a habit that never ceased to annoy him. He glared at her, but she turned her head from him. So, he left. Her voice echoed after him. "Lord Jesus, he no easy."

The family cemetery was not far behind Edward's home, halfway down a hill that leveled to a plateau. Rocks spit dust into the night air marking his passage. The overcast moon scowled. Nathan paused at the stone marker of his grandfather's tomb. Edward stood calmly on the other side of the small cemetery, with his back turned toward Nathan.

"I still know what you did, even if I don't have any proof. You know as well as I do, Jamaicans, especially Jamaican police, aren't real fussy about proof," Nathan shouted.

"Did what?" Edward asked. He turned, revealing a joyless smile as he slowly walked toward Nathan.

"Kill Poppa," Nathan's voice softened. He wasn't sure at what point his grandfather became "Poppa" to him. Edward stepped closer.

"I don't know what you're talking about." Menace laced Edward's calm measured words. Nathan took a few steps backwards.

"I bet you don't. I won't stop, you know. The will can be contested. Better yet, Aunt Karen wouldn't sign anything over to someone she suspects killed her father."

"You haven't learned anything, have you? You're in my country. My town. Your laws do not apply. Here, my will is done." Edward's hand patted against his side, toying with whatever hung there. "It's a shame that I couldn't find you sooner."

"Sooner?"

"'You hear how your people dem behave? Those rasclots from de shop got a hold of you. It was all I could do fe chase dem after dey tief you.'" Edward mimicked the gossip he would spread. "If only you hadn't been so determined to come on your own. I, for one, was greatly saddened. Family is supposed to *take care* of family."

Edward pulled his machete from its scabbard, the dim moonlight glinting off its razor-edged blade. He stood between Nathan and the road, blocking the path. Nathan dashed into the banana tree grove. The leaves cut into Nathan's soft flesh as he ran. Still in beach attire, he cursed himself for not dressing more properly. The sand in his clothes scraped as he ran, rubbing his skin raw. The wind ripped through the leaves, creating the illusory sound of a deluge.

Nathan stumbled blindly through the trees. Edward stalked close behind him, slower, but with sure footfalls, like a man who knew the grove like the back of his hand. A truck banged loudly along the road behind him. Above him. Beside him. He didn't know. He felt the truck rumble past as if his own stomach suddenly grumbled. Nathan's breath grew ragged quickly. The trees thinned ahead. Nathan hoped that was because they led to the back of the house.

The trees opened into an isolated clearing.

Wan moonlight weakly lit the area. Nathan's arms swung wildly as he ground to a halt. As he regained his bearings, he realized that the house was at the top of the next hill over. He swallowed deeply, his breathing little more than short, dry rasps. Nathan heard a tuneless whistle from behind him. Edward gripped the machete's taped handle firmly, tantalizingly slicing the air in front of him. He feinted to one side, letting Nathan flinch impotently, for the sheer joy of extending his game. Nathan's exposed skin rippled with gooseflesh. Nausea pooled in his belly, threatening to overwhelm him. The hair on the back of his neck stood up as if he had backed into a socket. Edward halted and looked around. He felt it, too. Something approached.

The shadows stirred nearby. A forlorn wail erupted all about the trees. Birds fluttered. All else seemed to fall silent. A harsh grating echoed closer, like a train braking in the woods. Edward craned his neck from side to side. The clanging of huge chains dragged in the distance. Nathan felt the blood in his veins freeze with terror. A foul, dank odor seared his nostrils. It accompanied the nearing cacophony of a maelstrom of metal.

A shape slowly materialized into view.

Twin, red pyres peered through the night. The abomination was twice the size of a bull. It was mostly black, with white patches, approximating the shape of a hornless goat. It had no mouth. A collar strained against its thick neck, attached to a series of chains that dragged along the ground. One of its front feet looked like a horse's hoof; the other, a human foot. Its back legs were reminiscent of goat legs. A cow-like tail swooshed broadly over its back. The raw stench of wet fur gagged both Nathan and Edward. The grotesquerie seemed to have absorbed all manner of life in its travels.

The rolling calf galloped faster than any living horse. Nathan simply fell and scampered backwards as fast as he could away from the horror. Nathan shrank away, hiding in the shadows, praying it wouldn't notice him. He watched in horror as the creature chased down Edward and cornered him. Edward swung his machete haphazardly at it, for all the good it did him. The rolling calf pinned Edward with its front legs. The horse hoof planted squarely in Edward's gut, the human foot pressed against his neck. It had no mouth, but it bent its face low toward him. Whatever awful exhalations it expelled choked Edward. Nathan saw the comically quizzical expression on Edward's face as his skin shriveled, as if his insides had been sucked dry. Even as he closed his eyes, Nathan still heard the snapping, the rending, the sounds of ... breaking. Then the dull thud of a machete hitting the ground. When he opened his eyes, Edward had vanished without a trace.

The rolling calf turned toward Nathan.

Nathan cringed against a tree, his arms thrown up, waiting for the inevitable to play itself out. The rolling calf snorted its dreadful cough. Nathan's mouth dried, as if hot sand filled it. His throat closed as a scream died on his lips. Each desperate gasp pained his chest. His muscles convulsed into seizing knots. The howl of the wind fluttered the banana trees, creating their rain-like patter. The rolling calf stopped just short of him. Its flame-socketed eyes locked onto Nathan's primitive pendant. It exhaled with a frustrated humphing of a donkey's bray as if it were reminded of something. The whole area grew hot with each breath, its snorts exuding blue flames, far hotter than the tiny flames should've produced. The rolling calf fixed its gaze toward Nathan. He peeked from behind his shielding arms. He saw something familiar, like the essence of country geniality hidden among the horror.

Nathan closed his eyes. He waited for the pain that never came. When he chanced opening his eyes, he found himself alone. Except for the red scarf that lay at his feet. That was when he knew: the farm had to be worked, but obeah was the true family business. And it was his turn to run it.

Read Me Up

Von and Earl Duperon glided past each other in the kitchen, knowing each other's moves. A choreographed dance of reaching for hand towels, opening the refrigerator and trading off frying pans they alternately stirred then tasted, all the while without touching each other. All the while in silence while she strained to think of something safe to talk about. Earl was the first to break the silence.

"Are you nervous to meet him?"

"Who?" Von was careful not to make direct eye contact with him. These days, such an act seemed too intimate. A challenge. A careful dare to search for anything familiar, anything that once was. Or worse, only finding a stranger's eyes peering back at her. He stirred his Alfredo sauce, an attentive eye to its color and texture, but all she knew was that he never made meatloaf much these days. He would rather conquer some new recipe, attempt some exotic dish than fix something she enjoyed. She liked meatloaf. No need to dress it in some fancy sauce. Just plain old meatloaf.

"You know who. Your new stepdad." Earl piled dirty dishes into the dishwater without consideration. He slammed the last plate into place. A blue, plastic one from the set they bought the year they were married. Their everyday set. Scratched and water-worn, the color bled from them. "God, why do you have to make each conversation like pulling teeth?"

"He's not my stepdad. He's the guy my mom married."

"That's awfully long to put on a Hallmark card."

"Let's just get through this. She's only in town, hell, in the country for a month. Two good visits and I'm back to being the favored daughter."

"The bar's not that high. Your brother and sister still aren't talking to her."

"I know. But I thought only one visit would seem ... obligatory." Von dried her hands as she swept the kitchen one last time for anything out of place. She tried to tell herself that it was the obligation of family that made her agree to allow her mother to visit. That it was the duty of the firstborn to protect their siblings, even if it meant hosting their mother. But while that all sounded good, the real reason was guilt. Forty years worth of her mother's hooks in her compelling her to accept a visit or else be tortured by the idea of being a bad daughter. The whole prospect made her more nauseated than she already felt.

"But two is okay? I'd hate for you to do the bare minimum to keep a relationship going."

"The key is to space them out. You know, make it seem like there's more to the relationship than there is."

The soft knock at the front door severed their dueling glares. Von wiped her hands on her pants and took a deep breath. She chanced a glance at Earl, who nodded.

Isabelle Bogle (now Isabelle Aster) loomed so much larger in Von's memory than did the diminutive woman who stood before her. Von hugged her with the awkward embrace of a security point pat down.

"Yvonne, it's good that you found time to fit me into your schedule." Her mother still insisted on calling her Yvonne, despite her legal name change. She smiled with the predatory gleam of a shark. "This is your new dad, Neville."

"Don't do that. It's a lot of pressure," Neville said, and concentrated on wiping his feet on the doormat, probably to dodge the awkward "do we hug or shake hands" dance. The thick gray of his hair was cut low, and he nearly matched Isabelle's burnt honey complexion, despite her orange glaze of foundation. He pushed past them into the house with a portly waddle, his expansive belly nudging the both of them. Like with aging, with death men got the better part of the bargain; there was a social cachet to men who were widowed. The cloak of sorrow made them sexy in a way that the stigma of divorce couldn't. Divorce meant someone or someones had failed. Widowhood meant someone had stuck it out to the end.

"Anyway, if I want a dad, mine's just down the street." Not that Von had seen him in months, but the ability to be absent from another's life was what the two of them had in common. She probably owed him a phone call. "This is my husband, Earl."

"The 'Ville's in the house!" Earl shouted, and reached out in a wide arc to grab Neville's hand. Earl had a wild swagger to his grin, a contagious charm when he wanted. A forced light danced in his eyes, but, if Von closed her eyes and listened to his laugh, she heard her father's chuckle.

"Too much, honey," Von tugged on his arm, a plastic smile plastered on her face.

"Earl." Isabelle pronounced it like some gauche mistake, so beneath her delicate sensibilities, so utterly … American. Except for his color, Earl behaved exactly like her father. When he walked, his bearing and shamble was so similar that the fact that her mother never commented upon it spoke volumes. Earl no longer worried about pleasing his mother-in-law and engaged her as little as possible—a series of head nods and "uh huhs." Similar to the way he handled Von these days.

Isabelle glanced about the house, crinkling her nose as she inspected the place. Von expected her to run a gloved hand along the bookshelves, with her other hand free to speed dial her friends to report on the state of the house. "Oo-wee," Isabelle clucked in conclusion, the house not kept the way she would have.

When they arrived in the living room, Isabelle and Neville took separate couches, dividing them by sex as Von joined her mother. Distance didn't stop Isabelle and Neville from bickering, correcting, and talking over one another without heat, as they discussed the best directions to get back to their hotel, whether to use a whole sheet or scrap of paper to jot down a note, whether it was warm enough to wear a jacket. Each married over 40 years before divorce or death caught up to them, they understood the rhythm of relationships.

Von hoped to disguise the appearance of her boredom by tapping at her laptop. Earl fixed his gaze on her. She exited her programs without meeting his eyes.

"Is it almost time for tea?" Isabelle asked.

"Somewhere over the Atlantic, I'm sure," Von said.

Von's mother was only conveniently British. Though born in Jamaica, she did her schooling in England. Tea time became a sort of game they played, as if any of their relatives in England still practiced high tea. Today it would have to be 1:00 p.m. rather than 4:00 p.m. because Isabelle wanted to eat at MCL Cafeteria to take advantage of the all-too-American senior citizens' discount rather than eat with them. Which was fine since, rather than "biscuits" or scones, she'd have to make do with day-old chocolate chip cookies. From McDonald's.

With the ease and forgetfulness of two people for whom the rest of the world disappeared, the chatter between Isabelle and Neville lapsed into thick Jamaican patois. Von believed in her heart that this was partly designed to exclude Earl. She rolled her eyes and headed toward the kitchen. Earl followed.

"You were chatting with him again." Earl's whisper had the steel of accusation to it.

"Him, who?" Von turned the heat up on the kettle of water. She attempted to find matching mugs but couldn't. Too many had broken over the years. She gathered the two remaining from their original set, a *Star Trek: The Next Generation* one, and another commemorating Prince Charles and Lady Diana's wedding. She couldn't believe it had survived all these years.

"We're going to do this again?"

"I ended it. I keep telling you it was nothing but an internet ... fling. I guess." Von rifled through the cabinets to find something suitable to serve tea from.

"So, what had you so occupied on the computer?" His arms folded over one another, Earl leaned against the counter.

"Work. Hell, taking my turns at Scrabble would preoccupy me if it meant," Von lowered her voice another notch, "not having to pay complete attention to my mom."

"Work? You expect me to believe that?"

"Yes. Are we going to go through this every time I log onto the computer?"

"Yes. Shit. No. I don't know. I'm still getting my head around it all. How you could get feelings for ... a set of 1s and 0s?"

Von prayed he didn't notice her wince at the dismissal of what she had shared. It was all emotional, that was as far as it went, she had told him, and it was over. She eyed the bottle of vodka in the glass-doored cabinet above the kitchen sink. Her mouth watered at the thought of a drink, but she knew she shouldn't. Not until she made her choice. She slid a stack of saltine crackers alongside the cookies, hoping they would settle her stomach. "There's nothing to get your head around. It's over."

The kettle whistled, sending them to neutral corners. Von arranged the cups on a tray. She used the champagne flute from their wedding as the creamer. She poured some lumpy brown sugar into a small, faded, blue plastic bowl. She slammed the tray down in front of Isabelle harder than she intended.

Serving himself, Neville said, "Add raisins to your brown sugar. It keeps it from going hard." He was one of those types that was an authority on everything. "The Chinese keep buying up all of the sugar fields in Jamaica.

They process the sugar too fine. Not enough molasses left in them, and that's what's good for you."

Reminded of something, Isabelle snapped her fingers and dove for her purse. She fished around in the huge thing for minutes. Finally, she withdrew a photograph. "Look what I found."

Her grandmother—who had forced everyone to call her "Aunt Mame" instead of anything warm like "grandma"—posed beside, yet apart, from her daughters. They stood oldest to youngest in descending degrees of misery, bitterness plain in all of their eyes.

Earl leaned in to see better. "How many brothers and sisters do you have?"

"There are 16 of us. No, 17. Aunt Mame insisted that we count Zaccie even though he never made it to term."

"You look like your mother when she was younger," Neville said to Von.

Von resisted the urge to spit in his eye. "It's like looking at the ghost of future past."

"The dying are travelers, going on to a better world. Sometimes they get lost. A duppy haunt me up once." Isabelle sipped her tea without blowing on it first. "Back when your father and I were having problems."

"So, for forty years?" Von asked. Earl shot her a "don't poke the crazy" stare.

"Hmpf." Isabelle's face twisted in an odd expression. "I was asleep, and suddenly this weight was on my chest. I tried to swing my arm out to wake your father, but I couldn't move. I couldn't catch my breath. Then suddenly it was gone. I turned on the light, and your father wasn't even in bed. He was downstairs watching television."

"Don't mind her," Von said to Earl, "she has a *duppy* story for every occasion. Treefoot. Rollin' calf. There's a whole menagerie of Jamaican bedtime folk tales. Any excuse to tell one of their stories."

"It's better than any obeah man." Neville stretched his arm out along the couch and settled into it, leaving his tea untouched before him. He dabbed his forehead with a red handkerchief that didn't match any part of his outfit. "They tell you stuff you don't want to hear. Stuff you don't want anyone else to know. They scare me sometimes."

"What's obeah?" Earl asked.

"It's like the Jamaican version of voodoo," Von stage-whispered.

"Like my sister Carmen," Isabelle said. "When she gets sick, before she go to the doctor, she go see an obeah man. Her daughter, too. Me, I don't truck with no obeah nonsense. I remember walking into town once with my mother ..."

Von closed her eyes, the way she had when she was a little girl and her mother started one of her stories.

Isabelle was back home for a visit. A cock crowed in the distance, but, by six in the morning, Isabelle and Aunt Mame were well on their way to the cave to collect water for the day. Isabelle balanced her basin on the nest of long plaits on her head. A thick mist rolled in from the hills. The wind stirred the trees, the banana leaves whispering.

Someone beat a drum. The arrhythmic pounding echoed from all around them, the sound scattered by the early morning fog. An old woman carried a lantern, its wan light smothered by the cloud. She swatted the drum she cradled in the crook of her other arm. She wore a blue gingham dress with dirt smudges along its front. A red bandana tied her hair back.

"Isabelle!" she said sharply.

Called by name by the stranger, Isabelle froze. Aunt Mame didn't move either, but she didn't show the apprehension of being approached by a complete stranger.

The woman took Isabelle by the chin, turning her head side-to-side, her hand with the grip of a vice despite her age. "You have the mark of God on your forehead, but you're disobedient."

Aunt Mame nodded. She followed the old woman along the washed-out road, pausing long enough to turn around to call after Isabelle. "Come, nuh, gal. She to read you up."

They approached a dingy shack of gray planks. Some of the boards had been painted sky blue at one time, as one wall was still washed with the faded color. Log stumps raised the house from sitting directly on the dirt mound. Stones strewn throughout the yard, looking more like they'd been accidently unearthed rather than forming a deliberate pathway. Barefoot children with their unbuttoned shirts or their one-piece dresses, scampered about, not noticing the rough ground. They said nothing, only watched as the trio entered the house.

Isabelle was careful not to run her hand along the rough-hewn banister for fear of splinters. She took a seat on a dilapidated vinyl chair in the gloomy living room. A card table was turned off to the side. Knickknacks, a random assortment of kitschy figurines, lined the shelves.

The woman hung the paraffin lamp in the corner and, without a word, began beating her drum. She bucked and jerked to the erratic rhythm, dancing as invitation for the spirits, though it looked to Isabelle like the dying spasms of a madwoman. The old woman's skin seemed so much darker indoors; her face was a filigree of wrinkles polished by sweat. Without buildup or crescendo, she stopped.

"Put two shillings into my hand," the crone said.

Isabelle suspected that the woman wanted to see if she wore a wedding ring. But Isabelle wore her band on the wrong hand, not wanting anyone to know she was married unless she told them. The woman's claw of a hand was thin but so alive as it wrapped Isabelle's own.

"There is a man in your life." The woman fixed her large, piercing eyes on Isabelle, their intensity unsettling. "You are conflicted."

"I'm here for you to tell me something," Isabelle said, avoiding the obeah woman's fishing.

"The spirit can't go through because you're too tough to break." The woman turned to Aunt Mame. "If you put ten shillings in my hand, I could go further."

Aunt Mame dropped the coins into the woman's palm, all the while complaining about her stubborn, willful daughter who ran off with the first man she found. Off to America, away from her family. Her roots.

The woman pressed the coins to her forehead. "The spirits have something to say," she said in an all-too-knowing tone.

"Lord Jesus," Isabelle said. "Duppies not dead out if they get paid?"

"Don't vain the name of the Lord," Aunt Mame said.

"You have a brown boyfriend," the woman said. *"You lived near a burial ground."*

Isabelle nodded, even though everyone lived near a burial ground since they buried on their property.

"Your boyfriend has another girlfriend. And there will be an altercation." The woman slumped into her couch as if spent. She waved them off.

Aunt Mame gave her ten more shillings.

"Come," the woman led Aunt Mame to a back room.

Isabelle wondered who the woman pretended her ancestry from. All of the healers and mystics claimed to be descended from Abyssian royalty, Jesus, or John the Baptist. The door to the back room creaked open. Aunt Mame emerged with a smile on her face. She smelled of spiced olive oil.

"A whole coolness has come about me."

"When you're rubbed down with oil, it'll cool you down," Isabelle said.

"A spirit haunt your mother. The oil will protect her," the old woman said.

"You too foolish. Come on, I've had enough." Isabelle grabbed her water basin with one hand and Aunt Mame with the other. The old woman followed her out of her shop and down the street.

"They will all leave you. Your every relationship will sour. You will be a poison to your own." The woman stopped and convulsed for a moment, sputtering nonsense in a strange tongue. Isabelle and Aunt Mame paused midstep. The woman ceased her tremors and stared at them. *"Someone is going to have an abortion, and then someone is going to die. This is curse you to the third generation."*

"To the third generation?" Earl asked.

"The woman did love her threes. Those obeah cons love to try to shame you when they don't get their money," Isabelle said.

"The third generation?" Von repeated Earl's question. "Does that start with Aunt Mame or you?" Von asked.

"Either way you'd be included, Yvonne. Besides, I had to have two abortions, and I'm just fine."

"You did?"

"I'm sure we've talked about this. I wanted to have six children, one right after the other, but the doctor said that it was too high a risk for me. That's why there's the large age gap between you and your brother."

"Why didn't you ever tell me about this before?" Von asked.

"I'm sure I did. What does it matter?" Isabelle sipped her tea but crinkled her nose at it now that it had cooled. "No one believes that crap."

"'Crap?' That's awfully American sounding," Earl said. Von shot him a glare.

"Don't be foolish. Anyway, the obeah people them, they just con artists. They try to get a read on you and twist your greatest fears against you."

"Why are you so dismissive about what she said? What she predicted came true," Von said.

"What do you mean?"

"I love him, but Daddy wasn't the most faithful of men. And you did get into that shouting match with that one woman who tried to sue for child support."

"Hmpf," Isabelle said without commitment. It wasn't her most dignified moment, and she hated to be reminded of it.

"Obeah works through belief. Either you have a spirit in you, or you don't. You have to choose." Neville folded his red handkerchief and tucked it back into his pocket.

§

Gentle snores drifted across the gulf between Von and Earl, the exigencies of life reduced to the way of slumber. In bed, in dreams, anything was possible. She could go anywhere she wanted to and start anew. Like clearing away dishes after a tea party: she could give the illusion of tending to someone's need without any real exertion or risk on her part, even if the someone in need was herself. Beyond this place of misery and anger, surviving the wounds of childhood, but not wanting its scars to last the first, second, or third generation.

Her mother made sense to her in a way. Von thought of the story she told herself about her life, like she were cursed and bad things hunted her like a hungry lion hot on the scent of a wounded gazelle. But it all came down to a choice. That was what her mother was, a series of choices, the choice to strangle relationships to within an inch of their lives, the choice to remain in a bad marriage, in a situation that made her miserable. Von thought about the picture of her grandmother, mother, and aunties and saw her future. Bleak. Miserable. Bitter. One day she might stumble into the living room of her child and mutter about her ingratitude, the refrain to her same, sad family song, ticking off the litany of offenses, both real and imagined. Each slight clung to and nursed like a coddled infant at her venomous bosom. She didn't want to join the ranks of sad desperation. She wanted to be free from it all, to go where she could heal from the mistakes of her past, to be someone ... whole.

To the third generation, the voice now whispered.

She would be the master of her fate, not the legacy of her mother's fears. And she dared anyone to tell her otherwise. It was her choice.

Perhaps it wouldn't be too late to create a life of joy with Earl. She wasn't sure he even much liked her these days. Nothing would spite her mother like her finding happiness. For a brief moment, Von wondered what life would be like if everyone told the truth. Whenever words landed in a way that cut. Whenever actions failed to live up to expectations or frustrated. Whenever life hurt or the heart was denied. To live in the open, in complete honesty, to forge life from truth. Life was messy, and there were no easy answers, especially after so much deception. She pondered how to begin repairs to correct the mistakes of the past and move forward. She just wanted a chance at finding happiness. If not for herself ... her thoughts drifted off while ticking off mistakes to correct.

She patted her belly and dreamed of red.

Cerulean Memories

Blue was her favorite color.

He touched the glass case one, last time before returning to the desk, but his handprint lingered on, an ethereal smudge above the backlit, cerulean shadow of her face. No matter how often he tried to write their story, he couldn't shake free of the lies he had built around them. He suspected that even if he could discover the truth, it would pass him by unrecognized, as ephemeral and false as a balladeer's concept of love. Love knew you better and could hurt you worse. Where fear faded so did love, and he nurtured a delightful terror, a trembling fascination bred in tales. He wanted to reach her and make her understand, but all he had left was the elusive call of memory.

A decade out of fashion, his pin-striped suit hung well on him. A man of occasion, his father would have called him. A head full of gray hair, a filigree of wrinkles around his gray eyes, his manicured nails adjusted his tie one final time before his appointment. The door chimed fifteen minutes earlier than expected. If he didn't have to inspect the merchandise, he wouldn't have bothered. The living offered little except their stories.

"May I help you?" he said.

"You the old dude who buys stuff?" A young boy looked past him with heavy-lidded, half-upturned eyes. His camouflaged hoodie, drawn up, shadowed most of his face. He under-enunciated his words.

"I am. I'm also quite busy. I have a one o'clock appointment."

"Yeah, with me. JaQuon Wilson."

"I see ... JaQuon. Shouldn't you be in school?"

"I should be a lot of things." The bulk of the hoodie hid his husky frame, and JaQuon allowed his wrinkled clothes to hang from him in calculated slovenliness. His book bag, half-slung over his shoulder, slid into the crook of his elbow before he hitched it back. He avoided eye contact all the while clutching a skateboard to his chest, protecting it as if it held all the secrets of childhood.

"Is that the item in question?"

"Yeah." JaQuon gripped the skateboard even tighter.

"It won't do. I have quite ... specific requirements."

"I know what you want. You think I'd be caught in this creepy joint if I didn't have what you wanted." His determined eyes half-pleading with him, JaQuon puffed up his chest and stepped broadly, all bravado and empty swagger.

"Come in."

The man's hard-soled shoes sat by the doorway, one pointed in the opposite direction of the other so no one knew if he was coming or going. Walking barefoot into the room, he checked his watch, age spots, like tiny scars, on the back of his hand.

The great thing about wealth was that things mattered less. Not the trappings of power. Not the social jousting of civilized behavior behind smiles like gleaming swords. Money excused eccentricities, and only the dreams mattered. That was the last lesson his father had taught him before he went away, leaving behind a blood-splattered envelope—addressed to him in exquisite calligraphy—shaded by the slumping body with the large hole in its head on the couch.

Thigh-high clusters of golden ropes of grass, their pallid color from lack of water, provided beauty in their dying. Burrs and brambles clung to his pants and socks, scraping his thin skin as he walked without care, a boy with the blush of ruddy peach in his cheeks. Resting in the crook of a low-lying branch, he daydreamed of the castle atop a hill he would one day build for a princess.

Glass enclosed the porch. He dreamed of tending hydrangeas, lilies, and morning glories. From the patio they would sit and watch the sunsets together. The paint fresh and the wood polished, the furniture stopped short of being inviting, museum pieces meant to be stared at and appreciated, but not for too long. Serviceable rooms held little decoration as not to give too much away. No knickknacks, bric-a-brac, or curios; no pictures, no portraits. Thick curtains didn't rustle when he moved past them, a ghost in his own home.

"Your house is bigger on the inside," JaQuon said.

"Is it? I hadn't really noticed." He leaned down, and whispered, "It lies, you know. The walls have ears and move to confuse you when you aren't paying attention."

"You ain't right in the head, old man."

"You're the one trying to sell me your skateboard," he said. "Tell me about yourself."

"Ain't much to tell. I go to Persons Crossing Elementary. I'm nine years old."

"What's that? Fourth grade?"

"Yeah, I stay with my grandparents. My mother doesn't come around much anymore."

He thought he'd seen JaQuon before: a latchkey kid, after a fashion, who punched in the code to their garage probably because he so often lost his key. JaQuon wandered about the sitting room, without shame or pretense, directed by the insatiable curiosity of childhood.

"So, what's your deal anyway?" JaQuon studied an empty curio cabinet.

"My ... deal?"

"Word is you buy stuff people died on. That's the story, anyway."

"Stories take on a life of their own, fireside tales spun into morbid tapestries of death and loss and remembrance. That's the point of them, isn't it? Voices of the past, grief working itself out in patterns of familiarity. Objects hold memories of a life lived, but the memories of the death outweigh the memories of the life."

"You talk funny."

"Do you wish to hear this or not?"

JaQuon nodded.

"It started with the couch my father died on. My mother set it outside to be hauled away, but I had it brought to my study. She never came near my room after that. When I curled up on it, I could still feel his presence. At night I still smelled him, the scent of loneliness and pain."

"Dang." JaQuon gave the word an extra syllable for emphasis.

"My collection has grown over the years. That chair over there? A grandmother of seven fell asleep while knitting and watching her stories, to never wake up. A man stroked himself out on the toilet, not to put too crass a point on it, straining during his morning sit down. It reminds me that death comes at anytime and there is no place safe from it."

"You're making that up," JaQuon said.

"Like most stories, some parts are real. But the stories comfort me."

Death was separation, leaving unchanging echoes of the people they used to be. He was the caretaker of a grove of memories, his and others. Kept like a scrapbook, taken out and revisited, an echo chamber of death. Grasped onto like a skateboard he couldn't bear to let go of.

A time of remembrances, of the day, of days past, of summertime dresses and walks along the canal, of hands held. Her leg brushed against his, and he still received the same thrill from her presence as the first day he saw her.

A farmhouse had stood on the field when he finally bought it. He covered her blue eyes as he walked her to the spot.

"This will one day be your castle," he said.

"But it's such a beautiful farmhouse."

"We raze history when the memories become unbearable."

She smiled with her upticked chin, leaned into him, and kissed him on the cheek. She filled his spaces. That was what love did.

"What am I going to do with a skateboard?" he asked.

"What did you do with the couch?" JaQuon said.

"I can sit on the couch."

"You can skate on the skateboard. You can sit on the motherfucker for all I ..."

"Language."

"What?"

"Watch your language. You have plenty of words to choose from in order to express yourself. Why limit yourself to the basest ones. It's so ... common."

"You a weird, old dude."

"You haven't told me the story of the skateboard."

JaQuon peered at him, his eyes suddenly seeming too large for his face. His legs quavered, and he sat down on the couch without thinking. His thin legs about to give out on him. "It was my brother's. I loved my brother, Demarcus. I was the oldest. It was my job to protect him, you know. My mom used to always hover over us. Wouldn't even let us walk down the two courts to our friends' house."

"It's a mother's job to overprotect. It's difficult to let their children rush off into the dangers of the world. As if they can keep you safe by force of will and control."

"Sometimes, it was like she wasn't happy unless we were rolled up in bubblewrap before going outside. Playing on the lawn only where she could see us.

"Demarcus really wanted this skateboard. We tag-teamed mom for weeks, wearing her down. Demarcus was in third grade, so if she let him have a skateboard, she'd have to give me more room to ... be. She bought him this board. Plus knee pads. Elbow pads. Mouthguard. Cup. And a helmet. The next two weeks she insisted on watching him learn to board. And we counted down the days until we'd be able to run free. She began to let us go. Just a bit. We could go over to the next court to play. She even stopped driving by ... like we wouldn't notice her car. Though a couple times, I swear I saw her peeking over bushes. Eventually, she trusted us to return. 'Don't worry about it, mom, we just ride around on sidewalks, and we just sort of push ourselves along.'

"No one wore a helmet. Definitely not our friends. That stuff was for babies.

"Demarcus wasn't even going that fast. He turned the corner, and the wheels stopped when it hit a break in the sidewalk; but he didn't. It threw him from the board. I watched him fly through the air, his arms flapping like a drunk bird. He landed head-first into the sidewalk, and I laughed.

"I laughed.

"It was like one of those funniest home videos. But then he didn't get up. They said it did something to his brain, and I had laughed."

JaQuon didn't wipe away his tears, probably wasn't aware that they trailed down his face. "So, you want to take it off my hands?"

The man leaned forward. In this chair a man cheered on his favorite basketball team and had a heart attack. "Five dollars."

"I can do better than that."

"I didn't amass my wealth by throwing good money after bad. I make wise investments. Hold onto it for a while. Offer's good. Whenever."

It wasn't about the money. JaQuon couldn't bring himself to allow it to go out in the trash. For him to let it go was to begin to let go of his brother, and, as painful a reminder as the skateboard was, forgetting his brother was worse.

Death was the pruning shears of childhood. Sometimes, to grow, you had to lose something. Sometimes, you had to force people to grow and change, shock them back into life, or else they may become a ghost trapped in a museum.

She found the first stray by the back door, sick and wounded. A large, white husky with eyes the color of overripe persimmons. She couldn't leave it behind: she had already pledged her heart to it. Rivulets of blood streaked when she shifted its matted fur from unseen wounds. Its head heavy in her lap, it didn't move, but simply closed one eye. A sullen nod of its head, its tongue lolled across its lips in pathetic repose. She hand-fed it pieces of torn chicken collected from her plate into its bowl. Stroking its fur for its pleasure, then for hers, as she nursed it back to full health.

He bought the dog a mate, and they patrolled the grounds, fiercely protective of her.

A cat park had once circled the outer gardens, but she was allergic. He loved cats, but he loved her more. Each cat was buried in a carpeted casket under a brass nameplate. His shoes click-clacked, click-clacked, click-clacked *along the plated sidewalk each day.*

"Come upstairs. I have something I wish to show you," he said.

"I ain't going upstairs with you," JaQuon said.

"You've already come into my house."

"You could be a pedometer."

"True. And you are wise to be cautious. I was going to show you her bed."

"I for damn sure don't need to go to your bedroom with you."

"You're right. I don't know what I was thinking. I just get so caught up when I tell the stories. I guess I just miss her."

"Who?"

"Helen. My wife. I was going to show her to you. I'm not going to touch you. I just need someone to know. Someone who'd understand."

An unspoken knowledge leapt between them. JaQuon nodded. The old man led the way up the stairs without any tiresome soliloquies about the state of his bones or kidneys.

The first time he saw her, she captivated him from the stage of the vaudeville show. She had yellow hair straight out of a fairy tale and eyes the color of a frost-covered pond. Her smile, a melancholy upturn of her lips. She wasn't the strongest dancer, her steps too pensive and calculated, like clunky prose that flowed from the head, not from the heart.

He just wanted a chance to be near her, to watch her up close. Every time you see a beautiful woman alone, someone was tired of being with her. That was the secret men told themselves. He dared asking her for a dance. Hers was an inexhaustible beauty. He feared touching her. She might have consumed him. The difference in their age was nothing, he told himself.

She loved to swim and spent hours picking out her bathing suit from J.C. Penney's. He would build the largest pool in Indianapolis. Large enough for a hotel, but just for them. Far away from ogling eyes. The inside painted blue and lit from underneath, its glow lent a bilious tinge to the hillside. They swam in the summer months, often sharing too many glasses of wine. Lost in their moment, an eternity in routine.

They stopped in front of a set of double doors.

"Is this your bedroom?" JaQuon asked without any nervousness.

"It was her favorite room in the house." He rested his hand on the door handle, attempting to gather the strength to open it again so soon. "When we got married, her father stood up during the reception. He wanted me to take care of his little girl. All of her. They had a tradition of saving everything. He handed me a box. It had all of her baby teeth."

"That shit is weird."

"I remembered thinking, Thank God I didn't marry their son. I'd have his bronzed foreskin or something in here."

JaQuon stared at him for a heartbeat then stifled a chuckle.

"Do you know how the Egyptians preserved the dead?"

"They were into mummies and stuff. My mom took us to the Children's Museum back when ..." JaQuon trailed off.

"Their funeral rites were the ritual re-enactment of the acts that raised their god Osiris from the dead. Life, even death, boiled down to ritual. The act of remembrance, more than the process. They took a long hook, shoved it up the nose, and took out the brain. They cut open the side and emptied the abdomen then washed out the cavity with wine then stuffed it with myrrh and frankincense."

"Ain't that the stuff they brought baby Jesus?"

"Yes. Then they sewed the body back up and wrapped it with bandages of fine linen cloth smeared with gum to glue it to the body."

Like a cloth coffin? Sounds like they were cheap. Wrap someone in a bed sheet and call it a day."

"Except that they then put them in coffins. They wrapped each of the organs and put them in Canopic jars. Each one shaped into the form of a head of the four sons of Horus, who were charged to protect them."

"That sounds cool."

"You young lot want the scares and blood of it all. Always with the blood, never enough evisceration for your prurient minds. But for us, the old folks, ones who have lost, we cling to the hope of contact with the other side. We all want some ... consolation. Consideration. Something from that place. To let us know it's okay. That it's all worth it. But the dead stay silent and keep their secrets to themselves."

Their first Christmas together, he spent three weeks in the woods hanging lights. Cobalt lights, purchased from all the stores in the city, strung in the trees surrounding the house. When he turned them on, the shimmer haloed the treetops for miles around.

The lights bathed them in sapphire luminescence when they stepped in. JaQuon twirled, wide-eyed, as he took in the room. A bank of shelves lined the wall. Jars, like soldiers at parade rest, awaited inspection. Dark shapes bobbed in clear liquid, like raw meat drained of their color. The serpentine coil of intestines piled in one jar. Kidneys floated in another. Liver. Stomach. Lungs. On and on, a collection of viscera cleaned and preserved. Attending their distant mistress. On a stand next to her glass coffin was her heart.

"They couldn't get her eyes right. They were the most delicate shade of blue, but they lost something in the process."

The old man ran his hand along the glass surface, the reliquary of memories, wanting all the things he had left behind. The finest linen bandages held her together, dipped in preservatives and molded and shaped to her body. He couldn't imagine her sprayed, sliced, waxed, painted like some sort of museum piece doll. Wanting her preserved, a beautiful snapshot of how she was in life, he wondered if she cared what color he would dress her in. She lingered. A forgotten pair of glasses here, her favorite pen there. Afraid to disturb anything. Hoping in vain that it wouldn't hurt as much tomorrow.

"I don't want to get to know who I am without her." He left one hand on the glass sarcophagus, a lingering touch before turning to JaQuon. "I think I'll purchase your skateboard, after all. It's all right to let him go. Five hundred dollars suffice?"

JaQuon nodded absently, his silent revulsion rooting him to the spot.

"I'll know when my collection is complete. I thought I knew what I was looking for. You know how there's a word on the tip of your tongue, just out of reach." He pressed the bills into JaQuon's hand then checked the time on his broken pocket watch, his age spots like tiny scars on the back of his hand, knowing that the time was always theirs. His and Helen's. "I suppose it's time for you to go."

§

Writing filled the days, scribbles that scratched toward the truth, each second a graveside marker, a matter of figuring out how to end the story. He lived a life steeped in regret. Not the man, the husband, he was meant to be. Neither able to do right by her nor live without her. He drifted until he found comfort in dead things and found purpose, knitting together some of the broken bits inside of him by simply not letting go of any part of her.

The first time he told her he loved her, she said she didn't believe him. Trust was a razor, she said, and belief had to be earned. The threat of competition, the possibility of her absences reduced his breath to hollow gasps. He mourned her loss though she was still with him. The memory of her, a ghost that wandered the hallways. His heartbeat, an aching flutter whenever she neared; her presence, a shadow within him. His thoughts drifted to her. Her skin the smell of crushed dandelions and jasmine. Her touch along his arm, the gentle tread of a spider along its web. He had words to describe his love.

§

[But it was the love written in the margins of journals. His alone.]

The Volunteer

Everyone called the church "The Underground." It began as a joke, as their services were held in the basement of United Presbyterian Church. The building was everything he loved in a building. Mostly that it was old, over a hundred years old. Things that withstood the rigors of time had been tested and found true. It had turrets, a slate tile roof, its design held prisoner by an architect's demented whimsy. And it had character. Like all old buildings, it had personality. Hallways that went nowhere. Nooks and crannies and misplaced alcoves that served no purpose. He volunteered for so many programs, such as the Exile and Restoration—the E/R, they liked to call the ministry—as much to be in the building as to be with *her*.

She waited at the top of the stairs, head held high. Not asking for pity, nor accepting it. The old building had been grandfathered in, not having to meet the code for being handicap accessible. The people rushed to carry her down the steps, held aloft as a queen in procession. Every night, the same routine. It took him weeks to screw together the courage to talk to her.

"What is that you're wearing?" he asked when she noticed him staring at her. She noticed everything. Her eyes were cerulean. They weren't really, but he believed the word cerulean wasn't used nearly often enough.

"An asymmetrical caftan, cut on the bias."

He didn't know what that meant. He only knew that her dress had a kente cloth pattern. A bead necklace draped her, long loops bunched around her neck like a high collar then swooped along her top. She jangled as she moved. With her accent, her English was succulent. No, it wasn't the right word, but it described the sensation he felt when he heard her speak, which made it the right word after all.

She toyed with the edges of her caftan, tugging at it in an unconscious way, drawing attention to her chest and he found himself staring. He leaned against the wall in an awkward posture, hoping to not loom as tall over her. Nor did he wish to seem like he was constantly trying to look down her top. She didn't appear to care either way.

Her feet were hooks. He pretended not to notice and figured it impolite to ask. Not everyone was comfortable with some of the refugees being vampires, but the church's mission wasn't to judge.

"How long have you been in this country?"

"A very long time. I was the first. I made the way for the others. I look out for them. That is my role, sweetie."

With practiced ease, she punctuated many of her questions with endearments: "You still doing okay, honey?" or "Can I get you anything, sweetie?"; as if she learned English by being a waitress in a local diner. He could never be that familiar with people he barely knew, much less strangers. He barely shook the hands of the people he did know well. But he loved the way she said "honey" and "sweetie" as if she meant them just for him. He bathed in the words, allowing them to soothe him.

"Are you all ..." Twirling his finger as if waving a wand at the rest of the people who milled about in the church basement, he realized that he did not know how to finish the question about the nature of her people. Words had traps he had found, because he was no good with words. Often, without meaning to, he insulted those around him. After a while, he found it safer not to speak at all.

"We are one people though different groups. Different bloodlines. Each with their own history and ways of doing things. In the end, we all serve the tribe. My mother was Asante. My father was Fante. So I speak Twi and Fante. And English. How many languages do you speak?"

"I'm doing good to speak American."

And she laughed. Never had he seen someone laugh or smile more. "My name is N'Kya."

N'Kya.

Such a beautiful name. He had to have her say it because his tongue was far too clumsy to pronounce it correctly. N'Kya. From her lips, her name had music. As he saw it, she made music with her lips. *Say her name ... N'Kya.*

He had a name once, he remembered when he mattered to people.

The E/R had the run of The Underground for the last few weeks. The ministry worked with people displaced from their country for one reason or another. He had been displaced from his home when his wife declared that he wasn't a man because he couldn't provide for her in the way she wanted nor was a fit example for their children. His dreams were the toys of infants long overdue to be put away. With no warning or fanfare, he found himself displaced. Not that E/R could've helped him. Unlike the clients of E/R, he had food, clothing, transportation, a place to stay, and spoke English so he didn't need many of the services E/R provided. Still, he was an extra set of hands to help care for the people.

"So, what do you do?" The words tumbled out of his mouth, clumsy and awkward. "For *them*, I mean."

"I sew." The words leapt from her mouth with such conviction. As if she were the embodiment of sewing. Colors for eyes. Fabrics for her body. Needles for fingers. Thread for vessels. Her hands trembled against the armrest of her wheelchair. His mother's hands shook like that when her blood sugar dipped too low and she needed to eat. Wizened, useless things that seemed so dark against his. Not that he dared to touch her. "Back home in our village, sewing was an important skill because clothes are very important. Not just to protect but also to define. Clothes set people apart, but first they have to be made. We brought that skill with us."

"I wish I had a skill," he said.

N'Kya laughed, but not in that hurtful way that his wife used to snicker at him when he shared something about himself. No, N'Kya's laugh was a revelation. "Come, let me show you what we do."

He fell into a seat beside the table, as if the force of her request compelled him to sit. The surrounding ladies glanced up at him with hungry eyes. Hungry, but not predatory. Their faces possessed a stoic grimness like the beauty of porcelain figurines, watching without comment as N'Kya wheeled behind him. A young woman whose face seemed ancient when he glimpsed her out of the corner of his eye, piled a bolt of fabric before him.

"We aren't little children waiting to be taken care of or exploited," N'Kya said. "Pick a piece, sweetie."

"Which one?"

"Whichever one speaks to you."

"How will I know if I get it right?"

"It whispers to you and you alone. How will we know if you got it wrong?"

He flipped through a velvety material; though he enjoyed the texture of it, it wasn't quite right. Then a kente cloth pattern with green as its focal color, but that wasn't for him. He settled on a black fabric broken by strands of gold. The material was lush, but not like velvet. "This."

"Good." N'Kya ran her hand through the material then along his fingers and up his arm. "You're a natural."

He nearly stopped breathing.

In high school, he loved a girl once. Her name was Amanda Fisher. During French class, she sat in front of him. And when their teacher—who never wore a bra and always stood beside him giving him a clear view of her—passed out homework, Amanda's hands brushed against his. He froze every time, holding the memory of that contact for as long as he could or until the kid behind him snapped him out of his moment.

N'Kya rolled close to him, filling his empty spaces. Her presence brushed along his neck.

"I think I'm supposed to say something, but I don't know what," he said.

"Then don't say anything. Sometimes silence is the greatest wisdom."

"Is that a saying of your people?"

"Our people have many sayings," N'Kya said. "And even more secrets."

"Tell me a secret."

N'Kya smiled. Two of her teeth had lengthened, her tongue lolled between the protrusions. Her mouth matched her eyes, hungry but not predatory. It was an exquisite smile. "You've been chosen."

"By who?"

"By us. By me."

"Why?"

"Because you're lonely, too. But you're also not ready yet. You haven't found your place."

She had been out of place, too, once upon a time. Her wheelchair was superior to the old wood crutches she got by on in her old country, she said. There, she had been abandoned to beg for a living. Until one day she was called and, when she was ready, turned. She became one of the tribe, and though her body changed, it was not made whole. Had she been a child, she would have remained a child. Or had she been an amputee, she wouldn't have suddenly grown a new limb. Still, she made the choice and joined her people to minister to their souls.

He remained unafraid.

"Did you dream that your life would be like this?" he asked.

"I expected to grow up in a village."

"No one expects to grow up in a village." He tried to picture a village, but all he imagined was dirt and straw-thatched huts held together by dry mud.

"Why, because your massive cities are so wonderful?"

"Well, yes." He knew that "yes" wasn't the right answer and that the question itself was one of those traps of speaking, but he didn't have anything clever to say instead.

"That's why your American Dream is doomed to fail, sweetie." She could condemn his lifestyle, values, and national illusion all she wanted, as long as she ended it with "sweetie."

"Why's that?"

"All your country is about—all your churches try to protect—is based on two parents and their children. Even if there is only one child in that family, that's not enough to support your way of life."

His way of life involved going to work and then coming home to watch television while his father ignored him from the other room. Though displaced, he had a place to stay, even if it had meant moving in with his father. That wasn't so bad, as he never had much of a relationship with his dad. He liked taking care of his father, though the elderly man went out drinking every night. Although the volunteer occasionally wrote checks for things he didn't remember buying or using, his was a sedentary lifestyle perfectly supported by his own efforts. He asked, "How so?"

"Not enough support. Your relationships become as disposable as any other material object in your life. Like poorly chosen fabric. Now in a village, you have parents, children, grandparents, aunts, uncles, and cousins all together, bracing one another. Different and many threads weaving together to create a stronger tapestry. It's all about family."

Family sounded wonderful when she spoke about it. For him, family meant more people to eat the things he bought and put in the refrigerator. And more people to turn the heat up too high in the house. And more people to argue about what to watch on television. Which she agreed with, but made it sound like those were exactly the things to be treasured.

§

Church at The Underground was on Sunday evenings. Some people objected to the time because it didn't feel like church time. Saturday nights they could live with and call it the Sabbath. Sunday mornings were the expected church time. But Sunday nights interfered too much with their football game viewing schedules.

The church service lasted an hour. For the first twenty-five minutes, the congregation sang: pop choruses reminiscent of seventies rock ballads for the regular attendees; Negro spirituals in an attempt to make their African guests feel more at home. No one knew the words or understood the melody, a congregation united in awkward singing. For the next twenty-five minutes, the pastor went on about shame and choosing to live by lies you came to believe about yourself.

The last ten minutes were for Communion. A large wedge of freshly baked bread. *The body that was broken for us.* Two sets of shot glasses. The colorless ones were filled with grape juice. The pink ones were filled with wine. Not everyone wanted wine. *The blood that was shed for us.*

The volunteer checked the time. When the service started, there were only a handful of folks. Though they were encouraged to attend the services of the hosting church, none of E/R's refugees had bothered to attend. But there was a meal afterwards, so a few refugees, joined by the local homeless, drifted in as the service wrapped up.

They also always arrived at this time, a murder of crows roosting at the periphery of their community. He didn't need to turn around to know who had entered as a shiver of fear rippled across the refugees.

Kwame.

His name had no melody no matter who said it. Tall and elegant, a curtain of night falling onto a stage. His skin tone ran toward mahogany, dark and rich. His pupils were too white against his skin. And he never smiled.

They were overdressed for the service. Clothes told their story. Most of the regular congregants arrived in shorts or jeans or whatever casual wardrobe they had. Perhaps misplaced empathy, not wanting to make the homeless feel out of place, guilt by privilege. The homeless didn't particularly notice or care.

The volunteer didn't have anything resembling fashion sense. He didn't believe in wearing clothes that had ads on them. If he were going to be a billboard, he wished to be paid as such. He was not made for low-cut or hip-hugging anything. His midriff remained quite concealed, thank you very much, beneath a crumpled blue T-shirt that read "Superdad," a Father's Day present from his children before he was displaced. He couldn't picture their eyes. He also had a pair of jeans whose brand he had forgotten, but he only had the one pair. That was the thing about jeans: few people looked closely at them. They were just jeans. Every pants.

To him, Kwame was just a man in a fancy suit, but when N'Kya spoke about clothes, he paid attention.

"He hasn't changed," N'Kya said. "He sports that same turn of the century look of when he first ventured from home and spied gentlemen of leisure. Dark gray saque jacket, like smoke, double-breasted with peak lapels. His sleeves worn short."

All the volunteer knew was that he hated the way Kwame wore the clothes. So regal. So commanding. The people stared at him with awe-tinged fear. A suit all too American on its surface and yet not, cinched too tight around the arms and waist, drawn too tight at his calves. Bold, square buttons. Colored inner lining fabrics. The matching pants flared a bit at the calves, accommodating the heavy boots he wore. He knew what those boots must have hid.

"The fabrics were a dance, honey. Materials conjoined together to tell a story about the article of clothes as much as the clothes told the story of the person who wore them. Look at Kwame's chorus."

Three women shadowed Kwame, a blur of lime green and fuchsia. They walked tall and proud. Walked was too small a word. Their bodies glided between shadows with a mix of grace and sensuality, the way a tongue licked along the top of a lover's lip in a languid brush. The curves of their bodies demanded to be noticed, yet with the menace of excoriation should a glance linger.

"They have remembered that modesty protects and inspires allure. There is a sensual mystery to fabrics. I designed that look for them," N'Kya continued. "Three different dresses, one story. All of that lime green, Dutch wax print edged in fuchsia tabs. The fabric itself an artificial construct. Colonization, imitation, assimilation. Patterns used to set them apart and define prestige. The tangled history of Europe and Africa all in the simple play of fabrics. It is only fitting that we ended up in America."

"They were pretty dresses." He loved their boots. They went all the way up to their knees. They reminded him of superheroes.

"Even their boots hold secrets." N'Kya eased back in her chair and shifted her weight. She drew her legs under her and draped them with her dress. It felt like a private moment, and he wanted to allow her space without embarrassment. Embarrassment wasn't the right word. If he had the correct cloth, he would sew something regal and proud, with a high collar that shielded all but deserving eyes. It was the only time he ever saw her slump, even in the slightest. "He won't make me jealous."

Perhaps he called himself being chivalrous or protective, perhaps he simply didn't want to let his jealousy get the better of him. Either way, he found himself stepping to Kwame. "Can I help you?"

"I've come to look for any of my people who may have arrived recently. Those forgotten by their own. Those who would die a slow death trying to fit into your world. Those whose needs you might not wish to meet." Kwame stepped to him and leaned in close. His voice was decadent. That was definitely the right word. To the volunteer, it sounded like an entitled basketball player who got into too much trouble. His breath smelled of hot iron.

"We have food. You and yours are welcome to join us for dinner."

"We hunger, but you don't want to feed us," Kwame said.

"We also have clothes, if any of your people need them."

"I don't want any of your clothes."

"But they're perfectly good clothes." The volunteer reached for the donation box. On top was the red sweater his grandmother made for him. A garish shade of red, like a prostitute's lipstick, with three bears across the center, each wearing a Christmas stocking. He hated the sweater and never wore it.

"They are an insult," Kwame said.

"It's Indiana. It gets cold."

"What does that matter to us? We haven't seen the sun in a long time."

"You ought to be grateful you have any clothes at all." There was no trap in Kwame's words, except the one the volunteer not only created but fell into himself.

"Grateful?" Kwame turned his dark, unwavering eyes to those gathered around them, directing his comments to the volunteer without deigning to meet his eyes. "I, for one, don't want to be part of your feelgood effort. You clean out your garages, give from your excess, and call it charity. You are emptying your refuse on us. To truly give, you have to sacrifice."

"That's enough, Kwame," N'Kya whispered, though her tone carried the threat of thunder. "What do you want?"

"More of the tribe have found us. We have need of your people's services. Of you."

"To brand our people."

"To set us apart."

"Aren't we set enough apart?" N'Kya asked.

"This is not who we were meant to be." Kwame held up the volunteer's grandmother's sweater, then tossed it in front of the wheel of N'Kya's chair. The sweater crumpled on the floor, bear side down. "We must find our own place here. We must find our own way."

Kwame's words touched a chord in the volunteer. Thinking back, he couldn't remember the last time anyone or anything stirred his heart.

"Come with us. You do not belong here."

The volunteer hoped Kwame had been talking to him.

"We are of the tribe," N'Kya said.

"I am Asantehene of our people. I trace my line back to Okomfo Anokey himself. I need a Mamponghene. Come with me."

"And you wish me to play second to your first? I belong with my people, sweetie." N'Kya wheeled away from him. "I'll need time. And measurements."

Kwame turned up his nose. Waving his fingers, the woman in the cocktail dress produced a piece of paper. "Find us when you're ready."

§

The story of the immigrants were all too similar. One way or another the story was always about one story moving against another. When stories clashed, one had to be eliminated. That was the story of people. The government moved against the people. The military needed to take over a land or another resource because people only had limited value as a resource. The authorities burned down villages, separated families, forced them into labor or battle or sex. Men, women, children faced elimination so they ran away, ran away, ran away. Hiding and going, resting and going, going and going, until a refugee camp became home. Over and over the same story with different details.

Indiana was one of the top settlement states. Who wouldn't settle for Indiana over extermination? And it had corn. And room for different ethnic groups, even from the same people. And churches on nearly every corner. A church for everyone.

"Kwame and his ... followers. They are different from the others," he said.

"You'll have to forgive Kwame. He's gruff, but that's his way. He is the shepherd of our people," N'Kya said. The others look to her for guidance. Yet they also fear her. Maybe more than they did Kwame. Perhaps they had never heard her say her name. Their people had been lost, scared, and the future was a great unknown that yawned into the horizon and threatened to swallow them whole. N'Kya brought them back from the brink and gave them purpose. A circle of women sheared fabric into patterns. Another group hunched over sewing machines, delighting in the thrum of the stitch. In their work, they found self-confidence and worth. They found personhood. Freedom. A look of longing filled the volunteer's eyes. "We rarely mingle with outsiders."

"You have no choice now." The words sounded like a puffed-up chest.

"You are so presumptuous, sweetie."

"I don't mean to be."

"Americans rarely do. You believe your ways to be superior to everyone else's. After all, the world turns to you for help, never the other way around."

There was another trap in her words. He wished he were smarter, more handsome, so that she could see him. He handed her a lunch tray. "The corn is fresh."

"We have our ways, our traditions, our stories. We're still a people. With history. And secrets." She turned up her nose at the food, then seemed to chide herself for seeming ungrateful for the gesture.

"Tell me a secret," he said.

"I thought people would welcome us, maybe have some tea with us."

"I like tea." He didn't, but it was a good lie.

She smiled. "You have a rare gift with the fabric. You have the eye, the heart, for the craft. And people. I could use your help."

"Anything."

"You should understand the cost before you choose, honey. I go through a lot of helpers."

"I don't care."

"Then let me have your hands."

§

The news reported that a jogger went missing at Eagle Creek Park. A pretty girl, Elementary Education major. When she started her run that evening, she probably never suspected that she would end up as prey. She was the kind of college girl who would have stared past him as if he weren't even there. He wasn't mad. He knew that he was ordinary, and commonplace things were easily ignored. Every man.

§

He and N'Kya found a secluded workroom down the hall and around several corners from the sanctuary of The Underground. He wasn't too certain the hallway actually connected to the room and hoped they'd be able to find their way back.

Craning his head back as if caught up in a moment of writhing ecstasy, he presented his neck. He counted the cost. Closing his eyes, all he could picture was a cat revealing its belly so that it could be pet. A most delicate undertaking. A declaration of complete and utter vulnerability. So exposed, someone could do untold damage: tear though muscle and trachea; leave him gasping for breath, wet and throttled.

The body that was broken for us.

His decision. It wasn't much of a decision. No one would remember his displaced life. He would disappear into the night and be unremembered. All that he was, all the mistakes he made, would be gone. Like moving to a new land. He wasn't going to get any older, and that thought made him sad.

He entrusted himself to N'Kya. The neck was a thick muscle, its veins throbbed against her hungry mouth. To have her tongue lap along the corded vessels of his throat like an antiseptic swab before an injection. To know both pain and delight in one piercing. Her hands—wrinkled though rough-hewn, like tree bark—scraped against the other side of his face. Her canine teeth were so pointed, he expected her to lisp when she spoke again. But she didn't speak again. She ran her teeth along the thickness of his neck. Images flickered through his mind as his life drained. The last bits of an umbilical cord falling brittle and black. The plucked eye of a doll, its vacant gaze staring like black buttons. A backseat copulation, awkward and hurried, with the attendant spill of a virgin's blood. The smoke of a crack pipe smoldering, like the remaining embers of hope.

Baptized in the sweat of the suffering, they were joined: conceptual artist and the performance. He'd never felt anything so wondrous. Like a blissful, unscratched itch.

The blood that was shed for us.

He was chosen, and he accepted.

A drop of crimson daubed his collar.

§

N'Kya hovered over him, always busy in that mysterious way cats were. He hunched over the bench under the column of light provided by the dim bulb dangling from the overhead fixture. A spider skittered across the pile of fabric. With a casual flick, he knocked it to the ground. He had nothing against spiders, but he knew N'Kya was terrified of them. Everyone was afraid of something. Still, he apologized to it before he reduced it to a black smear on the carpet.

"Tell me a secret." He rubbed his feet. The bones slowly ground into one another as the flesh tightened and morphed. He assumed it would be over when he first transformed. But not being of the tribe, the transformation took days. He concentrated on the boots he would have to make for himself.

"In our land, there are many people. The Ewe fear the creature known as the adze. They come to you as a firefly. In its 'human' form, it has a hunched back, sharp talons, and jet black skin. In an instant, it can kill you then drain you of your blood, then devour your heart and liver."

"Does your tribe fear anything?" he asked.

"We have our own night monsters. And we bring them with us, for where the village goes, so goes our nightmares."

"What do they call their monsters?"

"The sasabonsam." N'Kya touched his hand. "It's time."

"What do I have to do?"

"Some are hunters. Others are caretakers. In the end, all gifts serve the tribe. Open your mind, sweetie. You have to prepare yourself for the task to come. Consider this the communion of the creator."

"When do I start?"

"When the cloth speaks to you."

He had never been good with his hands before. Once, he labored with the act of folding paper to make an airplane for nearly an hour to get the folds correct. But when he described a pattern, the look of it, the interplay of fabrics, her words brought his hands to life.

He thought of his father's skin, having persevered, ready to be sloughed off before death, ready to be flensed from his bones.

§

Indianapolis was a crazy quilt of old and new, concrete and green. The concrete and metal spires of downtown gave way to dozens of incorporated concerns and communities which made up the city. On the northeast side of town, with its fashion malls and congested traffic, Allisonville had been swallowed up leaving only Allisonville Road to remember it by. On the west side, Speedway—home of the Indianapolis 500—was its own city within the city. A preserve for a people who were about their cars. On the northwest side was Eagle Creek Park. A nature preserve of 3,900 acres of land surrounding 1,400 acres of an eponymous reservoir.

"It was a perfect place to hunt," N'Kya said, when the fourth person went missing over there. "You must deliver the package there. Tell them you are ready to serve."

At night only an honor box attended the gate of the park. Few came at night fearing the predators within the woods. People were lost in Eagle Creek Park all the time. He believed the trees moved. Waiting beneath a stand of trees, the glow of the moon marked him. It whispered lonely things to him. He made it a point to ignore the moon. It was prone to lie. Night congealed, thick shadows surrounded him.

Flanked by two other men, Kwame glared at him. He wore a double-breasted purple silk suit with a notched collar. The two men each wore single-breasted suits: one, a burgundy velvet suit with the same angled flap pockets and a shawl collar; the other, a red one with a notched collar under a bow tie. Their pants were wide in the leg, giving room to their black boots. Kwame snatched the package of new outfits from the volunteer. His mouth unfurled into a terrible grin. His teeth glistened, thick iron bands worked by his bulging jaw.

Some friends mentioned that he tended to observe the people around him rather than interact with them. A writer's posture. He couldn't remember his friends' names. N'Kya and Kwame were different kinds of old things. Tested and true, she endured. She persevered. She was holy. All personality, Kwame was a character. Not to be confused with having character. He was a long, beautiful hallway that went nowhere.

"What are you?" he asked.

"You mean, what are you now?" Kwame said. "The Sasabonsam. We endure. We persevere. We thrive. New shores. Old ways."

Kwame gestured to the surrounding trees. Three shadows in the trees undulated under the play of moonlight. Their forms, a cross between a woman's and a bat's. Short arms scratched at the night. They ringed the space, their wings unfurled like rooms of cloth spanning twenty feet. Mewling in chorus, their cries were wet and needy. "And we hunger."

"My place is to serve."

"By N'Kya's side?"

The volunteer nodded. Kwame cocked his head to the side as if giving serious thought to an ancient song. He appeared to be somewhat remorseful. Sad. He's not especially good at it. He nodded to the man in the red suit. The air whistled as he leapt into the air, disappearing into the gloom of night. After a few moments, the man's boots landed beside the volunteer. Hands snaked about him, and he was drawn into the air. The man in the red suit hung down like an empty sleeve and hoisted him until his inverted face met Kwame's. He dangled as if he were a boneless cat toy, but his struggles ceased when he saw the man clutched to the overhanging branch by the hooks that formed his feet. Kwame licked him with his sharkskin tongue.

"I have loved her for an eternity. But she has only ever looked at me with pity. She said that I'm not ready. So, I will love her for an eternity more. Or not. And our tribes will end one another."

"What will happen to me?" the volunteer asked.

"She has chosen you over me. You will pass out of one story into the next," Kwame said. "You have been set apart. And with us you have haven."

That didn't sound too bad. It had been too long since he called a place home.

Futures

The Electric Spanking of the War Babies
(with Kyle S. Johnson)

Everything was inextricably tethered to the box in George's closet. He stood on his tiptoes and let his fingers find the familiar edge of the old shoe box on the top shelf in his closet. He pulled it down carefully and carried it over to the bed where he laid it with quiet reverence. Though it had become a weekly routine, George never lost sight of how important the ceremony of dressing was to him. Clothes made the man.

After a moment of silence, he popped open the lid and withdrew his most prized possessions: his well-worn-yet-still-fresh pair of robin's egg blue quad skates adorned with rhinestones in geomantic formations. They were his talisman. His key.

A Dr. J poster hung next to one of his namesake, George "The Iceman" Gervin, behind him. They were his childhood heroes. He had grown up wanting to ball just like them. The ritual, however, felt every bit as if he was turning his back on childish things. He was ready. His two-toned blue bell bottoms hugged him tight in all the right places. His sideburns trailed down to his chin. He tucked a pick into his sculpted Afro, leaving only the raised fist that was its handle visible. All that remained were his shoes. He slid the first one on, the familiar wave swept down over him. Before he lost himself, he paused and shouted toward the crack in his bedroom door.

"Going out for a while, momma."

From behind a curtain of beads that separated the rooms down the hall came a muffled cough and then her voice, weak and half-asleep. "Oh, is it Thursday already? Where has this week gone?"

"Yeah, it's that time again."

"Be careful, baby. The war is almost here," she whispered.

"What you say, momma?"

"You have fun now, okay? Don't be out too late."

"Sure thing, momma." George tried to ignore how tired she sounded. She'd been hustling all day to feed his brother and sisters. He couldn't help but think they'd be better off with one less mouth around. George returned his attention to the second skate, sliding it on easily. Pulling the laces tight, he rose to his feet. The energy coursed through him. He felt blue electricity. He felt alive. He felt free. Looking himself over in the mirror, George tugged the wide collar of his polyester shirt and watched himself disappear into the person he became every Thursday night. He was no longer George Collins. The transformation was complete. He was Shakes Humphries, the baddest mofo on eight wheels.

§

The Sugar Shack was an oasis in the riot-torn city. No matter how angry folks got, burning buildings and tearing up their own stuff, they left the Sugar Shack alone. It was sacred ground, but it wasn't a place for heroes. Everything was so dark and gritty in those days, one long shadow drifting into an endless night.

This wasn't how it was supposed to be, a broken world filled with broken people who reveled in their brokenness. A world populated by anti-heroes, misunderstood villains, and heroes with feet, legs, and torsos of clay, where those who stood tallest fell first. Part of him remembered an echo of how things used to be, of a time where men and women were proud and bold, which confused him because this was all he ever knew. He put it down to a childhood dream, to something he'd read in a comic or seen on the television in his youth. Something he'd lost himself in, lying on his belly in the living room, while momma was at revival meeting.

The street lights burned to life on either side of the street, guiding Shakes in like the open arms of a neon goddess. A few kids ran past him trying to make it home or risk getting the switch for being caught out too late. Though rough, the neighborhood was home. Whether he was George or Shakes, he stood as tall as the world would allow, had always done everything he could to help out his little brothers and sisters. He felt like the 'hood thanked him in its own way by keeping his momma and him safe. But from the moment his skates touched the asphalt, he knew he was being watched. He scanned the shadows, anxious but not wanting to betray his cool. Whatever stalked him waited.

"They're spying on us." A man knocked over a trash can in the alley. "With their satellites and drones and eyes in the sky. We can't hide from them." *Don't look up.* "That's how they capture your face and run off with it to another world." The man stumbled toward him. "Can I get a dollar, youngblood?"

"What for?" Shakes knew his answer from the booze on the man's breath.

"Information about the revolution isn't free. No one believes me, though. No one ever believes me. Belief is the key."

"Don't look up. Got it." Shakes handed the man a dollar. The old drunk stuffed it into his pocket and offered daps, an appreciative smile, and a slurred "Good looking out."

Shakes accepted his offerings. "Stay strong, brother."

Shakes hustled into the skating rink. His name rang out as soon as he entered. The neon pink words Sugar Shack bathed the back corner of the rink. A mural of the solar system covered a full wall of the building, lit up by the cascading lights. George rapped with some of his boys, slapping palms and clutching hands in the secret handshakes of the initiated. The DJ raised his fist in salute, the rhythmic bobbing of his head persistent.

"Our very own star child, Shakes Humphries, is in the house. Show him some love, boys and girls, 'cause this is an aaaaall skate!"

The strains of the Bar-Kays bumped from the speakers. With a series of crossover moves to remind them of who he was, Shakes eased into a groove, and his boys fell in step with him. They soon formed a train, imitating the intricate dance routine of The Temptations in precise lockstep. They made that rink grunt.

A series of figures stepped from the shadows. It took Shakes a few seconds to process what he was seeing. The brother at the front was protected by a hard plastic shell adorned with panels of little neon lights and buttons. Everything was fiery pink. Despite the seeming bulk of the suit, his movements were smooth and natural. Where a face should have been, Shakes saw only his reflection in the obsidian sheen of the orb fastened to the raised neck of the armor.

Who is this dude? Some kind of spaceman?

The others emerged from the darkness, their suits identical but for the yellow color. Each held what appeared to be a child's toy, like Nerf guns except with hard purple polymer for their carapaces. Despite the resemblance, Shakes knew that playtime was over.

"Sweet Christmas," Shakes muttered.

Two of them covered the front door, another stood by the rear exit. No one reacted to them, as if only Shakes could see them. Three more emerged from the shadows by the wall of lockers muttering a low chant. "Psychoalphadiscobetabioaquadoloop. Psychoalphadiscobetabioaqua-doloop. Psychoalphadiscobetabioaqua-doloop."

The rink was covered by a thin layer of mist that rose like a flood, reeking of lemon-scented Lysol.

The leader spoke behind his mask, the voice modulated to sound high by an otherworldly theremin. "Your time's up, sucker. High time you come with us. Make it easy on yourself. You don't want it getting tough out here."

The head spaceman fired into the air. The rink erupted in chaos. Tables overturned as people scurried for cover. People tripped over one another, rushing about blindly. Screams drowned out the music except for the throbbing bassline.

A hand clapped down on Shake's shoulder. He turned to find a fine sister wearing a fox fur coat and pink hot pants, revealing her bare midrift. Her matching pink sunglasses, trimmed with glitter, tucked into her Afro puffs. For all of the surrounding panic, she was ice.

"My name is Mallia Grace." She held her hand out to him. "Come with me if you want to funk."

§

Mallia melted, her skin sloughing like wax giving way under its own weight. Shakes raised his hand, but it pooled, rain streaking a windshield in a hundred rivulets. He tried to take Mallia's hand, but they merged together, their bodies falling into a commingling mess. He tried to hold onto her, find some grip on her reality, knowing they'd mix into a single bowl of cosmic slop to be poured down the drain, discarded and forgotten. He resigned himself to their ultimate dissolution, hoping, maybe this time, the light hanging at the end of the darkness would be kinder ...

Shakes opened his eyes. His head pounded, his stomach queasy, but he tried not to throw up on the chair. His throat tight and dry as the pants clinging to Mallia's behind. And with that image jolting him to full consciousness, he forgot his thirst and tried to find his cool. His chair faced out over a throng of people in the club beneath him. He wasn't in the Sugar Shack anymore. The place was too packed, too clean. The building seemed like a hollowed-out warehouse. Metal gleamed along each of the three tiers of space like the polished rib cage of a huge beast. Gaudy lighting—fuscia, olive, purple—flashed, pouring over the sea of bodies beneath him. Every last person was dancing, moving, loving, and grooving. Far removed from judging eyes, they were people who knew they were out of sight. Everything was sweating, even the room beaded with condensation from the rising heat. Shakes realized the room he was in was a huge, clear bubble, suspended somewhere above the third level.

The stage was at the far end, the six-piece band on it wove through an uptempo rendition of "Pop That Thang." A double stack of what appeared to be Marshalls, triple stacks of Ampeg SVTs, a chorus of speakers pulsing as one great wall of music. On a separate stage above the fray was an oversized set of drums—but like no kit he'd ever seen before. Nearly translucent, each pounded kick produced rhythm as color. It had been the bassline that brought him back around, a defibrillator shockwave through his chest. Like the thump-thump-thump of a brand new heart.

He knew Mallia watched him, so he strapped on his cool again and turned his head back slightly. "You didn't have to drug me. I'd have come quietly."

All business, she passed on the lingering innuendo. "Oh, baby, I didn't do a thing."

"My man, you flat-out fainted. You missed all the action," a brother in a pink coat and chartreuse bell bottoms said. Stars and crescent moons had been shaved into his head, as if his skull streaked through the cosmos as he bobbed his head. But the rings on his bare feet seemed too affected, as if he were trying too hard to create a look he wasn't entirely comfortable with. He was slick with perspiration and trying not to show that he struggled to get his breath back.

"Don't make it sound so glamorous. It got thick in a hurry. We lost one of our own back there, and we don't have many of us to spare," Mallia said. "Shakes, Weary Nation."

Weary gave him a head nod. "You look a little rough. You may have caught some of their steam. That shit'll fuck you up like a blast of LSD."

Shakes caught his next words in his throat and turned back in full toward the people below, whooping their appreciation as the tune ended. "Who were they?"

"Afronauts," Mallia said, with a matter-of-factness to her voice. "But don't you worry, sugar, the man's gonna be up to see you in a minute. Just sit tight and it'll all be explained."

The lights changed, stayed there, bathing the masses in an otherworldly green. The band wasted little time, the horns bleating out, jumping right into some Tower of Power.

"Aw, I love this song, man. Love it."

Shakes turned toward the heart of the bubble room, toward the figure striding to the long zebra-print sofa in the middle of it. He was lithe and graceful, majestic in a shimmering golden vinyl jumpsuit that seemed painted on him. The platform shoes he glided in on made him tower like a golden titan.

"How'd it go?" Mallia asked.

"They tightened that ass," the golden man said.

"Yeah, I bet they were stroking on that," said a man in a buccaneer hat from which long braids snaked. He wore matching buccaneer boots, but the only other items he sported in between were a diaper and a smile.

In a long chain of motion, smooth enough to have been rehearsed, the golden man snatched a drink from the hand of the buccaneer, knocked it back, and flung the glass away before reaching the couch. When he got there, he stopped and looked it over like it was offending him, shook his head in disapproval, and turned to face Shakes. The table between them sat low and was covered in LPs. *Hot Buttered Soul. Mother Popcorn. Stand! Innervisions.* The essentials.

"It's a fitting tune, ya know? For this situation we have ourselves here. So, I just gotta figure it out. You drunk as a skunk? Maybe you're loose as a goose? Or maybe, maybe, maybe, you're high as a fly?"

"I don't have a damned clue what you're talking about." Shakes swallowed the saliva pooling in his mouth from his still-sour stomach.

Hands on his hips, the golden man leaned over the table and inspected Shakes. Something in his face softened. To Shakes, it almost looked like surprise or maybe relief. "Or maybe you're the real deal."

He turned to the buccaneer who had taken to inspecting his own muscles in the doorway mirror and shooed him out. When the door closed, the golden man reached behind his back and yanked a string from the vinyl jumpsuit, releasing the hidden girdle built in. His midsection bloomed, a full belly pressing hard against the gold and stretching it to its limits. He sighed and plopped himself down on the couch, throwing his feet over the stack of records and sending some spilling to the floor.

"So, you probably want it straight. You have no idea. Yeah, I can dig that." The golden man stroked his belly as if in his final trimester, still getting used to his bulge.

"What the hell is going on here?" Shakes asked. At the steel of his voice, Mallia took an aggressive posture, but the strange man waved her off.

"Shoot. You really have no idea who you are, brother?"

"I know exactly who I am. Never been in doubt."

"No, you don't. Not even close. You just one of them cats. You practically glow. You ain't Shakes. Yeah, I know about that name. Know your momma called you George, too. But that's not how I know you, oh no. No, you are the inheritor of the Funkenstein spirit. Intergalactic Master of the Funk, Emperor of The Groove, Ambassador of The Rhythm, The Heart and Soul of Rock and Roll, Martian Prince Come Down From His High Obsidian Tower on Mount Bump, Dr. Funkenstein. And I've been looking for you for a long, long time."

"You higher than a mug," Shakes said.

"We don't have much time." The golden man planted his feet firmly in the shag carpet, stiffened his spine, and leaned forward.

He was going for serious, Shakes knew, but the whole act played just an inch shy of cornball. It was when the strange man took off his star-framed glasses and Shakes saw it there in his eyes that he shut his mouth and opened his mind.

"I'm tired. Every night I go out there to that crowd, tripping off the music. We're out there, doing our thing, every night making promises. All about that sanctified testimony. They never ask questions, you know, because they want to *believe* it. So they believe us, believe the things we say, and we let it grow. When we hit the break, we let the whispers start. 'I think I hear the mothership coming.' But I'm just out there faking the funk, man. All hype, no love. Was a time when I could hear that mothership coming, too. But that's been a long time now, and now I'm an imposter. All because we need them to believe."

"Believe in what?"

"In all of it. In the mothership connection. The funkentelechy. In the Star Child. In you. Their groove powers us. We want to go home, and we need you to lead us there." He pointed a multi-ringed finger out to the bouncing masses. "They're the fuel. You're the engine."

Prophetic pronouncements never went down well on an empty stomach. Shakes never thought there'd come a time where he actually craved Sugar Shack's chili fries. He didn't know how he was supposed to feel. Hearing the story reminded Shakes of this one time at the barbershop when he was a kid. He'd listen to all the older men, huddled in a corner as if they all belonged to a club he wasn't a part of, discussing mysteries of life he'd never understand. Mostly women. They'd said things with such certainty, like how ladies loved full beards. All George wanted to do was grow a full beard, to prove that he could hang. But his hair came in patches. He'd study his face in the mirror, lift his chin, examine his soul patch on the side of his face. "Next time you have to go to the bathroom," the men at the shop said, "dab some pee on your face. Hair'll come in thick then." Of course, he believed it. He came out stinking of piss to peals of laughter from the men. Wasn't often that he was taken for a sucker after that.

"Look here, Agent Double-O-Soul..."

"We can't explain it to you." The golden man looked tired all of a sudden. "You have to experience it. I'm into something I can't shake loose. Mallia?"

"Don't be scared. You ain't no punk." She motioned for Shakes to follow, and he'd follow her shake anywhere.

Mallia led him toward the crowd below them. The buccaneer moved to the golden man's side, cinching him back up into his suit in preparation to take the stage. When they reached the smaller bubble that would transport them to the first floor, Mallia leaned into Shakes' ear.

"I can see why he believes in you. The Star Child's been talking you up, and I didn't really believe it. But now? Yeah, okay, I'm on board."

"Yeah?"

"Fo' sho."

"How do you know?"

"It's just one of those things. Can't explain it. You just know when you know."

§

The crowd hushed, a track on pause, waiting, breath bated as the Star Child slithered to the microphone like a whispered word, his fingers wrapped slowly around the mic stand, taking it as surely as he would his manhood, confidently, sex everywhere, everyone turned on, and his lips moved, forming the hiss, "Shhhh ... y'all hear that," and they roared their approval that they could, oh yes they could, "I ... I think I can ... yeah, I think I hear something way, way up there," oh yes, they heard it too, "it's out there," finger erect pointing up toward space, "Can't you hear it moving out there behind the stars, it's looking, and oh, it's powerful, but it needs a little help," they swayed in anticipation, wanting to know how they could aid the cause, "Oh, you see, the mothership relies on a sense of smell, that's right, and it needs to pick up your funk," kinetic, the band hummed behind the Star Child, kept them on their feet, the pulse of the bass not giving them a chance to sit down, their words brought to life, their feet stepping with them, sacrifices to the altar of The Funk, "We need this funk uncut if you want the mothership to find us, children," their eyes rolling back, their mouths moving, like the Holy Spirit falling down on them causing them to speak in tongues, chanting the words, *Psychoalphadiscobetabioaquadoloop, Psychoalphadiscobetabioaquadoloop, Psychoalphadiscobetabioaquadoloop,* his voice rising, "No, no, I don't think you understand how far out there it is," moving faster, "So far out there, so you gotta Funk it up better than that," the crowd writhing, building toward it, "I wants to get funked up, we've been down here for so long, too long we've been trapped in the Zone of Zero Funkativity, so long now, from way back, kings and queens and presidents and cabinets and dictators and real fakers and," the crowd fed it back, thrumming like an organic bass drum, setting the tempo, "OH MY LORD," he exploded, the crowd swooned, the chant burst forth, *Psychoalphadiscobetabioaquadoloop, Psychoalphadiscobetabioaquadoloop,* the words hit Shakes' ears and found familiarity there, something distant, some far-off place, somewhere proud, the crowd hit its mark, achieving climax and riding it down on the hook of the backing band's bassline, and the Star Child turned his back to head off-stage with a little more dip to his hip, with a little more bounce to the ounce, picking up a little bit more of what he was putting down, smiling to no one in particular.

They crowded around Shakes off-stage, maybe without meaning to, maybe on purpose, his gravitational pull absolute. Their eyes tracked his every twitch and breath, their gazes filled with something expectant, as if even to watch him was to be enlightened. Shakes flinched but didn't buckle. Their scrutiny unsettled him, leaving him with feelings of both vulnerability and being creeped out, like having garden gnomes watch him undress. Like they'd scoop him up and slam him down onto an altar at any moment, plug the knife in, and cut a bit deeper, draw some more blood for the good cause. But he had plenty of practice putting on cool that he didn't have anymore.

"You ain't from around here," Shakes said.

"No, we're not. We're reality explorers. Funking cosmonauts," the Star Child said.

"Afronauts. Like the ones that jumped us?"

"No. *Funkateers.* We're about peace and the groove. Afronauts, they're a different school of cats entirely. We all access the groove the same way. *Psychoalphadiscobetabioaquadoloop...*" The Star Child closed his eyes, lost in a moment.

"... to different effect. They take our message for weakness. They see love and dance as a plague ... and they're the cure."

"The war crept nearer ..." Shakes whispered.

"At this point, no one remembers what incursion into whose space started things. There's always been a rivalry between the Star Child and Professor Bereft of Groove," Mallia said. "They're both Leos."

"Man, we were like brothers back in the day. We came up together in the same band. We had all these hopes and dreams, wanted to make music no one had heard before. And we were good, too. No one could get with us. Then everything got funked up—and not in a good way. We got caught up. We each had a song to sing, had to go solo, do our own thing. It tore up the group. All anybody seems to remember after that is the hurt." The Star Child's attention drifted far away, seeing it all again, feeling it once more. For, as accomplished as he was at faking the funk, he couldn't hide his pain. "Our reality was obliterated. We pushed through what we could, and whatever made it into this world resonates as things of music, of fiction."

"There were stories. Rumors of a child, sent down..." Mallia started.

"Just hype." The Star Child didn't want to go into it any further, but Shakes could sense something. "All that's left is dance and rhythm and making love and partying past your momma's curfew. That's all we've got left, and we're hoping it's enough. There are some out there who are attuned to it. Agents of the Funk. Music, love, the groove, it awakens something way down deep and lets them see glimpses of what we were. It lets them dream of what we could be again."

"We make the music to fill in the gaps, like holes in our DNA. To make ourselves whole again."

"To believe us into reality," the Star Child said. "I have a relic from our world that I need to show you. It will ..."

Psychoalphadiscobetabioaquadoloop. Psychoalphadiscobetabioaquadoloop. Psychoalphadiscobetabioaquadoloop. Psychoalphadiscobetabioaquadoloop.

The chant seemed to come from all around them. The lights fluttered. Darkness took shape, spaced folded on itself. Silhouettes shuffled in the night. A thick wave like dry-ice fog swallowed the dance floor, riding up George's legs and into his nostrils. A familiar smell, like citrus-scented disinfectant. Then a voice, like a wiggle in the ear, spoke.

"Citizens of the universe, we are here to reclaim the mothership."

§

They lie to you, George. You don't exist. You're nothing but a pack of baseball cards without gum. You are little more than the liner note drivel, ripped from the ravings of a fringe cult transcribed while riding shotgun on a bad LSD trip. This isn't the real world. But you know that, don't you? You aren't some savior figure struggling to come to terms with your messianic consciousness. Look at you, George, you are a boy, not a man, having a drug-induced dream. If your mother could see you now, you'd be the death of her, George. You know what's best for you, right? Get a nine-to-five. Get married. Consume. Obsess. Covet.

Never question. Never wake up. Never wake up. Never wake...

"... up, Shakes! Hump your ass!" Mallia had him by the wrist, dragging him behind an overturned table across the floor. Through the fog, all around him, he could see the trampled bodies, could hear the screams. His fingers scrabbled over the floor to gain some kind of hold for leverage, but his fingers only found discarded clothing, still warm, and the grains of sand that he knew had once been people. He felt sick, coming down off a bad trip.

"What's going on?"

"Damn it." Mallia leaned over, her breasts heavy on his chest, as she checked his eyes. "Their gas is still affecting you. I hoped you would be more immune to it."

"You're beautiful."

"Apparently not." Mallia palmed a rod in each hand. With a flick of her wrist, they extended into batons. She caught him staring at them. "For defense purposes only."

"Defending who?" Shakes asked.

"Get up! We need to get you somewhere safe. The Star Child's using the artifact to hold them off. I don't know how they found us. They didn't ..."

... think of your brothers, George. Of your sisters. Think of what would become of them without you. Think of your home. Think of your hood. Think ...

"... they're sending everything they got at us." A bad mama jamma, Mallia leapt into the fray, delivering a round house kick that shook the roof off that mutha. Then she battered him with the batons, twirling them with the ease of drumsticks. "That's Professor Bereft of Groove's lieutenant leading them. He must know that we've found you. He must know that ..."

... you can still have a future. There's something more out there for you, but you must stop this nonsense. Get back on board with the real thing, George. Get your head out the stars and come back to earth. You need to ...

"... snap out of it, Shakes. We're doing this all for you. You're the real thing."

"The words are gone." Shakes stared at his hands, making sure he had the appropriate number of digits.

"They're coming out of your mouth."

"Funk you. They're not there. They're not there, I'm telling you." Shakes trembled. "No, wait, somebody's in my head."

"Then fight him."

Unsteady at first, Shakes rose to his feet, letting Mallia's voice pull him through the noise. Through the smoke, the screams of the people rushing past as thick and clunky suits of brightly-colored armor chased them. The high squeal of a dozen theremins laughed at them, cutting them down with glee. One of the Afronauts stood there, his fiery pink and purple Bop Gun aimed toward Shakes' heart. He could sense the smile behind the obsidian orb, hear the cackling of laughter, and the mocking tone of his words.

I am transmitting ideas directly into your reality, crooked and unoriginal. You fell into my grandest trap. Prepare to become the greatest story ever untold.

The muzzle of the Bop Gun flared, but then the Star Child was there. He leapt, waving an object that looked like a flashlight. He screamed. He fell.

But all Shakes knew after that was the light.

§

Who am I?

Another pointless dream lost in a crowd of pointless dreams. Hunched over in the dark, gyrating, bumping, grinding, in dance to relieve that pressure. The ship. Hurtling through space. The ship was mother. My true mother. That knowing noise, the constant thrum, giving myself over to the music. The dance itself is the most intense rush, taking me out of this world to that place of possibilities. Holy funk, the engine of life and creation, like collard greens, KYs, and cornbread for the soul. Where everything that could happen, has happened, a cosmic conflagration, subatomic rhythms in collision. Where reality is the imaginary story.

I am ...

"... waking up. I'm making it up. I'm ... cosmically aware," Shakes said. "Sweet Christmas, this is deep."

Vibrations poured through his body, a deep soul spasm, and leapt from him into the surrounding walls then reverberated back to him. Panels along the walls lit up. The walls hummed to life. Neon everywhere, blinking to life like the eyes of long-dormant beasts. Somewhere deep within the building, something pulsed to life.

"This building ... it's the mothership," the dark Afronaut said. Shakes felt his fear through the modulation.

"Look here, Mr. Wiggles." Shakes turned to the black-clad Afronaut. Its onyx-domed body seemed frozen in time, space-locked. "Y'all think you so slick, so cool, but you nothing but a daggone fool. Everybody's got a little light under the sun."

Shakes felt his mind becoming a weapon of love, flexed it like fingers and reached into the Afronaut's mind. He was struck by the image of maggot-laced meat. Shakes heard the music in his heart, the pounding drum. The bassline kicked through his soul. His feet took off with the groove, skating in a circle about the man. His skates never seemed to leave the ground, round and round he went. Shakes opened his mind, allowing more funk to wash into his soul. He watched it crash down in a great pink wave. A torrent of groove washed out the silt of Unfunkiness, whipping beneath the surface, brushing out the dead and breathless at the bottom.

"No. No more. I hate water. I never learned to swim!" The Afronaut clutched at the sides of his orbed head, trying desperately to claw it open, and collapsed to his knees, then fell forward.

Seeing Mallia cradling the Star Child's head, Shakes rushed to their side.

"If I'm going to be down with you, I'm down to the bitter end." The Star Child's eyes grew distant. "I can hear my mother call. I can hear my mother call. I can hear—"

§

Shakes stood within the bubble bridge of the mothership. Earth filled the viewscreen, growing smaller and smaller.

"We're prepared to leave orbit," Mallia said.

"I know. I was just taking one more look." He thought about his momma, about his brothers and sisters. Had they known all along? Would they be safe without him? He couldn't say, couldn't worry about it. He shifted and turned to Mallia. "What's the plan?"

"We find more of the Funkateers, gather our forces. We will spread funk's glorious message across the cosmos if we have to. Then we'll bring it straight to Professor Bereft of Groove."

"In other words, we take it to that sucker." He nodded, turned back to the blue marble on the screen. "Where'd you learn to fight, anyway?"

"Shortest kid in the band and four older brothers." Mallia slipped her hand into his and joined him in staring at earth. "It all seems so big. I don't know where or how to begin."

Living and jiving and digging the skin he was in, Shakes stretched his mind out, touching so many, awakening them to the possibility of everything. He turned to her.

"Free your mind ... and your ass will follow."

Pimp My Airship

"Who Stole the Soul?"

"Citizens of the Universe, do not attempt to adjust your electro-transmitter, there is nothing wrong. We have taken control to bring you this special bulletin."

"Aw, hell nah." Hubert "Sleepy" Nixon paused mid-keystroke on the pianoforte. A system of pipes ran from the back of the instrument to the ceiling, steam billowing in mild tufts from the joints. The low, arrhythmic notes slowly faded into a dull echo as he turned to the gleaming carapace of the electro-transmitter with mild exasperation.

A phlegmatic gentleman by nature, some mistook Sleepy's somnambulant demeanor for muddle-mindedness. Given nuanced consideration, this was rather true after a fashion. Sleepy reached for his pipe, tamped the side to even the spread of chiba leaves, lit them, and inhaled. Holding the smoke in his lungs for the span of three heartbeats, he exhaled a thick cloud of noxious vapor. Only then was he prepared to amble his considerable girth toward the faded tapestry that concealed the descending spiral stairway. Wide-shouldered and bulbous framed as he was, each step creaked under his weight as he slowly made his way into the subterranean hollow. The basement smelled of a privy pit.

"That's right, today's mathematics is knowledge. Let me break it down for you: Know the ledge." A glass-fronted cabinet contained a rotating cylinder that gyrated up and down. A series of antennae lined the top of the device, electricity arcing between them, the charges climbing the spires like tendrils of ivy. Pipes splayed like pleats of a fan, groaned and gurgled as the home kine burned. In the undercity, Fortune—as much as the government allowed—favored a neighborhood possessing a single kine or two, much less a home laying claim to its own. The voice emanated from the darkened corner of the chamber and belonged to the spindly-framed gentleman behind the strange apparatus. Barely seated on the many-times-patched ottoman, was (120 Degrees of) Knowledge Allah.

Knowledge Allah's strong, handsome face was eroded by despair. His distant eyes had stared into the abyss of anger and hate for too long. A gold band pulled back his thick braids giving them the appearance of interlocked fingers. His thick cravat was tucked into his vest. The difficulty of Knowledge Allah was that one had to decipher the code of his thought language before he began to make any sense. Such a task rarely proved simple while under the effects of the chiba.

"You don't know who you are," Knowledge Allah's self-secure voice rang with steel. "Take on your true name. *A*rm. *L*eg. *L*eg. *A*rm. *H*ead. You are the original man. You are gods. Yet, you sit there, blind, deaf, and dumb to your potential.

"Few realize who they are, and those that do—and seek to wake the people from their neglected truth—are incarcerated by this grafted government. The Star Child, leader of the F8, is due to be executed in a few days, but none of you could be bothered. The time for revolution is at hand, brothers and sisters. The time is at hand. We only await a sign.

"I exist between time outside time. In the between places. I am the voice of truth in these troubled times."

The clockwork gears ground to a gentle halt as the spindles of the machine wound down. The electric arcs sputtered, and the entire apparatus darkened. Knowledge Allah stooped from behind the glass cabinet, daubing his sweaty brow with a handkerchief, a smirk of zealotry on his face.

"What the fuck, man?" Sleepy asked, his insistent steps catching up to him as he found himself winded. He eased himself into the nearest chair. Knowledge Allah poured him some brandy from a nearby decanter before pouring a glass of water for himself.

"Are the mysteries I strive to illuminate too deep for you, my brother?" Knowledge Allah clinked Sleepy's glass with his own then downed his water. He often regaled Sleepy with the idea of forming a band, being the frontman to the capacious Sleepy's music with the hopes of using their act to spread his message. Like many of their ideas, it collected dust due to inaction.

"The only mystery is my need to get high." Sleepy ran his pick through his blond-streaked Afro, his beard barely tamed by a comb. His nose was too flat and too broad for his face, as if he'd been punched with an iron. His teeth, likewise, were too small for his mouth. Against skin like burnished onyx, a silver stud protruded from his chin. He puffed out another cloud. "Mystery solved."

"They set snares that have been prepared for you. Snares meant to lead you from your path of righteousness. You've let them cave you."

"They, who?" Sleepy asked, forgetting his oft-repeated lesson of not asking Knowledge Allah questions. The answers were rarely of any use. However, Sleepy couldn't help but think there was an undercurrent of derision to Knowledge Allah's tones, as if the other man stared down the thin beak of a nose at him.

"Your so-called grafted government's behind it," Knowledge Allah continued. "The next phase is to destroy us. You think it stopped with Tuskegee?" The Tuskegee Institute. One of the few schools allowed in the undercities. The name sent a chill along the spine at the memory of the experiments done in the name of science. "No, they just got slicker. We don't have poppy fields. We don't have dirigibles. We do have wills sapped by opiate clouds."

"Sounds like we don't have shit," Sleepy said. "Speaking of, I thought we agreed on no more broadcasts until we got our act together?"

"The truth cannot go unvoiced."

"Shit." Sleepy pronounced the word as if it possessed three syllables. "You one of them long-winded niggas who just like to hear themselves talk."

"Look at how quickly you let their hate speech drip from your own lips, betraying your own. Don't get caught up in the game of the 85. We need to—"

"Blah, blah, blah, nigga. Blah. I hear you talking. What I don't hear is a plan. You got all this 'righteous knowledge' ... What we going to do?"

"I'm going to free the Star Child." Knowledge Allah stood up for maximum dramatic effect. "You driving?"

Sleepy remained seated, as the implications of the words reverberated in his mind; their import required a few moments to digest. Knowledge Allah beamed, obviously quite pleased with himself, and wrapped his great coat around himself and nodded topside. Sleepy fastened a cape around his long, blue eight-button coat, the image of a flabby martinet.

Smoke stacks belched poisonous clouds. The oppressive sky, gray as prison-issue uniforms, cloaked their furtive entry onto the streets. The air, redolent with a ferrous rock, was heavy with the stink of coal and sweat. He had bathed for an hour and a half to scrub off any trace of soot from him. Even the poor clung to their dignity. In the shadows of the steam trams of the overcity, a Hansom whisked by, held aloft by rusty trellises. Neither man dreamed of catching a cab in Atlantis, especially at night. A police trawler slowed as it neared them. Other denizens scurried away like rats caught in the light, quick to return to the burrow openings they called home. The pair held their ground, hard eyes unblinking at the passing vehicle. Sleepy spat a black-tinged wad of phlegm. Once out of eye line, Sleepy opened his garage door.

The metal gleamed even in the wan moonlight, polished to a glassy sheen every day. Twin brass tubes formed the body of the car, curving down on both ends stitched together by copper rivets. Headlamps, jutting cans, burned to life. The suspension bounced and lurched in a frenzy of steam belches, jolting them up and down. The bemused pair enjoyed the weight of stares from their neighbors. The 24" rims, whirring fans, continuously shuttered like deployed armor. With a roar, the car took off, spumes of steam left in its wake.

"Fear of a Black Planet"

The slow and winding White River neatly carved the undercity in half as the Victorian architecture of the overcity known as Indianapolis gave way to the more dilapidated homes in the undercity the natives dubbed Atlantis. Billboards of smiling, brown faces endorsing opiate use sat next to adverts of money changers offering promises of quick loans. Both preyed on desperation and ignorance. America shone as the most prosperous colony in service to the Albion Empire. With its plantation farms and free labor force, America was the dirty sweatshop engine that propelled the Empire. Even the upper crust of the American social strata were held in tacit contempt by the Albion proper, unwilling to acknowledge how they kept their hands clean. The force of her colonialist spirit had long ago reduced the issue of slavery to a low simmer, and the much talked about threat of an American Civil War never came to pass. With the rise of the automata, however, the economics of the unseemly endeavor proved too deleterious, and the slaves were released.

Those of an African bloodline, no matter how much or little ran in their veins, were relegated to a state of vague emancipation. Not living in the massive, industrial overcities, but dismissed to ghettos—pacified by legalized, free-flowing drugs—a terra incognita somehow lost between the cartographer's calipers. Or, they were imprisoned.

Viceroy George II, who pandered without shame to the interests of the Empire, currently governed the land. Though high-born and privileged, he was no nobleman but rather a spoiled bloodline of nine generations of insular breeding.

The buildings crumbled into screes of pebbles along rotted sidewalks under an air of imminent decay. Gas lamps produced forlorn shadows from the steeped darkness. Old men huddled in puddles of light, drinking brandy and smoking cigars blunted with opium by wan moonlight. Their garrulous conversation of the most impolitic kind filled the night with the bluster of oafs. A twinge of jealousy at not being able to join in fluttered in Sleepy's chest.

Knowledge Allah directed him to a two-story brick, Queen Anne home guarded by a wrought-iron fence. The house stood out from the rest of the neighborhood's squalor as if someone had staked a claim to retake this spot. Drab green with fine terra cotta ornaments and lacy spindles, its conical-roofed turret had fish scale slate shingles. Stained glass sat atop curtained bay windows.

"Whose place is this?" Sleepy asked.

"An inventor's."

"He down with The Cause?"

"Do you even know what cause you serve?"

"I was just asking."

"You assume a lot. *The Cause* is more than attitude, affect, and wardrobe. You need to be open to the mysteries life offers," Knowledge Allah said.

"Like what?"

"Like the inventor."

Knowledge Allah rapped on the large obsidian knocker. The door swung open. A poor simulacrum of a person greeted them with the smooth manner of a well-rehearsed marionette. Its inner workings whirred—pistoning brass and steel gears—over the gentle hum of whatever powered it. Its face— dull, unpainted metal—held no expression and little attempt at humanity. Wondrous and intricate, a flawless design, it projected a knowing discomfort of the other. Sleepy suddenly grew terrified of the mind of its designer. With a mime's gesticulations, it offered to take their hat and coats and escorted them. Twin lanterns burned in empty spaces as optical receptors, a mechanical stare masking its inner workings. Its disjointed consciousness lacked imagination, the ability to create story, the power to question its being or its place in the greater scheme of things. It moved without the gift of ancestors and the weight of history. At best, it held the illusion of electric dreaming against the cold void of blackness.

Sleepy envied its uncomplicated existence.

The double-door entry opened into the foyer of the opulent home. An elegant, curved staircase separated the living and dining rooms on the right from the library on the left. Walls, alight with whale oil-filled lamps, created an erudite glow. A lone settee perched alongside a fireplace on the opposite side of the room. A deck of cards sat on a piece of silk atop a table. Sleepy cut the deck at random and saw a card inscribed with the number XVI over the picture of a tower struck by lightning. The building's top section had dislodged from the rest of it; two men were falling from the crumbling edifice. Filled with sudden disquiet, Sleepy set the deck down.

The automaton paused, like a bellboy awaiting a gratuity.

"One nation under a groove," Knowledge Allah said.

A bank of books parted to reveal a maw of shadows. The automaton withdrew, closing the library door behind it. The civilized façade of the pews of books gave way to the vaulted chamber of the laboratory. Rows of workbenches lined with test tubes, flasks, and beakers gurgling over Bunsen burners. Though a langorous whir of fans vented the air, the room roiled with the cloying smell of steam and coal, hot metal and ozone. A skirling of flutes emanated from a boiler, groaned under the strain of power and settling. A lithe figure bent over a metal frame of eight, jutting arms spinning from a central mass, a mechanical arachnid contraption. Sleepy expected rolled-up sleeves, moleskin trousers, and a grimy leather apron.

Instead, beneath a cap, goggled and draped in a lab coat, the figure welded a few more joints, testing the articulation as the work progressed, lit to a haunting blue hue behind the jet of the torch.

Once the goggles had been raised, the inventor took a step backward and nodded. Sleepy realized he regarded a woman. A green velvet jacket beneath the lab coat, with no décolletage or hint of femininity; the inventor held the bearing of a strict governess. She admired her handiwork and snugged her gloves. Her face retained an aqua tint in the dim electric glow. Wrinkles filigreed the corners of her eyes, belying the youthfulness of her face. A product of miscegenation, she radiated the afterglow of light-skinned privilege, despite her secretive life ferreted away in her laboratory. Upon noticing them, she stepped to Knowledge Allah, and the two clasped hands.

"You're a lady of odd enthusiasms," Sleepy proclaimed. He managed to hold his affable leer awaiting an introduction.

"I don't have time for social niceties." She ignored his proffered hand.

"Cooking stuff up in the lab," Knowledge Allah said.

"Just like 'Yacuub,' good sir."

Unabashedly vital, her high cheekbones framed an aquiline nose against her sallow complexion, tea with too much milk—just light enough to be on the fringe of polite society. With a rigidity of face and a hardness in her hazel eyes, she possessed a noblewoman's airs. She probably had an A-level education, which meant her parents had money or connections. The mirth of aristocracy barely masked an anarchist streak. Her terrible impertinence of dressing like a man covered a repressed gaety to her Victorian effect. She polished her spectacles in a handkerchief.

"'Bout time we got some ladies representing," Sleepy said.

"He rises in my estimation, Deaconess Blues." She shook his hand.

"It's nice to see not all of us had to struggle."

"Do not talk to me about struggle while you thoughtlessly squander what money you manage to scrimp together on instruments and automobiles worth more than your hovel." Her wan smile soured to a grim line. "My mother had been a governess, a high rank for Negroes, though she tried to program me with how it was unbecoming for a lady to fill her head with designs and equations. Though no mother would phrase it as such, she wanted me to be vapid and colorless. I had other ideas."

Though now he whiled away his days as a coal shoveler rather than as an artist or poet, Sleepy never fancied himself an anarchist by any stretch. Not like the deaconess who decided that she, if not the rest of society, was past male supremacy's notions of womanhood. Her body and mind were hers to do with as she would.

Sleepy pulled a hair from his chin, closing his eyes at the fresh sting of pain. A nervous habit anxious to remind himself that he could still feel. He didn't know who he was—a man out of place, a crowd of one. Jamaican-born, but England-educated—through C-levels, the bare minimum for a citizen, appropriate to his station—and America employed; a one-man triangle trade. His father was a man of dreams and ideas. And causes. Sleepy joined the struggle in his youth and paved the way for the F8 through civil disobedience. "Life ought to be lived outside of yourself," he often preached. But Sleepy's passion for music provided release from his miserable existence, embued with anger and vitality of the dwellers of the undercity; not the staid tones enjoyed by the ranks of nobles. Sleepy tapped percussive melodies lost in the rhythms of his thoughts.

"Am I boring you?" Deaconess Blues asked.

"Nah, I'm just waiting to hear the deal."

"All in good time."

"Funkin' Lesson"

Deaconess Blues led them back to the library where her automaton had spread out the accoutrements of high tea. A silver teapot poured a heady brew. The aroma filled the room. A tray of crumpets and other delicate pastries lay before them, as the blank-faced automaton attended to etiquette in Deaconess Blues' fragile dance of civility. Going through the motions of refined breeding, protocol—appearances were paramount—despite being excluded from upper society.

"Are we all that's left of the F8?" Sleepy asked. He stifled a rheumy cough, slipping a trail of gray sputum into his napkin.

"I do not know, sir. We compartmentalize ourselves so that no one person knows too much about our organization." Deaconess Blues tilted her head with a glimmer of maternal concern. "You look troubled."

"I just don't know what we're doing and ..." Sleepy paused. "What's the point?"

"Has it ever struck you that we aren't as ahead technologically as we should be?"

"Knowledge and the reflection of knowledge equals wisdom," Knowledge Allah said. "Knowledge and wisdom equals understanding."

"Then if you *knowledge* my wisdom, you will understand what I'm saying," Deaconess Blues said. He nodded as if they shared the same gibberish wavelength. "Knowledge is built on the back of itself. Those who come along later stand on the shoulders of those before them. That great capitalist machine called slavery robbed mother Africa of generations of scientists, artists, and creative minds. Think of where we'd be without that holocaust."

"We'd have flying cars," Sleepy said "and show tunes."

"We *have* show tunes."

"We'd have had them sooner, you feel me? What? A black man can't enjoy show tunes."

"He isn't ready. He still needs verbal milk," Knowledge Allah said.

"Then this meeting is premature. I am ... resources. Not propaganda."

"Time is of the essence. The Cause demanded this level of meeting."

"My job is to oppose the state," Deaconess Blues scowled. "I care about the liberation of my people."

"Your people? You a high yella, bougie dilettante." Sleepy shifted, uncomfortable with how defensive he sounded. Deaconess Blues remained unflustered. Strains of classical music reverberated from the large horns encircling the room, surrounding them with sound. With another dollop of chiba, the pungent sting of burnt weed sent his mind adrift among the clouds and made him much more receptive to high-flung ideas.

An obviously delicate eater, Deaconess Blues drew a long sip then set her cup back onto its dish. "I'm black like you. I resist. I seek to end the chains and the extermination of all oppression."

"You don't talk like a scientist."

"I am an anarchist, insurrectionist, and a scientist. A scientist searching for knowledge and proof. For truth and meaning."

"You're a scientist of God," Knowledge Allah chimed in with a tone of deference.

Sleepy raised an eyebrow. He wondered if Deaconess Blues was one of the alchemist spirit riders whispered about, those who combined science and the ancient ways.

"With the revolutions in engineering and science and industry, we have yet to see any in our social systems. We might as well dress up the automata in minstrel outfits and paint them with bright white eyes and red bulbous lips for how we are seen." Deaconess Blues poured herself another cup of tea. She stirred in milk and sugar as her words settled in their ears, their eyes anxious on her, though she was unhurried. "We've been promised universal enlightenment, an end to war, and a rationalist utopian ... as long as everyone knows their place.

"We are at the intersection of class and race, class and sexuality, and class and gender. Any class reduction will face critical resistance. We have sold our souls in the service of commerce. We toil in the embrace of the machine and become a concubine of industry. So we rage against the machine, and we must take extraordinary steps to defend ourselves. There must develop solidarity among our people, a swell of anti-colonial resistance."

"I feel you. I'm angry, and I know y'all are angry, too. So, what're we going to do about it?" Sleepy asked, not one for the intellectual stuff. "Civil disobedience?"

"I've no interest in begging for scraps from our presumed master's table."

"Let me lay it on you like this: blood for blood," Knowledge Allah said.

"Now we're talking," Sleepy said, stirred from his settling ennui.

"And you know that." Knowledge Allah outstretched his hand that was received with blitheness by Sleepy, as if he'd finally earned a spot at the table.

"You'd be happy with any militant action," Deaconess Blues sniffed.

"Blowing shit up is a plan," Sleepy said.

"I understand your anger and how you may think of *blowing shit up*—given your coarse leanings—as revolutionary. But it is the beginning of a plan, not one unto itself. There must be a greater vision. There must be a catalyst for change."

"Niggas are in a state of emergency. Got to start wilding out."

"You are a ruin to language," she said with the exacting manner of a spinster aunt.

Sleepy chafed against her civilizing influence. The discussion, though somewhat diverting, left him with the sensation of being out of his depth. Maybe it was Deaconess Blues' subtle condescension. Or perhaps it was the disconnection between the lofty ideas of the Cause and the practical reality of the people. Sleepy's views boiled down to pragmatism: the theory of struggle was great only insofar as someone actually was helped. It wasn't further argument he wanted, but action. "You rebel in your way, I rebel in mine."

"I dream of different but similar worlds. I dream of one where we're free, not under the heel of Albion. There is something profoundly unwell in their sense of entitlement." Deaconess Blues shook her head as if the very act of reflection was wasted effort. Her stiff, stately bearing was the picture of restraint. "Eating their blood sausages and tripe, their raspberry tarts."

"The Inventor has a plan," Knowledge Allah said, as if reading his reluctance.

"Oh?"

"The plan is the paragon of simplicity. The local penitentiary ..."

"The Ave?" Sleepy asked.

"The Allisonville Correctional Facility is a wretched place. Its serpentine bowels, and those of its ilk, incarcerate a third of our people. Little better than slave pens with us little better than beasts."

"Including Star Child and the rest of the F8."

"The Star Child is a powerful symbol of the struggle. Imprisoned for speaking of a better way. Of revolution."

"But the Ave is..."

"Impregnable? No, its design bears the fruit of the very hubris of its designers. Think of it: a lone spire, defying the heavens like the tower of Babel. All the guards, knights of the realm, gathered there more as symbol than actual need. Were it to come crashing down, our brothers and sisters would be free."

"Oops upside their head," Knowledge Allah said.

"Wouldn't they be trapped?"

"Don't you see? The same underground shafts that entomb them now also protect them. All we would need is a group of folks to shepherd them to safety."

"And something to bring down the tower itself."

Deaconess Blues stood up and strode to the coat rack. Donning a hat and gloves—though Sleepy distrusted the cock of her hat—she announced, "Come on. We need to be armed with a bop gun."

§

133

"Bop Gun (Endangered Species)"

"Citizens of the Universe, do not attempt to adjust your electro-transmitter, there is nothing wrong. We have taken control to bring you this special bulletin." The attenuated pulse of Knowledge Allah's voice echoed along the airwaves. "The Albion Empire bloated itself on its own myth—a proud, corpulent pustule of wealth—spreading across the land, a decadent cancer of corporate greed and industrial indulgence all in the name of national pride.

"Washington aristocrats with vested interest in our eternal domination, governing to their interests not ours. The Empire is a corrupt federal leviathan, swollen and lazy, and we are the cheap table legs propping it up. Revolution is inevitable. We are the First Cause. In our tiers of rage, we call for direct action. We resist constituted powers through property damage. We impede the flow of goods and capital, using their system against them and making the cost of perpetuating domination prohibitive. And it is time to co-opt their instrument of military guarantor to break out the F8. There's a party at the crossroads. Watch the skies. Freedom or Death.

"I exist between time outside time. In the between places. I am the voice of truth in these troubled times."

Escaped the low ceiling of the undercity. No sunlight, only the arc of electricity from the tram. A city of shadows consuming their bodies as grist to drive the Empire forward. The trio rode in silence following the banks' scenic greenway to the summer homes of the overcity. They quickly left the shadows of Atlantis to the sprawling suburbs of greater Indianapolis, careful to avoid the constabularies who might pull them over or otherwise detain them for not being where they were supposed to be. Deaconess Blues' fair skin granted her passage to casual observers. Soon, they reached an immense pole barn structure on property ringed with barbed wire. A mad grin danced on her face as she activated the lock controls via a sequence of numbers punched into an electro-chirographer pad. Gears winched, and the doors trembled before parting. Inside the makeshift hanger was an airship.

From the first day the sight of a bird in flight fired his fancy, man dreamed to one day take to the clouds, to conquer the air as easily as he conquered the land and the sea. Unlike the massive warships of Lockheed or Sir Halliburton, this one did not bristle with armaments. No mighty bombs would drop on unseen enemies or innocent school buildings nor would the blood-soaked dreams of nation states be enforced by it. A ridged watermelon with a hull of black with a red underbelly, gas-filled tubes ran along the outside of the ship and burned to life to ring the ship in a brackish green. A gold ankh, like an uplifted key, emblazoned its side.

"Where did you get it?"

"I am not a lady of unlimited resources ..."

"You stole it."

"We wrested it from the control of the military/industrial complex, who deemed this model a failure and relegated it to a barely guarded warehouse," Knowledge Allah said.

"Why didn't you say so?"

"Haven't you understood, yet? We proceed on a need-to-know basis. You didn't need to know."

"One man's failure is another person's treasure." Deaconess Blues climbed a scaffold. "Coming inside?"

The decks of the cabin divided into small rooms, tiny tombs in the greater sarcophagus, connected by tiny ladders Sleepy had little hope of navigating. A network of cables, ropes, and pipes ran throughout like capillaries. Pressure hissed from the valves of the Malcolm-Little engines. Mahogany bedecked the main cabin and retained the reek of stale cigar smoke. A luxurious box, a den of sorts, formed the sanctum sanctorum of noble breeding. A decanter of pear wine sat in the middle of a table spread with finger foods, as another blank-faced automaton whirred out of their way.

Knowledge Allah reclined on a bench, a gentleman of leisure. Deaconess Blues stood before an array of membrane discs and tuning forks, lost behind the steady cadence of whirs and clicks. A wave of nausea swept over Sleepy as he imagined himself squeezing into the small window seat, staring out over the sea of land.

"Wisdom is water. I'm about solar facts. God is the sun. It's all about the elements," Knowledge Allah said, a brutal curl to his lips.

"You and your outlandish expressions," Deaconess Blues remarked with admirable dispatch. "Your peculiar phraseology never tires." She moved about the cabin, examining the controls with considered elegance.

"The sundial speaks. We prepare to ride as Afronauts."

"So how does this all play out?" Sleepy asked. "We become the villains they assume us to be?"

"One man's villain is another person's Star Child. Do you know how we're seen? Human chimpanzees. Immature, in need of constant guidance. Emotional, not rational. Unreasonable and easily excited. Without religion, only superstition and fanciful mythologies." She nodded to Knowledge Allah. "Criminals with no respect for private property. Filthy. Excessively sexual. We are niggers left to fester and shamble in the undercities."

"Us and the Irish." Uncomfortable in the awkward pause left by his attempt at humor, Sleepy pulled another hair from his chin and examined the kinky strand against his fingertip.

"Their blue-eyed, blond-haired Jesus used to keep us in our place. We are but noble aborigines. Such is the result of their gradations of mankind. Here I am, too black for their tastes, too white for yours, trapped by their index of nigrescence." Deaconess Blues manned a station, the controls warming the dirigible to a full-throated bluster, pulsing with steam. Baffles and stanchions, ballasts and air ducts pumped furiously. "Where is our justice?"

"Justice? There is no justice, there is Just Us," Knowledge Allah said.

"Aluminum and iron oxide are elements of the fabric doping. This zeppelin ought to be filled with helium or another inert gas. However, as our purposes are of a more combustible nature, I've filled our little dirigible with hydrogen. I wouldn't advise any more of your chiba indulgences." Her stiff upper lip set to grim resolve, she remained unruffled by the chaos springing up about her.

"I ain't down with no suicide run," Sleepy said. "This brother don't go out like that."

"Yet, our best-trained, best-educated, best-equipped, best-prepared troops refuse to fight!" Knowledge Allah recited with an evangelical fervor and a sneer of contempt. "Matter of fact, it's safe to say that they would rather *switch* than fight!'"

"Who's going to fight for The Cause if our *best* keep taking themselves out?"

"An arm, a leg perhaps. But not the Head," Knowledge Allah said.

"I am not one to shrink from such deviltry. Besides, it's not suicide. We are meant to be among the stars, signals from the heavens, showing others the way home." Deaconess Blues stepped from her perch to meet Sleepy eye-to-eye. "Nor are we asking you to come."

"What?" Sleepy's sated gaze fixed on her.

"We accepted you because we saw your potential. Ancient tribes had truth tellers and history keepers and storytellers. You are like one of those ancient griots. We give you the space to tell stories. Our story."

"Vainglorious," Knowledge Allah echoed.

"I detest long goodbyes," Deaconess Blues said.

Sleepy glanced from one to the other, tasked and dismissed. His lips parted to protest, but no sound escaped. He backed out toward the rear of the deck, ignoring his sense of relief while wanting to feign the injured party. As if he was deemed unworthy to partake in his own struggle.

"You smell that?" Deaconess Blues called out, her skin like luminescent butter. A static charge hung in the air. "The air smells like freedom."

"Freedom or death," Knowledge Allah said.

"We fly into glory."

"Black Steel in the Hour of Chaos"

"Citizens of the Universe, do not attempt to adjust your electro-transmitter, there is nothing wrong. We have taken control to bring you this special bulletin."

Sleepy raced along the back roads desperate to beat the landing of the mothership. A great shadow filled the sky, the pride of the empire. Clouds blackened into banks of ominous dark swirls by the endless entropy of Night. The wind howled. The gleaming overcities and jutting spires must look so different from up above, Sleepy imagined. Air raid lights filled the sky, spotlights on the stage of the night sky. The dirigible, their Bop Gun, moved with implacable grace, an airborne whale, strident and regal.

"My message is simple. Tonight the Star Child... all of us will be free. By any means necessary. Freedom or death."

"I exist between time outside time. In the between places. I am the voice of truth in these troubled times."

By the time Sleepy pulled up, a throng of people had gathered, held in check by too few constabularies. The Ave's tower, impregnable and arrogant, saluted them. Slowly, the ovoid silhouette of the Bop Gun came into full view. The crowd burst into a roar of applause and cheers. As if in response, the behemoth canted forward in a sharp downward arc. Sleepy stared, filled with profound apprehension. The crowd became a pantomime of motion and fury and panic. Knowledge Allah stood before the grand bay window.

Backlit, his grand gestures were perfectly visible to the spectators as the ship careened earthward.

He raised a clenched fist. "Vainglorious," Sleepy whispered.

Everything happened at once, a series of images broken into shards of memory one tried to forget. The roar of the crowd, an exhalation of panic. An explosion. A billowy fire cloud, a phoenix springing toward the heavens. The smell of India rubber burning. Shrapnel of stone. A body, encircled in flames, stumbled two steps then collapsed. Fiery scraps blew about in the night breeze. The injured structure suddenly unable to bear its own weight, the tower collapsed. The terrible crash, thunder flattening the eardrums. Smoke and flame, thick and choking, burning the lungs with each inhalation.

"Revolution"

Watching the skeleton of the Bop Gun continue to burn—its tattered shell buckled upon itself—Sleepy waited, carried along by the undertow of the crowd. The constabularies, with their thick night sticks and steel-riveted riot shields, cordoned off the scene. Fear glazed their faces. He spied no one immediately fleeing and prayed that the prisoners had been moved. He feared that they remained trapped beneath the ground, escaping slaves caught in a cave-in. Soon, among the wreckage and destruction, black bodies scrambled from the underground, a stream of ants fleeing their hill. Some of the constabularies fired at the escaping prisoners. Something stirred inside Sleepy. The caustic smoke stung his eyes, his vision little more than watery blurs. Soot-tinged spittle dropped to the ground.

The voices rose into a chorus. Knowledge Allah. Deaconess Blues. His father. Lost in the din was his voice. Sleepy felt the anger. The urge to join the fight. To retaliate. Blinking through a haze of pain, he ground his heel into the desiccated earth and punched the nearest guard, a tacit signal to the crowd to surge forward. The horde spilled in every direction, blind fury, pent-up aggression in search of a target. A mob of chaos, arms swinging blindly, clubs battering senselessly. Sirens sounded. Bodies clambered through barbed wire. In the ensuing mêlée, Sleepy was arrested. To the chants of "Let him go," the constabularies clapped him in irons, his expression more frustrated than fearful. At the precinct house, the questions came fast and furious. "Who were involved in the organizing?" "How did you get involved?" "How many were there?" "Who were the leaders?"

Sleepy fought his revolutions his own way.

And raised a single fist.

The Valkyrie

Second Lieutenant Macia Branson leapt into the dark abyss and descended into a purgatory of red tracer fire. The night sky held her close as the air whipped about them, reducing her world to the deadening screech of white noise. She plummeted toward the earth, not knowing where they might land. In trees. In water. Into the midst of a Heathen patrol. All she knew for sure was that they would land somewhere in Holland. She prayed that she would be at least close to her drop zone. She was deployed in service of The Order and had a duty to perform.

The church was mother, the church was father.

A grassy knoll rushed toward her, and she braced for the jolt of impact without looking down. The rush of the ground toward them, despite their training, could still send a jolt of panic through a soldier. Besides, she enjoyed holding onto the peace of the horizon for as long as possible to steady her.

Her knees slightly bent, she dropped her chin to her chest and tensed her neck muscles. The earth slammed into her, her body twisting and bending in automatic reaction, giving in to the crash, a rag doll carried by the current of momentum. She slid down an embankment before coming to a halt. Slogging through three inches of pooled water, she knew what she'd find when she checked her gear. Nothing would work right. Her flight suit was only designed for controlled descents. The best tech went to the evangelical deployments. The rest of the church's military was left with equipment full of glitches, if not flat-out defective. With so many theaters of operations, the troops' equipment had been rushed into production and not battle-tested. Like many of her fellow soldiers. Her hard landing smashed the communication relay, and her leg bundle, full of extra ammo and rations, was nowhere to be found. At least the familiar weight of her Stryker XM9 pulse rifle, though it was a generation out of date, comforted her like the embrace of an old friend.

Above her, tracer fire continued to crisscross the night sky, the light of exploding flak almost reminding her of fireworks. Almost. The proximity alert lit up on her rifle.

"Fishes," Branson challenged.

"Loaves," a familiar voiced responded softly from the shadows. "Your comlink down, too? Where the hell are we?"

No one was happier to see Prefect Sergeant E. Kenneth Dooley than Branson. Short, quick-thinking, and ugly as a catfight, when Dooley first joined the ranks, the older soldiers took to calling him "Doo-Doo." That lasted until the first time they saw him in a firefight. He stalked a battlefield with defiant determination, daring the Heathens to hit him.

"I'd guess five to seven miles from our DZ, judging from the firing," Branson said.

She didn't bother to check the digital telemetry or maps in her helmet subsystem. Half the time she found the continual stream of information and dogma sermons more hindrance than help. "Which way do we head?" Dooley asked.

"Where else? Toward the firing."

They both knew it was a bad drop. The navcom signal was down across the board, so they set about cobbling together their unit the old-fashioned way. They spread out, slow and tentative. When unfamiliar soldiers joined them and saw Branson—many replacement soldiers filled their ranks for this mission—a sense of relief lit up their faces. It was as if they sensed they were in good, experienced hands. Other officers complained that she was friendlier with the enlisted men than she was with them. She didn't care. The front line was where she belonged; she even volunteered for patrols. The uniform meant something to her.

Branson watched with weary eyes as this latest batch of green recruits checked through their rucksacks and readied their weapons. She waited for them to regroup before taking final stock of what the service had her working with this time.

"When are we gonna see some action?" asked a square-jawed, broad-shouldered glamor boy with curly blonde locks. He still stank of military school.

"Who're you?" Dooley asked, with the casual contempt mixed with pity of a boxer who wholly outclassed his opponent. He had little patience with replacement soldiers.

"The name's ..."

Dooley bit into a well-chewed cigar stump and swished it about in his mouth until it found its comfortable crook. "Stow it. I don't wanna learn your name. Learning your name is the first step to getting attached, and I sure as hell ain't getting attached to no replacement. From here out, you're Goldy."

"What do they call you, ma'am?" Goldy turned to Branson.

"Second Lieutenant Branson. You want to try to call me something else?" Her stare made him turn away.

Goldy spied the ink along Dooley's arm. "What's the tattoo?"

Dooley pulled up his sleeve to fully reveal the image of a woman astride a white horse on his arm. Long, blonde hair covered by a silver helmet, with blazing blue eyes peering from underneath it, she carried both a spear and shield. "A Valkyrie."

"What's a Valkyrie?" Goldy asked.

"Collectors of the favored dead. They chose the slain heroes to be taken to Valhalla. If a warrior saw one before a battle, he'd die during it. I want the Nils to always see one coming."

"You got to be careful with all that myth talk. You don't want to be seen as a Nil or a sympathizer."

"A Heath. They're Nils if they have no gods; Heaths if they worship the wrong ones."

"Still, choosers of the slain? Nice ..." Goldy's voice trailed off. Dooley had turned his back and stalked off to be about his business.

Branson pretended not to have noticed the interaction by studying the maps on her view screens as Goldy approached her. "How'd it go with Dooley?"

"We're dutch," Goldy said, without any trace of irony. "We hit it off swell."

"Give it time. Newbies have to learn how to slip in between the seams."

"I get it, ma'am," Goldy said, obviously bored with the lesson.

"Pack 'em up, we're moving out," a new voice shouted out. First Lieutenant Gilbert Meshner. "Mush" behind his back.

Of course, he'd been chosen for this mission. Branson spat.

Meshner wandered through their makeshift camp like a distracted tourist. A mop of black, greasy hair and dead, gray eyes gave his face a grave severity. He was little more than a petty dictator who used vindictiveness in the guise of discipline. Rumor was that, when they'd parachuted into Chiapas, Mexico, a Nil had charged Meshner. By the time the rest of the men got to him, the two had played "kata tag," and the Nil lay dead at his feet. But otherwise, Mush'd long since developed a reputation for taking long walks away from the action. The men tried to joke it off as Meshner's luck masking as skill, but no one knew what to make of him.

"We're marching until high ground." Meshner eyed Branson with something approaching scorn.

Not a single man stirred. They turned to Branson in a tacit double check of the orders.

"You heard the man. Let's go, you scrotes!" Branson echoed.

§

The hills of Holland were supposed to be beautiful. The war had reduced them to greenspace ambush sites for the Nils and Heathens. The church embraced a holistic approach to fulfilling her mission: politics, technology, and the military. The Evangelical States of America already ruled their hemisphere, along with parts of Africa and Asia. The United Emirate of Islam controlled the rest of Africa along with Asia. Europe was up for grabs, a self-declared safe haven for atheists and heretics. Not that Branson cared. Nation. Religion. Tribe. Cause. There was always some supposed big idea to fight for, but in the end, all that mattered was that orders were obeyed and the mission carried out.

A dense fog crept along the field, and an eerie silence embraced them. Pulse rifle fire left a distinct odor in the air, a mix of ozone and seared flesh. The smell of death. High ground took them the rest of the night and most of the next day to find. Patrols detected Heathen troops nearby. The men marched in silence, the only sound filling the air, the steady stamp of their boots slogging muddy earth. The waiting was the worst; that was what broke people. The constant state of alert, their minds imagining horrors behind every point of cover. Branson shoved that all aside.

The momentary peace gave her a chance to read up on some of her newbies. Goldy held particular interest. His body was a stew of experimental psychotropics. For all of his country boy persona, he had once been a serial killer with a penchant for skinning young girls before his conversion. Fortunately, the church left nothing to chance when it came to one's sanctification, even if it had to overwrite existing memories with new ones. Everyone needed redemption from something.

Praise be the blood.

"Where's Goldy?" Branson whispered.

"Making out with the toilet." Dooley thumbed toward some bushes. He shifted his unlit cigar to the other side of his mouth as if suddenly aggravated.

"My back teeth were floating," Goldy muttered, as he caught their eyes watching his approach.

"Tell the men to fix their katas. We attack at first light. 0530. Meshner's orders." Branson withdrew her edged bayonet and fixed it to the front of her pulse rifle. The high-tech stuff was good for attacking an enemy at a distance, but the final cleanup was always up close. She would always know the face of her enemy. God have mercy on her soul.

"Tell her what you told me," Goldy said to Dooley.

"What?" Branson held her gaze on the sergeant.

"Nothing. Just campfire stories that old soldiers tell." Dooley cut his eyes at Goldy, a silent cursing which he'd vent at some later opportunity.

"I like stories," Branson said.

Dooley shuffled, flushed with mild embarrassment like a child caught speaking out of turn, which Branson found amusing. "You've already heard this one. During the American Civil War, a general kept getting these reports about how his men were afraid to be left for wounded on the battlefield. Not just afraid, but absolutely terrified, especially if they had to lay wounded at night. Try as he might, the morale of his troops kept sinking to new lows every day, but no one wanted to talk about it. The only thing any of them would say was that, if you fell in combat and you wanted to survive until morning, you should hide your breath so no one knew you were still alive.

"One night, after an extended engagement with the enemy, the general walked his line. He often did this after a battle. You know, to pray for his men and clear his head. He saw some movement on the field between the two warring camps. A lone mook. He couldn't tell if it was Yankee or Confederate, walked among the bodies. In the morning, the medics found the fallen bodies decapitated. Swore it was a woman with a sword."

"Don't that beat all?" Goldy asked.

Branson knew the story. She'd heard it many times before. From Meshner. "You and Lt. Meshner close?"

"Not really. He just took a shine to me is all," Dooley said sarcastically.

"Must be your special brand of charm and wit."

"Yeah, temper got the best of me again," Dooley said. "Back in training camp, I threatened to kick his balls into the following week if he gave me any more bullshit jobs instead of letting me fight. There was this long pause. Thought I was done for, either booted out or thrown in the stockade. But he just got this strange grin, like a gator smiling at you. Said I was all right. I kinda took him under my wing after that. You know, we have to raise these lieutenants right."

"Speaking of our esteemed lieutenant and long walks, where is Mush?" Goldy asked.

Branson' eyes shriveled the grin on the replacement soldier's face. Meshner was still their commanding officer and Branson's job was to enforce discipline among the men. "I'll go look for him."

Praise be the blood.

The Blessed Sacrament. Thanks to the sacrament, a combination of human growth hormone and nanotech, she remained about the physical age of twenty-seven and in peak condition for fighting. Truth be told, the wars had begun to blur together. She hardly noticed when one ended and another began. Tour of duty after tour of duty, her body repaired and rejuvenated. "Through the blood we have life," a familiar refrain, never truly aging, only knowing war. She tried not to think about how many test subjects that the church's science division had gone through to perfect the gene therapy. Or worse, that they had occasionally remanded those burnouts back to the field. Like with Goldy.

"Fishes." The challenge sounded with a tremble of nervousness. Meshner's pulse rifle swung toward Branson, who stood in the shadows. "Fishes."

"Loaves," Branson said in a low voice, calm and focused. She tried to speak with as little venom as possible, but she couldn't always hide the distaste of addressing Meshner. "What are you doing out here, sir?"

"Just checking out the Nils' lines."

"I just came from there. Everything's under control." Branson staggered a little from exhaustion. Her ARM XS monitoring system pumped stims into her system, steadying her.

"War is a grave matter, the province of life or death," Meshner paraphrased Sun Tzu.

Branson, not impressed by his book learning, finished the quote. "'War is like unto a fire. Those who will not put aside weapons are themselves consumed by them.'"

Meshner sucked from a small silver flask. He tipped it in obligatory offer to Branson, who waved it off. Meshner continued drinking. "Do you know what the curse of war is?"

"Sir?"

"The loss of tears. The stress. The loss of so many. The things ..." Meshner's thought trailed off. "Most men drift through life unaware of what they truly are. Only another soldier knows how hard it is to keep his sanity doing this dirty business. What did you do before all of this, Macia?"

"This is all I do, Lieutenant. I find it easier not to worry about the person I was." She preferred war's clean and uncomplicated emotions; giving into it, leaving behind idle dreams of family or could've beens. Her father was what they called an "indigenous leader," a colony planting novice-in-training, killed in the mission field. After her parents were killed, the church took her in. The church was mother, the church was father. So joining the Service of the Order was natural. The church birthed her, and war made her in its image.

"Because the person you were might not be able to live with the things that the person you've become had to do? Or because you don't remember anything before the war?"

"That's the life of a soldier, sir," Branson said.

§

"Weapons on me. We're moving out," Meshner shouted. Once again, the men discreetly glanced toward Branson.

"We're expecting some of the Nils' best." Branson slung her weapon to readiness, not meeting the eyes of the men, treading the minefield of leading while appearing to follow. Morale was bad enough without the men wondering who to follow when the shit hit. Technically, Meshner was the ranking officer, but the First Lieutenant's role was more administrative. A liaison ensuring that the will of the church was carried out through her military arm. First Lieutenants were usually hands off, opting to work more behind the scenes. They knew the theory of war. Branson and Dooley, they were war.

The land itself struggled against them. Mud sucked at their boots as they marched toward the hedgerows that lined the town's perimeter. Flak lit up the starless night from a town more than 10 miles away as drones passed overhead. The gloomy woods and endless fog followed them. Isolated them. Sound echoed and bounced back, carried oddly by the whims of the hollow.

They tromped along the base of a hill that hid them from the road above. Meshner held up his fist. Branson cocked her head at the distinct sound of biomech marching on cobbled roads. A lone Heathen soldier. Branson kept one eye on Meshner, the other on her squad. This was the dangerous time for green soldiers. She knew how their hearts stammered so hard they might not be able to catch their breath. Trying to maintain their composure as they stared into darkness. Trying to distinguish between normal and abnormal shadows. Praying that their anxiety for something to happen, anything, just to get the nerve-jangling waiting over with, didn't make them do something stupid.

Goldy had wandered too far from the squad before they could do anything about it. Maybe he figured he had a better angle to see their situation from his position. Slinging his rifle over his shoulder, he was climbing up the hill to sneak up on the Heathen soldier.

"Hey, buddy," Goldy said, in a mock-conspiratorial whisper.

The Heathen soldier had little opportunity to react before Goldy's kata slipped between his ribs. His body crumpled to the ground. Goldy turned to them, pleased with his actions, but failed to notice what Branson had: this wasn't a lone soldier separated from his unit. He was a lead advance scout clearing a path for the entire tactical unit, replete with two biomechs supporting the newcomers. The stutter of pulse fire shattered the night, muzzle fire like angry lightning bugs in the darkness. Goldy dove off the road.

"Get up that hill, or I'll have your balls for breakfast!" Dooley yelled, above the whine of charges building to fire, focused light spat out as hot teeth. Dooley roared up the hill, the men quick on his heels.

A shot whizzed by Branson, and she nearly choked on the accompanying adrenaline rush. She tumbled into Dooley's position and returned fire. "You're going to get me killed."

"Not you," Dooley smirked with a knowing grin. "Not today, at least."

Dooley's eyes betrayed his attempt at humor. He was reveling in the slaughter. There were no innocents to consider, no waxing on about misguided soldiers. They were all, "Heathen bastards that had to be killed," and be they men, women, or children, they would die if they stood between him and accomplishing his mission.

There was something monstrous in Holland that night.

One of the replacement soldiers took a bullet right through his mouth, sending his helmet flying and spilling him to the ground. Branson crawled over him to get to a better position. A battle still had to be fought, which left no time to mourn him. She shut down another piece of herself and wondered how much she had left to shut down.

One of the Heathens broke through their ranks. Branson intercepted him. No matter what The Order preached, there was no honor in battle. Fights were not won by adherence to rules of some imagined, gentlemanly engagement. Violence was the most primal language of humanity. Pain was the universal translator. Branson jammed her right index finger through the Heathen's eye socket. When he recoiled, she punched him in his genitals with her left. She grabbed her pulse rifle and hammered his head with its butt.

§

The shooting eventually stopped. MK-241 incendiary attacks left scorched trees. Holes pockmarked the earth. Branson prayed that they hadn't wasted these men on a bloody joyride.

All Branson wanted was to reach a command post, get a shower, and feel human again. Dismissed, she went to check on Dooley.

"How's the leg?" Branson asked.

"Just practicing to be the dummy," Dooley winced. He had caught a ricochet, but Branson knew that he wasn't going anywhere.

"It's all such a waste."

"I'll be patched up and ready to go again before chow time."

"All for the church to claim another bit of real estate, to justify the use of the sword to fulfill God's kingdom."

"Careful. Questions like that might make some think you're losing your beliefs."

"The only belief of mine anyone needs to worry about is my belief in following orders. I'm just ... tired."

"Yeah, we all get tired like that sometimes."

Goldy huddled over a body hidden in the shadows. Branson tried to make as much noise as possible when she walked toward him in order to avoid spooking him, but Goldy whirled at her approach, weapon ready. Branson calmly raised her hands. "A little jumpy?"

"I guess, ma'am."

"Got anything good, kid?"

"Good?" Goldy demurred, not quite hiding his guilt at being caught.

"Souvenirs."

"I found this." Goldy pointed to a fallen Heathen soldier. "He's the seventh body I've found like that. Most nowhere near any shelling."

"Maybe someone's collecting more ... exotic souvenirs."

Goldy's face suddenly seemed too young to know the taste of war. "How do you do it, ma'am?"

"Do what?"

"Live with the constant fear."

How could she explain to him that each day was a struggle to believe that life was worth living? That people were supposed to be created in God's image, that there was a point to any of this?

"There's no fear on stage," Branson said. Goldy shook his head, not understanding. "It's like an actor's performance anxiety. Our holo-training, all that rehearsal, takes over. Resign yourself to your own death and you can do anything. Especially live."

§

Branson watched her breath curl languidly in front of her. The cold air stabbed at her lungs like a swarm of needles. The treacherous, man-made forests had been planted specifically as a defensive barrier. The unrelenting shelling reduced her squad to shadows backlit by burning trees. She could barely feel her fingers despite the flames erupting in the woods. A miserable downpour, closer to sleet than rain, left thick, slimy mud that slowed their every movement. The thick fog rolled in, damp and cold, leaving the men disoriented, isolating them in their own private Ragnaroks. The thought of roads seemed like bedtime stories told to give hope to the weary soldiers. The hours might as well have been days.

Branson heard the Devil's Whistle, the whine which made every soldier's blood run cold. Drones gave little warning before their attack. "If you can hear the shells, you'll be okay," she taught. She hugged the ground, certain that this time a missile had come for her head. The earth trembled beneath her, spitting dirt in its death throes.

Then the shelling stopped.

War held Her breath. After being fired upon all night, the silences proved just as eerie. The earth stilled. Gold flames illuminated the trees. Like prairie dogs, the medics popped their heads up to scan the terrain. They scurried out of their foxholes to tend to the wounded. With diabolical timing, the shelling started again. Bleeding limbs, shorn to their rent bones, lay scattered on the field, bereft of bodies to connect to. The smell of burnt flesh filled the air.

Branson feared for her men. She eyed every fog-dulled silhouette with suspicion, not trusting any sound. At a branch snap, she whirled, finger on trigger, ready to fire until she recognized the man's helmet. She breathed a sigh of relief. She'd just wanted to get them on the line and through a couple of days of combat. Then they'd be fine. They were good men, only green. The cries of the wounded filled her ears. But even without translation psi ops training, she understood prayers when she heard them.

When the fog lifted, decapitated soldiers littered the field. Bodies strewn about, half-buried in the mud. Blood from friend and foe alike seeped into the soil. Replacement troops puked their guts out at the sight of mangled corpses. Branson inspected the bodies. A hint of suspicion tickled the back of her mind. Many of the wounds should have left some of the men hurt but not dead.

Goldy stumbled about, sure that the last round of shelling was indeed the last. He was young. And inexperienced. And oblivious to the fact that the Heathens had all night to play in the woods with their special brand of toys.

Like sniper rifles.

"Stay down, kid! Keep your head down!" Dooley yelled.

The blast tore into Goldy's throat. His hands clasped his neck, a thin trickle of blood escaping through his fingers even as the shot cauterized itself. Men returned fire in the direction of the shot. A medic scrambled toward Goldy, not seeing the tripwire. The explosive device threw his body into the air like a discarded toy. The cloud of dust and smoke made it difficult to breathe. The medic struggled to stand up on just one leg. Dooley was the first to reach the still-thrashing Goldy. Branson dashed over to help hold him down as best she could. The medic was already dressing his own leg.

"Medic!" Dooley yelled. He fumbled about his jacket for his emergency aid kit.

"I'm sorry, Sarge. I goofed up. I goofed up," Goldy spat through his own blood.

"It's not that bad. Hang on, kid." Dooley slapped a bandage over it and injected him with morphine.

"Tell me about Valhalla," Goldy said in his treble rasp.

"It's a huge palace, kid. Big enough for all of the warriors. All you do is drink, eat, and tell each other lies about your greatest battles."

"It sounds great, Sarge. I'm tired of fighting." Goldy's head fell to the side in a relaxed beatitude.

A signature dull thrum in the ear signaled everyone to scramble for cover. Branson dove into a nearby hole. Its occupant whirled to face her. Each of them brought their weapons to bear.

"Lieutenant," Meshner said in a flat voice, not unlike a man sitting down for afternoon tea.

"Lieutenant," Branson responded, matching his nonchalance. She lowered her weapon, but only as Meshner dropped his.

"We're on hallowed ground."

"We are, sir?" Branson ducked down at the renewed thrumming and then fired in its direction.

"Tilled with the blood of our enemies."

"A lot of our blood, too, sir."

• "War has always been with us. She whispers to me. I try to silence Her, but She continues every night. I hear Her voice in the groans left in Her wake, and She only stops when the earth streams with blood. She whispers to me. She told me all about you. Her cup bearer. Always thirsty. I thought you were the one. It's in our nature. It's why we fight," Meshner raised the kata. "The same spirit in which Cain killed Abel. Where we walk, the earth groans with blood in our wake."

"Something's not right with you, Meshner." War did strange things to people. Sometimes Her whispers simply drove men mad. A glint of light from Meshner's side drew Branson's attention. A Nil's dress kata. Her stomach tightened like a clenched fist.

"We're both orphans of a sort, no family, no name." Meshner drained his flask, upturning it completely to capture the last drops. "I wasn't always 'Mush,' the paper pusher. I had skill on the battlefield once. Then, one day, the war was done, and I found myself back home. The white picket fence, the possibility of a normal life, was like ashes in my mouth. I had no interest in family. In friends. In any kind of social mask. What I did on the combat field was what I was. Nothing else mattered."

"There's blood on our hands." Praise be the blood.

"I know. Blood that rivers couldn't wash away," Meshner said. "So, all we're left with are our dreams. Mine are of you. It's always you. The two of us could ..."

Branson shook her head, her eyes wanting no part of whatever it was he offered. She had the feeling that he really wasn't speaking to her at all. She wondered if Meshner had been a burnout like Goldy. Perhaps, before conversion he, too, had struggled against an inner darkness, one that clawed at him just under his surface.

"You have many guises," Meshner said. "You die, you come back. But I can see you now. Cursed to fight and suffer over and over again. Like the others. We have sown nothing but death and blood."

"Praise be the blood," she said. Branson had been to the cliff's edge of madness herself. She knew how tempting it could be to give in and dive off into the awaiting embrace of the abyss. So many nights she thought she was losing that tenuous grip on her humanity. Every night it seemed harder and harder to choose to remain human.

"As you have sown, so shall ye reap. For now is the time for harvest." Meshner raised his kata.

Too many times she had lain awake imagining someone trying to butcher her. Her rifle blocked his kata thrust, throwing him off balance. In close quarters the rifle was otherwise useless. His strength superior to hers. Meshner continued to drive the blade down. Fueled by desperation, she found the strength for survival. Up close, the only sounds were their gasps as they struggled. He grunted when her elbow smashed into the bridge of his nose. They were reduced to animals as Meshner grabbed her head and drove his knee into her throat. He tried to get her in a stranglehold. She bit through his hand then butted him in the jaw. She jumped to the side and drew him backwards. She caught him by the head, her fingers gouging his eyes. She pulled his head backward. Planting her foot into the back of his knee, she threw her weight into him as he fell. He rolled over, freeing himself of her. His hand fished about, retrieving his kata. He stood up slowly, his head above the foxhole. A mad, feral smile glinted in the wan light. His blood stained his teeth. His mouth twitched as if itching for a drink.

His head exploded. Shrapnel of bone, brain matter, and blood sprayed her. The sniper round, more missile than bullet, had shattered his skull. His body dropped to its knees, and he fell forward.

Waump. Waump. Waump.

She recognized the sound as well as she knew the sound of her own heartbeat. The Heathens were launching mortar bombs their way.

An explosion, pure concussive force, smacked them like the backhand of God and showered them in a storm of dirt, dust, and stone. All sound became muffled, taking on a looped, distorted quality. The woods erupted in a tumult of fire. A thick haze of smoke rose against the backdrop of flame. Men advanced like ghosts along the horizon. Branson scrambled for cover.

Something hot burned through her three times. Her body betrayed her, and her legs began to give out. Blood splayed across fingers she no longer felt. She fell alongside Meshner, burying her face under him to hide her breath. Not every monster was meant for redemption.

Praise be the blood.

Voice of the Martyrs

A mist rose from the cool waters stretching out in front of me. For all of my training, open water terrified me. I viewed open water the same way I thought of God: majestic and mysterious from a distance; holy and terrifying when caught up in it. My body trembled, an involuntary shudder. The migraine following my regaining consciousness meant I was at least alive. Then I vomited, confirming it. My biomech suit was a self-contained unit long used to handling my various excretions.

Even in the gloom of the graying twilight, my surroundings danced on the nearly artificial aspect of my holo-training sequences. The large fern leaves, a shade too green, undulated in the wan breeze, and water dripped from their undersides to splatter on my visor. My arm clung to a piece of bobbing driftwood, a pillow tucked under it and clutched to in my sleep. Water lapped just under my chin, but my seals were intact. A tired ache sank deep into my bones, and I suddenly felt my true age. Remaining the physical age of twenty-seven every time I re-upped for another tour with the Service of the Order factored into my decision for continued duty. Vanity was one of the many sins I worked on.

I tapped at my wrist panel. The action caused me to slip from my precarious perch. I re-adjusted myself, half-straddling the shard of log, and bobbed in place. The seconds retreated, collapsing into a singularity of eternity as I waited for it to lock onto the beacon of my orbiting ship, the Templar Paton. I used its navcom signal to map my position relative to our colony site. The terrain's image splayed across my visor view screen. I paddled toward the shore.

Memories returned in fragments. Thundering booms. Balls of light. Clouds illuminated against shadowy skies. Ground explosions scattering people. Heat. The confusion of artillery bursts. Targets acquired. Chasing someone. Shots fired. A shelling run toward me. Bolting across a field. The sudden pressure in my chest.

Falling.

My biomech suit sealed me off from the world, shielding me from the errant breeze or the rays of the sun on my skin. It filtered sound through its receivers, the noise of which became muted when navcom channels engaged. The world appeared to me on my visor, scanned and digitized. Set apart, I was a foreign intrusion, and, like any other pathogen, the world organism raised up antibodies to fight off my presence.

I pushed through the thick canopy of leaves whispering in the breeze. A series of sinkholes replaced the metal cabins where our camp had been. Our fields burned to the ground with methodical thoroughness. Animal carcasses torn asunder by blade, the occasional limb scattered here and there left to rot. Insects worked over them in a low-lying cloud. The ways of death and reclamation were a constant throughout the universe.

Even without the proximity detector, I knew I wasn't alone. Despite the isolation of my suit, my psi ops enhancements functioned at high alert. A Revisio. Their eyes, too big for their head, their skulls smooth and higher, they studied us with their critical gazes, a mixture of curiosity and mild distain. The Revisio sentry skulked about the remains of our camp with a stooped gait as if he carried an invisible burden. Turning over scrap metal, scanning the rubble, it hunted me. It. Once a mission required judgment protocols, thinking of those about to be judged as an "it" made the work easier.

Despite its deceiving bulk, the biomech suit moved with great stealth. Dampeners reduced its external noise to near nothing, and its movements were as fluid as my own. It no longer mattered that I had lost my rifle. For up close work, I preferred my combat katas.

Though I came upwind of it, the native turned at my approach. It ducked the wide arc of my kata, the edged baton bashing only air. It tried to bring its spear to bear, a lazy gesture I blocked. I spun into it like an unwanted tango partner, thrusting my biomech-enhanced elbow into its gut. I grasped its wrist, praying the thumb lock I had it in was as painful to its physiognomy as a Terran's. Wrenching its arm up and behind it, I ignored the snap of its bone and held it long enough to deliver another couple punches. The creature slumped in my grip.

"Where?" I asked. This Revisio had no understanding of my language at all. That was why psi ops lieutenants were attached to mission units. Besides security, we provided translation. The metal cap, a socket on the back of my skull, pressed into its place within the suit. Repeating my question, I projected my intent. Spatial concepts were the most difficult to process between cultures. Few saw life the same way. The universe, our place in it, was a matter of perception and perspective. Where did he come from? Where were my compatriots? Were there any survivors? The questions were meaningless, but my intent clear. In the end it was about brain chemistry and interpreting signals. A complex swirl of thoughts bubbled beneath a barrier stifling my efforts. Had it been trained, it would have shut me out entirely. Along with its derisive sneer, I managed to perceive the direction from where it traveled.

The issue at hand became what to do with the native. We entered hostile relations. Once those conditions were met, military protocols were in effect. Casualties were expected.

I would pray for his soul.

My fears for this mission were being realized.

§

This wasn't how this was meant to be, but this was the only way it could end.

§

They dubbed the encampment Melancholia as the cyan sphere of the gas giant they orbited filled the sky. The name had more of a ring to it than its designation, CFBDSIR2149. The crew cleared a space for this camp along a crest overlooking a lake. Hastily constructed sheds broken down from the self-contained modular sections of the supply shuttles surrounded a central fire. Test batches of Terran agriculture grew outside our camp, green sprouts rising from dark earth. A thick grove of trees, lush with leaves the span of an arm's breadth, encircled our site. A mist swept across the ground. I longed to take off my helmet and smell the foliage for myself, but that would've broken mission protocol. Once deployed to the field, infantry had to maintain preparedness at all times. I patrolled in my suit. I slept in my suit. I wept in my suit.

"Magnificent, isn't it?" Novice Wesley Vadair pulled his blonde hair back into a ponytail. Three days of beard growth stubbled his long, angular face. His eyes squinted in an involuntary muscle spasm, but no one ever commented on his facial tick.

"What is, sir?" Novices were little more than glorified civilians, but he had mission command.

"The view. The potential. You can practically feel it on your skin. Well, I suppose you can't." He slapped my back in an alltoo-familiar way. Not that I felt it within the suit. He meant to convey a camaraderie we didn't share. "Professional hazard, I suppose."

He was already tap dancing on my last nerve. "Is this your first colony plant?"

"That obvious?"

"If I could detect excitement levels, your readings would redline."

"Good. Excitement is contagious." Novice Vidair began walking, waving an invitation to join him.

"Then, it's a blessing I'm in this suit, sir."

"I welcome your cynicism. I'll win you over, you'll see. I'm going to do things differently than other colonies. My dad was a planter. I grew up in a colony like this, so it's in my blood."

"Familial hazard, I suppose."

"See? We're going to get along great, you'll see. This colony won't be burdened with dogma. It will be more about community ..."

The novice went on to describe his vision, sprinkling it with all of the popular jargon and buzzwords of the day. Community. Conversations. Authenticity. But I knew this story would end the way it always did.

My parents were the vanguard of "indigenous leaders" novices aimed to raise up. They were killed in their colony. I forgave their murderers. At their funeral, I mouthed my prayer over and over. "They know not what they did."

Other indigenous leaders took me in and raised me. Then I witnessed how such colonies worked from the other side. Coming into our neighborhood, planters demanded that we act like them, speak like us, until there was little left of us, in order to receive their gospel. Eventually, their colony plants dotted the land like grave markers.

I joined the Service of the Order on my sixteenth birthday.

"What do you think?" The novice drew me back to full attention.

"Permission to speak freely?"

"Always."

"I've heard it before. If you didn't believe that, you wouldn't be a planter. But planting is what it always is."

"What is that?" the novice asked.

"A wealthy culture sending out well-intentioned missionaries using the gospel to impose themselves on indigenous cultures to create satellites of themselves."

"You make us sound like ... cultural bullies."

"It's a push or be pushed universe, sir."

"And what's your role in this process?"

"I'm your pusher."

I followed Novice Vidair from the settlement into the valley. He spouted the right words, but I had the evidence of history. My own history. Once in the Service, the Order selected me for Jesuit Training School, officer candidacy. I faced grueling studies in advanced mathematics, Latin (because all alien cultures need to be fluent in languages long dead on Terra), stellar cartography, astrobiology, logistics, strategy, game theory, and tactics. Part of me suspected the reason they took such a special interest in me was because I was reclaimed, a story of redemption they could point to. I was that rescued urchin from the streets with a tragic story. They could pat themselves on their backs for having saved me from the fate of my people. My parents.

"They know not what they did."

The valley was a potential utopia, but I knew that our leaders back home saw only desirable natural resources and a strategically positioned planet. The gas giant, CFBDSIR2149, absorbed most of the radiation emitted by the solar system's star, lowering the amount of UV radiation, so fewer mutations followed. It slowed evolution, leaving fixed gene patterns. Life took the hand it was dealt and would be required to play for a long time. Whatever life forms that dominated here were frozen midstep on the evolutionary ladder, but the transplanted flora and fauna displaced native species with ease.

"We're almost there," Novice Vidair said. "You can see me in action."

"Sir?"

"What do you know of this planet?"

"It's the moon of CFBDSIR2149 of the AB Doradus Moving Group. The planet itself is a gas giant," I said.

"Yes, yes, a rogue planet ejected from its system, cradled by its neighbor. But what understanding do you have of life on Melancholia?"

"I ..."

"Look over there. We call them Species A."

A group of natives milled about a cave entrance. Long simian arms rippled with burly musculature. Thick brows ridged deep, inset eyes. A hulking brute stopped and sniffed about, his protruding jaw set and resolute as if he'd had a bad day out hunting. Picking up a stone, he hurled it in our direction. We didn't budge. Satisfied, he joined the group of other males guarding the entrance.

"Aren't they magnificent?" He spoke of them the way I spoke of my cat back home.

Despite their primitive appearance, they were more human than I felt. Stripped of my culture and my people, not much of me remained. I wore the emptiness that came with a life of obligation and duty without passion and meaning. My neural pathways had been re-routed to accommodate the cap. I could sync up with a computer in order to download information, language matrixes, and action protocols in an instant. My physiognomy recalibrated with each tour of duty, slowing my aging process and knitting tired muscles back together. I hated and resented the Order as much as I loved and needed it. The Order gave me life and purpose. The Service left me without scars, physical ones, that is.

"Do they ... speak?" I asked. "It doesn't appear that they have reached the level of development necessary to grasp the intricacies of the gospel."

"Now who sounds elitist? I'm sure they have some sort of proto-language. If we can teach the gospel to children, we can reach these noble savages. We have an opportunity here, a people in the early stages of their development. With our help, their culture, yes, their entire civilization can be made in God's image. We will avoid the mistakes of the past."

§

The colony buzzed with excitement at the caravan's approach. Taking point, I escorted Novice Vidair. Fraught with possible misunderstandings, first contact protocols were the most dangerous part of the mission. Novices were trained to be opening and welcoming, but service members were trained to watch for and deal with threats. My parents had paid the ultimate price for the short-sightedness and arrogance of novices.

A delegation of four rode beasts similar to hairless horses. Three of them were armed with spears and daggers tucked into the sashes girding them. The last of them wore a tunic of animal skin. This aliens' musculature was smoother, closer to resembling ours. In my experience, the more a life form mirrored ours, the more nervous I became. Violence was our way, no matter where we found ourselves in the universe. My rifle, displayed but trained at the ground, showed that we had teeth. It helped establish trust as they knew what they were dealing with. Novice Vidair all but applauded with joy at their approach. With every step forward, the novice nipped at my heels. I placed my open hand in the center of his chest to scoot him behind me.

"Greetings," the head of the processional said. "I am Majorae Ha'Asoon."

As he dismounted, I processed the sounds through my linguistics database. My cap thrummed while reading and deciphering the intent of his words. I relayed the message's content.

"I gathered as much. 'Hello' is 'hello' on any world." The novice smirked at me with dismissive disdain.

"'Hello' is only 'hello' if not followed by weapon fire." My cap continued to process their language. Given enough of a sample with my psi impressions monitoring the emotional intent of their words, the cap sped up, relaying translation in near-real time. I conveyed the greeting on behalf of the novice.

Majorae Ha'Asoon turned his back to me to address Novice Vidair directly. "On behalf of the Revisio, we welcome you. You are not of ... here."

"We are of a far-off planet called Earth," Novice Vidair said, with the tone of a parent telling their child a fairy tale.

"You, too, can travel the stars?"

"Too? We detected no signs that you had such technology." The novice glanced toward me to confirm. I nodded.

"We don't require vessels to travel. We are star stuff. Flotsom carried in the void," Majorae Ha'Asoon said.

"I don't understand," I said.

Majorae Ha'Asoon kept his back to me. "Yet, you recognize us?"

"You look like the natives, the ones we have called Species A. Except ..." Novice Vidair said.

"Different. We, like you, are from another world. We, unlike you, have a natural claim to the *Derthalen*, as we have called them."

"What claim?" I asked. The steel of my tone caused Majorae Ha'Asoon to shift to his side, keeping me within his peripheral gaze and making a smaller target of himself. His guards moved in predatory lurches. I swung my rifle to my side.

"The right of first. We are children of the blue planet."

"We detected no life on CFBDSIR2149," Novice Vidair said.

"Perhaps not life as you measure it. We are ... what would you call us? A virus?"

"You look pretty big for a virus," I said. My cap continued to whir, locked in a processing loop, as if under a cyber attack of some sort.

"Floating unicellular things. I suspect, as you would measure it, each strain you would consider an individual."

"Some sort of communal intelligence," Novice Wesley Vidair said.

"This virus business, I still don't understand," I said.

Majorae Ha'Asoon sighed. "It's simple. We were carried here on the backs of asteroids. The *Derthalen* made for natural hosts. Understandable, since we are from the same star stuff. Once we take over, we mutate and spread. Each generation of the virus is a mutant strain of the last. The course of the infection has physical side effects, too."

"I noticed. You appear smaller," I said.

"No, you don't understand. They ... we have evolved." Majorae Ha'Asoon gestured to his men. "Look around you. We're not running around naked as beasts. Our form allows us a certain resonance with the minds of others."

My cap tingled again. The Revisio's "resonance" functioned as a low-level kind of telepathy. Each of them had the equivalent of my cap, though theirs operated naturally. Communicating with each other, gleaning information from us, interfering with my cap, it explained why they were so familiar with our ways. It also made them more of a threat.

"This is utterly fascinating. We've suspected and explored that potential in our own kind. There is so much we could learn from one another," Novice Vidair said.

"We had hoped you were a peaceful party," Majorae Ha'Asoon said.

"We are, I assure you."

"You are well-armed for peace." Majorae Ha'Asoon cast a sideways glance at me.

"Experience has taught us to be cautious when exploring new worlds and contacting new peoples. Not all missions end ... diplomatically."

I thought of my parents.

154

It was an Easter Sunday service. A group of "seekers" entered to learn more about the Scriptures. Seekers were my parents' favorite kind of people to talk to as they were open, questioning, and thinkers. But the seekers were actually members of the tarik, a group of faithful believers from a competing sect, armed with an array of weapons: guns, break knives, ropes, and towels. Towels. Because they planned for a lot of blood. No one told me what happened, only that my parents were killed in the line of duty. But the full truth resided in the reports that I had access to once I joined the Service of the Order. The tarik read from the Scriptures before the assault began. They tied my parents' hands and feet to the chairs.

"When you oppress the weak and poor of your own world, trampling their freedoms, there are consequences. For the oppressed and the oppressor," the tarik leader said.

They video recorded their handiwork, which I have never watched despite its still being available in the archives. The power of the stark words in the reports, combined with my imagination, was enough: ritual slicing of orifices, disembowelment, emasculation, decapitation. One hundred thirty-two stab wounds total. You never know what you really believe until those beliefs are tested, in that moment when you put your life on the line for them. My parents believed in a loving and just God. And I forgave the killers. I forgave them.

"If you got business with them," I leaned forward, letting him see the full bulk of my armament, "you handle it through me."

"Stand down, lieutenant," Novice Vidair said. "We're all about meeting new friends."

"Yes, heel," Majorae Ha'Asoon said.

I regripped my rifle, doing my level best to resist the urge to cram the butt of it into his ... its ... inviting jaw.

"We would welcome a conversation of equals." Majorae Ha'Asoon made a point of once again turning his back to me.

"Indeed. I look forward to it."

Majorae Ha'Asoon bowed slightly then hopped on his beast. With a swirl of his hand, he led his men away.

"That went rather well," Novice Vidair said.

"We need to prepare for an attack," I said.

"I appreciate your hypervigilance, but that's not the way to follow up a first contact."

"Did we not hear the same thing? They are a colony, too. An entrenched one, from what I gathered. And we are a threat to them."

"Lieutenant, nothing of the sort was said. Perhaps, we can establish a trade of some sort with them. Crops, maybe. We have much to offer them. And them us."

"I know a scouting party when I see it. They were taking our measure." I stared at him full on. "And make no mistake, I have killed enough people in the service of the Order to know how this story ends."

"Then perhaps all of the blood on your hands has made you paranoid. We serve God's will."

That was the problem with many novices. They existed in a bubble of privilege. They were used to people deferring to them simply because of their special calling. People were done no favors by being raised up coddled. It made them soft. People needed to fight off things: germs, people, life. It builds you up. If you didn't ... I thought of Species A, the *Derthalen* as the Reviso called them. Not even allowed to name themselves.

"God's will or not, this expedition will face troubles. My job's to handle them."

"You don't understand, this could be the miracle from God that we were looking for."

"Excuse me, sir?" I said, because "What the hell nonsense did you just spout?" would have gotten me court-martialed on the spot.

"You feared that Species A might not be cognizant enough to receive the Gospel."

"A notion you dismissed."

"Yes, before we learned of Species B. Perhaps we were meant to evangelize Species B in order to bring the message to both them and Species A."

"But the Revisio are a virus."

"Exactly. Imagine the Gospel spread by viral transmission. It would make our task so much easier and our stay shorter. The Lord's ways are not our ways. Just like our ways have you obeying the orders given you. My orders."

The Lord sure could bring out the stupid in some folks.

It all came down to the story we lived by. If the metaphor of that story could be changed, the individual could be changed. An ungodly people deemed less than human. Our people, holders of secret knowledge and power, could trade the Scriptures for land and resources. Evangelism encouraged by way of blaster rifles. My blaster rifle. The people traded one sin-soaked culture for another; forced to change their language, their names, their gods, their cultures. Suffer a slow death by assimilation. The story always ended the same way.

"Your ... orders." My set jaw began a slow grind, like I chewed on something distasteful. I peered down my nose at him. "Allow me to correct any misconceptions you may be laboring under: I'm not here to wipe your nose. I'm not here to diaper your behind. I don't cook, clean, or sew. You think I sings and dances real good, too? You need to get out my face and let me do my job."

Novice Vidair squinted at me. His facial tick intensified when he was angry. "Lieutenant, you are confined to your quarters for a day."

"I thought I 'always' had permission to speak freely."

"Until you cross the line. I give some people enough rope for them to hang themselves."

His order probably saved my life.

§

This wasn't how this was meant to be, but this was the only way it could end.

§

When I finally returned, they were all gone.

§

I tracked the trail of the attack party back to a series of looming structures, ominous shapes of deeper shadow in the night. I wasn't even sure what my mission was anymore. I had ignored my action protocols. I hadn't signaled the Templar Paton, not with a status update or report. I moved on instinct. I couldn't call myself investigating the native culture, though the biomech sensors recorded and logged everything. Without knowing if my party was even alive, I couldn't claim to be on a rescue mission. And if they were dead, the Order wasn't about vengeance.

The Service, however, was all about God's judgment.

Flexing my arm and wiggling my toes, I tested each extremity to make sure everything still worked. I craned my neck to each side, popping out the kings, certain that I should just name the knots in my shoulders since they accompanied me for so long. The pain focused me on the task at hand: I had bastards to kill. In Jesus' name.

Having lost nearly an hour finding a suitable blaster rifle, I crouched behind a fallen tree. No breeze moved the leaves. I detected no sounds of birds or any other night life I had gotten used to; as if the structure's very presence stilled all life to a respectful silence. The main building seemed carved from the very mountain itself. With its massive foundation and heavy fortifications, it could have been a temple or a citadel, the high arch of its entrance and formidable walls meant to convey a mixture of awe and intimidation.

Twin sentries patrolled the main archway. The entranceway lit by a series of torches, illuminating an area leading up to it that provided no cover. Even at full sprint I couldn't cover that distance and subdue the guards without raising an alarm. I skulked through the dense forest, circling the castle. At its side, a rivulet emptied into the lake below. Perhaps it was simply an underground stream, or a natural sewage line, either way my heart stuttered at the prospect of wading through it to make my entrance.

The force of the water's current slowed my progress, each lugubrious step an act of determined will. Steadying myself against each tunnel wall, the water rose past my thighs. My visor digitized my surroundings as much as it could through murky dimness. The lights on my biomech suit didn't penetrate the pitch. The cramped space pressed in on all sides, with no way to measure when my journey would end or if my progress would be halted by watery death. But I kept walking. Faith buoyed my steps. I had to believe in something, have a hope to grasp onto. No amount of faith could still the apprehension that gripped me as the water lapped my helmet. I only had a few more steps before the water overtook me. I couldn't help but rethink my plan. It made sense why this passage wasn't well-guarded. Only a fool would chance this.

Water filled the entire passageway. The biomech suit continued to circulate air as the emergency supply automatically kicked in. A timer on my visual display counted down how many minutes of air I had left.

I continued to march deep within the compound. Scant seconds of air remained. Shafts of light stabbed the darkness ahead. I gulped one last breath of air. The passageway opened into a bay of sorts with a grate above me. I punched handholds into the wall to scale my way to the top. I bashed though the metal mesh and pulled myself up. The biomech suit was designed to augment its occupant's efforts, but the work began with my own exertions. I collapsed, sprawled out along the floor while my re-breather unit replenished itself.

The room was a mechanical closet of sorts. Heat baked the room, a cauldron of molten metal rotated. Levers and switches cranked away. The way the cauldron revolved, its contents' heat could be used to warm the complex or be hurled as a distance weapon. I left it for the structural engineers aboard the Templar Paton to puzzle out. The floor was connected to the walls, rigged to fall into the antechamber below in case of emergency. Advanced thinking. It began to make sense, even to my simple infantry mind. The Revisio, no matter how advanced, how evolved, couldn't just drop tech into this world. Life on their own planet precluded them from building anything. To build they had to have, well, thumbs. They were essentially advanced minds. They may have evolved the *Derthalen*, but it would take a while to get their technology to the point where they'd have the tools necessary to advance their world. But it wouldn't take long. Within a generation or two, they'd rival us. I could only imagine what they'd do on our world with our tools and technology.

Scrounging a loose bolt, I tossed it against the door. I listened for a few moments before I retrieved it and threw it again. A guard opened the door. I expected as much. It stood watch against anyone going into the room, not coming out. I yanked him inside. Another soul I would have to pray for. Later.

Flickering pools of amber from torches created puddles of shadow throughout the long hallway. The biomech wasn't designed with indoor stealth in mind; however, it was built to carry armaments. I crept along the shadows as best I could, setting a charge as I went, praying none of the natives decided to turn down this way. I followed the sounds of garrulous chatter and laid two more charges. I may have lacked Samson's strength, but blowing a support wall would collapse a room or two if it came to that. I hoped my escape wouldn't come to another trek through the crawlspace. I took a measured breath then plunged into the room.

The room ran the length of a banquet hall, ringed by long tables. Behind them, male and female Revisio wore simple tunics of animal skins. In the center of the room, game roasted on spits. Musicians played in the corner while two women danced. Guards stood at attention by each table. My entrance halted the revelry. I fired once above Majorae Ha'Asoon's head. My blaster scorched the wall before I trained my weapon on the leader. "Where are my people?"

"Is this more of your diplomacy?" Majorae Ha'Asoon sipped from a tall cup, unflustered.

"You have our diplomat. I, on the other hand, am not ..."

"... very diplomatic. Do they not have manners on your home planet? You barge into our great hall uninvited and accuse us in our home."

"Our rules of etiquette don't extend to those who lay siege to a peaceful camp, destroy our property, and make off with our people."

"You talk to us of peace? You come to this world, armed, with no regard for our plants and animals. You comport yourselves in the way of your world, imposing them on ours."

"As you have with the *Derthalen*?"

"This is our moon. Our dominion."

"I'll ask one last time, where are my people?"

"We have ... exchanged ideas. They have been welcomed into our tribe. There have been some ... complications."

"They better be unharmed."

Majorae Ha'Asoon nodded, and a member of his guard departed. The others shifted positions, not grouping to surround me, but taking up more defensive postures. I eyed the nearest exit. Majorae Ha'Asoon's attention focused on my weapon, studying my suit with the glint of greed in his eyes.

The guard led Novice Vidair to the area just before Majorae Ha'Asoon. The novice averted his gaze, studying the ground. It had been not even half a day since the attack, but the novice's belly distended. His face gaunt, flushed with a grayish pallor, his eyelids had swollen shut. Wizened fingers dug into emaciated arms, scratching at the red splotches that ran along them.

"Are you okay, Novice Vidair?" I asked.

"They infected us." He upturned his hands. Maroon pustules blossomed on his palms like tumescent stigmata. When his eye spasmed, the muscle contraction tightened his entire face.

"We didn't know what effect our introduction would have on your kind," Majorae Ha'Asoon said.

"You mean, as you force yourself on us," I said.

"Your kind no longer embraces change."

The full implications of what he intimated settled in. Perhaps we had evolved as far as we were able. I swept the room with my rifle, stilling the slow encroachment of the guards. Their movements were subtle, professional. "We resist you."

"We're the future. We build. We create. We define. We have no need of your God. Or your Order. We have studied your Scriptures, and one 'truth' intrigues us." Majorae Ha'Asoon returned to his meal. He waved his knife about, light glimmering from its edge. "Your chosen people were called to wipe out nations and peoples before them. That is where we find ourselves, one story destroying the one that came before it. That is the 'gospel' message you have brought us."

I watched the glint from the knife. And thought of my parents.

The first shot of my blaster burned a fist-sized hole in the center of Majorae Ha'Asoon's chest. My next shot took off a quarter of the nearest guard's head. I fired and fired, backing toward Novice Vidair. Before I could turn to shove him toward an exit, he leapt on my back.

"Too late for us." His fists slammed into my neck attempting to divorce my head from my body. My biomech suit shuddered with the impact of his unanticipated strength. "We are joined. Not one of them. No longer us. We order you to join us."

I reached around and flung him from me as if tearing off a shirt I no longer wanted. Veins thickened and bulged along his neck. Peering with overly vesseled eyes, blood trailed from their corners like thick tears. He raked fingers across my suit, desperate to open a gash.

I raced down the corridor, pursued by a mad clamor of hoots and cries as the guards were let loose from their leashes. Backtracking to the room I entered from, I barred the door and disabled the room-dropping mechanism. My people had been biologically compromised by a hostile contagion. The Revisio had genocidal intent toward the *Derthalen*. Nothing remained of this mission except judgment protocols.

"They know not what they did."

I placed my remaining charges around the massive cauldron.

Synchronizing the timers, I gave myself a thirty-second window. I no longer cared if that allowed me enough time. God would see me through if I was meant to labor on. I dove for the grated opening into the waiting water. The torrent whooshed me along, flushing me from the compound like so much unwanted waste. The vibrations of the explosion rattled the passageway. I prayed the rough tunnel's integrity would hold, as the only death I imagined worse than drowning was being buried alive while I drowned.

The hillside shook, its contraction excreting me toward the lake. I dug my biomech enhanced hands into the earth until I came to a halt. The remains of the building collapsed on itself. I doubted there would be any survivors, but I would wait. Each step became more difficult as the extensive damage to my biomech suit caused power loss. Eventually, it would be inoperable. I would salvage what I could, but I needed to send one final report. With my suit compromised and the vector of the Revisio's transmission unclear, I submitted myself and this world as under bioquarantine.

From the cover of forest undergrowth, I could study Species A, the *Derthalen*. A pod of them groomed one another, the adults sheltering the young. No one escaped agents of change. If God was already at work in their culture, as we purport to believe, then these people have earned the right to find their own way.

As have I.

About the Author

Maurice Broaddus is the author of *Buffalo Soldier,* as well as the *Knights of Breton Court* urban fantasy trilogy: *King Maker, King's Justice,* and *King's War.* He is a co-author of the play, *Finding Home: Indiana at 200.* His fiction has been published in numerous magazines and anthologies, including *Asimov's Science Fiction, Lightspeed Magazine, Cemetery Dance, Apex Magazine,* and *Weird Tales Magazine.* Some of his stories are collected in *The Voices of the Martyrs.* He co-edited *Streets of Shadows* and the *Dark Faith* anthology series. You can keep up with him at his web site, www.MauriceBroaddus.com.

"Warrior of the Sunrise" was originally published in *The New Hero: Volume One* (Stone Skin Press, 2013)

"Rite of Passage" was originally published in *Space & Time Magazine* (November 2008)

"A Soldier's Story" was originally published in *Vampire Don't Sparkle* (Seventh Star Press, 2012)

"The Ave" was originally published in *Horror Literature Quarterly* (November 2007)

"Family Business" was originally published in *Weird Tales Magazine* #338 (January 2006)

"Read Me Up" was originally published in the *What Fates Impose* (Alliteration Ink, 2013)

"Cerulean Memories" was originally published in *Book of the Dead* (Jurassic-London, 2013)

"The Electric Spanking of the War Babies" was originally published in *Glitter and Mayhem* (Apex Books, 2013)

"The Valkyrie" was originally published in the *War Stories* (Apex Books, 2014)

"The Voice of Martyrs" was originally published in *Beyond the Sun* (Fairwood Press, 2013)

Also from Rosarium ...

"The stories here are diverse, but what they have in common is a clear and exuberant feeling of joy in their shared enterprise, of indebtedness and gratitude."
— *The New York Times*

STORIES FOR CHIP

A TRIBUTE TO SAMUEL R. DELANY

EDITED BY NISI SHAWL AND BILL CAMPBELL

Featuring: Junot Díaz, Thomas M. Disch, L. Timmel Duchamp, Hal Duncan, Eileen Gunn, Nick Harkaway, Ernest Hogan, Nalo Hopkinson, Walidaah Imarisha, Ellen Kushner, Isiah Lavender III, Kit Reed, Kim Stanley Robinson, Geoff Ryman, Michael Swanwick, Sheree Renée Thomas, and more!

"The SEA Is Ours is a subversive and rebellious addition to the steampunk canon and one that's been needed."

— *The New York Journal of Books*

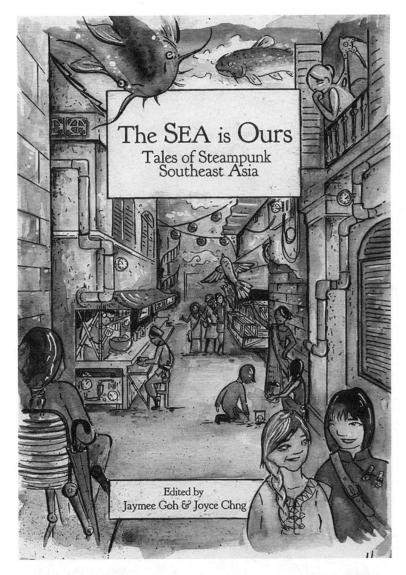

Featuring: Timothy Dimacali, Marilag Angway, L.L. Hill, Alessa Hinlo, Nghi Vo, Paolo Chikiamco, Kate Osias, Olivia Ho, Robert Liow, z.m. quýnh, Ivanna Mendels, and Pear Nuallak!